BELOW THE BELT

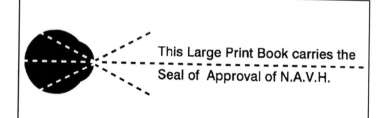

This Large Print Book carries the
Seal of Approval of N.A.V.H.

BELOW THE BELT

STUART WOODS

LARGE PRINT PRESS
A part of Gale, a Cengage Company

Farmington Hills, Mich • San Francisco • New York • Waterville, Maine
Meriden, Conn • Mason, Ohio • Chicago

LIBRARY OF CONGRESS CATALOGING-IN-PUBLICATION DATA

Names: Woods, Stuart, author.
Title: Below the belt / Stuart Woods.
Description: Waterville, Maine : Thorndike Press, 2017. | Series: A Stone Barrington novel | Series: Thorndike Press large print basic
Identifiers: LCCN 2016049527 | ISBN 9781410496652 (hardback) | ISBN 1410496651 (hardcover)
Subjects: LCSH: Large type books. | BISAC: FICTION / Thrillers. | GSAFD: Suspense fiction.
Classification: LCC PS3573.O642 B454 2017 | DDC 813/.54—dc23
LC record available at https://lccn.loc.gov/2016049527

ISBN 13: 978-1-4328-3741-9 (pbk.)
ISBN 10: 1-4328-3741-9 (pbk.)

Published in 2017 by arrangement with G. P. Putnam's Sons, an imprint of Penguin Publishing Group, a division of Penguin Random House LLC

Printed in Mexico
1 2 3 4 5 6 7 21 20 19 18 17

BELOW THE BELT

1

Stone Barrington landed the CJ 3 Plus smoothly at Santa Fe Airport at mid-afternoon. Holly Barker sat next to him in the copilot's seat. "Very nice," she said.

"Thank you," Stone replied, and taxied to the ramp, where a rental car was waiting for them. He transferred their luggage to the car, and Stone went inside and made arrangements for regular hangar space. Back in the car, he drove through the automatic gate.

"Excited?" Holly asked.

"I guess so, yes."

"If I had just bought a new house, sight unseen, I'd be terrified."

"It's not exactly sight unseen," he replied. "I've visited there a few times. It was owned by Ed Eagle's wife's sister."

"Are we going to have a bed to sleep in?"

"We are. I bought it substantially furnished."

"What does that mean?"

"We're going to find out in about twenty minutes," he said, turning onto the Santa Fe bypass. Twenty minutes later they turned off the main highway at the Tesuque exit.

"What street is it on?"

"This one — Tesuque Village Road." They passed the Tesuque Village Market, and a quarter mile later, Stone turned into a drive and reached out his window to enter the gate code into the keypad. The gate slid silently open, and they drove up a fairly long drive and parked in front of the house.

"From here it looks like every other house in Santa Fe," Holly said.

"It's true, all Santa Fe houses look a little alike — it's the architectural style and the mock adobe finish." He unloaded their luggage, carried it to the front door, and saw that the key was in the lock, as promised. They entered a long hallway and found a large living room on their right. The big pictures that had hung over the fireplaces at either end were gone. Otherwise, things seemed as he remembered them.

He gave Holly the tour of the kitchen, dining room, and his study, then led her to the master suite and showed her her bath and dressing room, where he left her luggage, then he took her into the bedroom. "Look," he said, "a bed to sleep in."

"Now?" Holly asked mischievously.

"Later. Unpack." He found his own bath and dressing room and unpacked his things, and they met in the study for drinks.

"Thank God she left liquor," Holly said, sipping her bourbon.

They had hardly sat down in the comfortable leather chairs when the phone rang. "I expect that's for the previous owner," Stone said, "but I'd better answer it." He pressed the speaker button. "Hello?"

"Mr. Stone Barrington?" a woman's voice asked.

"Yes."

"This is the White House operator. Will you accept a call from President Lee?"

"Which President Lee?" he asked.

"I beg your pardon, the former President."

"Of course."

"Stone?"

"Will, how are you?"

"Very well, thank you. How's the new house?"

"I moved in half an hour ago. How the hell did you find me here?"

"Didn't you know? The White House operators can find anybody."

"How's the other President Lee?"

"Thriving."

"And William Henry the Fifth?"

"Rambunctious. I wanted to invite you to something in Santa Fe tomorrow evening — a fund-raiser, actually, but never mind that. It's dinner at the home of friends, followed by an evening at the Santa Fe Opera — *La Bohème.*"

"Sounds wonderful, we'd love to."

"Oh, yes, and give Holly my best."

"Thank you, Mr. President," Holly said. "You're the only person at the White House who will talk to me."

"I'm not talking to you, I'm talking to Stone. We all have orders from the commander in chief not to speak to you."

Holly sighed. "Yes, I know." President Kate Lee had told her to take two weeks off and not to call the office, just to have fun. She had gone to New York to see Stone, but then he had bought the house and they had flown west to see it.

"We'd love to come," Stone said. "It's my favorite opera."

"It's everybody's favorite opera," Will replied. "And you and I will have to find a private moment during the evening. There's something I need to talk to you about."

"I'll look forward to it," Stone said.

"Six o'clock for drinks, followed by dinner. The opera begins at nine — sundown."

"See you then," Stone said, then hung up.

"I'm annoyed," Holly said. "The White House will talk to you, but not to me."

"That's because Kate knows you well enough to know that given an inch of access, you'd take a mile. It would be as though you weren't on vacation at all."

"I'm unaccustomed to vacations," Holly replied. She was the national security advisor to the President and, as such, chaired the National Security Council. "And there's no telling what those people are screwing up in my absence. I'll probably return to find that the nation is at war."

"Remember, you chose many of those people. They're perfectly capable of running the council in your absence."

"That's not what a girl wants to hear," she said moodily.

"I think what you need is another drink," Stone said, picking up the bottle and refreshing her glass.

"You're a mind reader." She took a gulp. "I'm hungry."

"That's because it's two hours later in New York. Let me see what I can find." He went into the kitchen and found the refrigerator well stocked and returned with some cheese, crackers, and salami.

"That's better," Holly said. "What are we

doing for dinner?"

"We'll go up to the Market. It's a grocery, a restaurant, a pizzeria, a bakery, and, not least, a bar."

"Everything we need for survival," she said.

Stone saw an envelope on his chairside table, addressed to him, and he opened it and read it aloud.

Dear Stone,

Welcome to your new home! Everything you see in the house is now yours. My L.A. house is already furnished, so all I took with me were my clothes and a few pictures. You'll have fun shopping for replacements. I've attached a list of numbers for the best restaurants, the maid and cook, the gardener, a handyman, and others you might need. By the way, the hot tub is set to 100 degrees. Feel free to call for advice, and enjoy yourself!

Gala

"That was sweet of her," Holly said. "I like the sound of the hot tub."

"Then let's go find it," Stone said. "Bring your drink."

2

Stone and Holly found the house with his rental-car GPS; it was big, set into a hillside, and had quite a lot of guest parking. He found a spot and they walked toward the front door. A figure stepped out of the darkness: "Mr. Barrington?"

"Yes."

The man showed him a badge. "Secret Service. May I see some ID, please?"

Stone showed him his New York driver's license.

"Got anything federal-issued?"

Stone showed him his pilot's license.

"This way, please. Just you, not the lady."

"Holly, will you go ahead inside? I'll join you shortly."

Holly climbed the steps, rang the bell, and was admitted. The agent led Stone to a large black SUV and rapped on the window. The door opened, and he motioned for Stone to get in.

"Evening, Stone," Will Lee said, putting aside his New York Times. "How are you?" The agent closed the door, and the only sound Stone could hear was the air-conditioning.

"Very well, Will."

"Forgive me for ambushing you, but once we're inside, everyone will be watching."

"What's up?"

Will turned his body more toward Stone. "I want to tell you a story, some of which you'll already know about."

"All right."

"Would you like a drink? We have Knob Creek."

"Sure, thanks."

Will opened a compartment in front of them and extracted two glasses, some ice, and a bottle of the bourbon and poured them both one. "Happier days," Will said.

"Are these not happy ones?" Stone asked, taking a swig.

"Think of this as the first day of the election season," Will said, "though we have a long way to go. The election season is never happy, just frenetic, and often depressing."

"I suppose you're right. What's the story?"

"It begins on a December day in Washington more than ten years ago. We were flying down to Georgia for Christmas, so we left

14

our house in Georgetown and drove up to Silver Spring Airport, where we kept our airplane, at that time a new Piper Mirage. As I was doing my preflight, a marine helicopter set down next to us, and a young officer got out and told me that the vice president would like us to join him and his wife for breakfast at Camp David.

"We arrived there and met Joe and Sue Adams, and after some small talk, Joe got serious. He told us that they had just spent a few days in New York, shopping and going to the theater. There was more to it, though — Joe had had some medical tests, most of them in their suite at the Waldorf, and the results were troubling."

Stone nodded and had another sip of his drink.

So did Will. "He told us, in the strictest confidence, that he had been diagnosed as being in the early stages of Alzheimer's disease, and that he hadn't told anybody else."

"I never knew that," Stone said.

"No one did, for a while. Remember, this was eleven months before the election, and the President couldn't run again. Joe was everybody's favorite for the nomination and the election."

"That, I remember."

15

"Joe told me that I was his personal choice for President, and he wanted me to announce almost immediately."

"A big surprise."

"An enormous shock. I'd given thought to running, but I didn't expect to do that for another eight years. Joe said that he would announce in another month or so that he would not be a candidate, but he didn't want anyone to know why. He was giving me a heads-up to give me time to get a team together for an announcement of my own."

"That was very good of him."

"He knew that George Kiel, the minority leader in the Senate at the time, would jump right in, and that he, being better known than I, would be the immediate favorite. Anyway, we went back to our airplane, flew home, and I talked with my folks about it. They were all for a run, and eventually, as you know, I came around. Something odd happened, though, while we were still at the homeplace. Kate received a letter there."

"Why was that odd?"

"Because no mail had ever been addressed to her at my folks' house. She borrowed the car, disappeared for about four hours, then returned. She said it was business, and I knew better than to ask any more. She was

16

deputy director for intelligence at the CIA at the time."

Stone nodded. "Did you ever find out where she went?"

"Yes, but not until after the election. The letter was from a man named Ed Rawls. Does that ring a bell?"

"Of course — a CIA mole for the Russians. He went to prison for it, and you later pardoned him."

"Right. At that time he was in the Atlanta federal prison. Kate had been responsible for exposing him, and she went to see him."

"Why?"

"Because he alluded to Joe Adams's illness in the letter."

Stone sat up straight. "But you had only learned about it that morning, right? And you and Kate were supposed to be the only ones who knew."

"Right again. You can see why she went to see him."

"I guess I can. How the hell could somebody in a federal prison know about this almost as soon as you did?"

"We never learned how he knew, but Ed was a brilliant intelligence agent, and he knew an awful lot of people, even if most of them weren't speaking to him anymore."

"I guess not. Why did he want to see Kate?"

"Because he wanted a presidential pardon, and he figured that if he helped get me elected, I might give him one."

"That must have seemed pretty breathtaking."

"It certainly took mine away when I finally heard about it. So, let's skip ahead a few months: I got the nomination, largely because Joe Adams called in some favors that helped us swing the California delegation at the last moment."

"I remember. I was at the convention, and it was a squeaker."

"Right. I was losing the battle for the nomination because I had sworn to accept the recommendations of a study committee on whether to close a huge base in California. George Kiel had made the same pledge, but he told a lot of California delegates that he would renege on that promise if elected, and keep the base open. Joe managed to find out that the committee was going to recommend that the base remain open, so George's promise became meaningless."

"How'd Adams find out about the committee report?"

"Ed Rawls found out and told Joe."

"Did you know about this?"

"Not at the time. All I knew was that everybody, including myself, wanted me to take George's offer to run with him on the ticket — everybody but Joe Adams. He urged me to turn down George's offer and go for the nomination, but he wouldn't tell me why. I took his advice. Then word somehow got out that the base would not be closed. Most of George's delegates from California swung to me, and I got the nomination."

"And, in due course, the presidency."

"Right."

"All because of inside information from a traitor to his country?"

"Right, though I didn't know it for a long time."

"Wait a minute," Stone said. "A while after you were nominated, the President had a stroke and died a few days later."

"Correct."

"And the vice president, Joe Adams, became President."

"Correct again."

"But he had Alzheimer's? And you *knew* that?"

"I did. I had a very difficult time with the decision, but for a lot of reasons I kept my mouth shut, and Joe served out the term with distinction."

"I never heard any rumors."

"Few people did, because Ed Rawls had a hand in keeping Joe's secret from becoming public."

Stone sucked in a breath. "And when did you find out about that, Will?"

"Yesterday."

"Who told you?"

"Joe Adams."

3

Stone sat back in his seat. "I don't know if you knew this, but I know Ed Rawls from Islesboro, where my Maine house is. We sort of worked together in solving a series of murders on the island."

"I didn't know that," Will said, "but that could actually be helpful in all this."

"All what? Let's get back to your story."

"Did you know that Ed Rawls was Kate's mentor at the Agency?"

"I may have read that somewhere at the time she exposed him."

"They were very close, and she was devastated when she found out what he'd been doing."

"What, exactly, had Ed been doing?"

"He got caught in a honey trap — photographs and all — and the honey turned out to be a Soviet agent. He was near retirement, and the Soviets blackmailed him into giving them CIA secrets. Ed was smart enough not to give them anything damaging, but they kept a close rein on him, and one evening when two of our people who had become suspicious were following him, they rumbled his Soviet watchers, shots were exchanged, and our two people died. That, in the end, is what sent Ed to prison, even though he had no knowledge of either the Soviets or Americans following him. Except for that, he might never have been prosecuted. When I learned of the circumstances, it made it easier for me to pardon him."

"I understand. How does all this affect what's going on now?"

"While Ed was in prison he wrote an account of his years at the Agency, including the end of his career and how he surreptitiously helped Kate's campaign. Apparently, he held nothing back, and his revelations could be explosive."

"How explosive?"

"In the worst case, think nuclear. He named names — government officials, military commanders, top journalists, senators and congressmen on both sides of the aisle, Agency personnel — and he related everything in intricate detail and backed it up with documentation."

"How'd he do that in prison?"

"He wrote the book from memory and hid the manuscript on a computer disc in the prison library, where he worked. Then, after he was pardoned, he went back to his retreat in Maine, where he had cached thousands of documents, and finished it there."

"I guess it wasn't published, or I would have heard about it," Stone said. "What happened to his work?"

"He gave the manuscript and all the backup documents to Joe Adams on computer discs."

"And what did Joe do with it?"

"Nothing. He still has it."

"Is he threatening to publish it?"

"Certainly not. Joe's Alzheimer's has progressed slowly, and I'm told by Sue, his wife, that he still has lucid intervals — hours or even days. During one of those, he told Sue he wants to give Ed's documents to me, and Sue wants them out of the house."

"Why you?"

"Joe appears to believe that some of Ed's revelations might hurt my legacy — or worse, damage Kate's chances of reelection. I'm not worried about my legacy, but Kate needs a second term to finish what she started, and that's very important to both of us."

"And how did you hear about all this?"

"Sue got a message to me to get in touch with Joe, but carefully. I used someone else's cell phone to make the call. That remains my only connection with Joe since he left office, and I want to keep it that way."

"What do you want me to do, Will?"

"I want you to visit Joe and Sue, accept the package from them, and hang on to it until I let you know different. That could be after Kate is out of office, one way or the other. I can't send a staffer for it or anyone the press might pay attention to."

"All right, I'd be happy to do that for you. Where does Joe live?"

"He's at his Santa Fe home, half an hour's drive from where we sit. He moves among his three homes seasonally. As a former President, he has access to government business jets." Will handed him a card with an address on it. "He's high up on the road to the Santa Fe ski area."

"When shall I do this?"

"Tonight. Stay at the party until we leave for the opera, then go to Joe's house. I'll meet you on the south side of the opera parking lot at, say, midnight. I'll be in this car. I won't be able to wait long — Air Force One will be on the ramp and ready to go."

"All right."

"You've met Joe, haven't you?"

"At the convention where Kate was nominated I sat in a skybox belonging to Strategic Services, and Joe and Sue were there, too. As I recall, Joe and I drank some bourbon. Sue, too."

"They both remember you fondly, and agreed to have you pick up the package. They'll be expecting you."

"Can you see that somebody takes Holly back to my house after the opera?"

"Of course."

Stone scribbled the address on the back of his business card and gave it to Will. "I'd better get inside and speak to Holly."

"She can ride to the opera with Kate and me and sit in our box, and an agent will take her home afterward." Will shook his hand. "Thank you, Stone. You're our good friend, and I don't know who else I could have entrusted this job to."

Stone got out of the car, pocketed Joe Adams's address, and was escorted to the front door of the house and admitted by an agent. He saw Kate Lee on one side of the room and Holly on the other. He went to the President first.

She greeted him with a hug and a kiss and whispered in his ear, "Thank you so much, Stone. Will and I both appreciate it. Is there anything I can do for you?"

"Be nice to Holly tonight," he said, laughing. "She's miserable from being shut out of the White House."

"I will be nice to her, but remember, it's for her own good, and yours. She needs the break, and you need to keep her . . . entertained."

"I will take it as a sacred duty," Stone said, then moved on so she could greet others. He went and found Holly leaning on the bar.

"Don't ask how many I've had," Holly said. "What was that all about with Will?"

"I'll tell you later," he said. "You're going to ride to the opera with the Lees and sit in their box. While you're doing that, I have to run an errand, and I'll see you back at the house. Will Lee will send you home with an agent."

"So, at least I'll have a date. Shall I ask him in?"

"Let's just say that, when I get home, I will fulfill any duties he might have dreamed of."

"All right," Holly said, "and I won't have my third drink. You got here just in time."

4

Stone set the Adams address into his GPS and followed instructions to the road up to the Santa Fe Ski Basin. As he ascended his ears began to pop, then, half an hour later, nearing the twelve-thousand-foot elevation, he saw the road sign and turned left.

He followed the unpopulated lane to an open gate at its end, and as he drove through it the front of the house was suddenly floodlit. A man in a suit appeared and tapped on his window. "May I see some ID, please?"

Stone showed him both his driver's and pilot's licenses.

"This way, Mr. Barrington." He opened the car door, led Stone to the front door, and opened it for him. "Mrs. Adams is waiting for you in the library, to your right."

Stone rapped on the door, and a woman's voice invited him in.

"Hello, Stone," Sue Adams said, rising

from a wing chair before the fireplace and greeting him with a handshake and a kiss. "Thank you so much for helping us."

"I'm happy to do whatever I can," Stone replied, taking the chair she indicated.

The library doors opened, and Joe Adams rode in on an electric scooter. "Stone!" he cried. "It's so good to see you!" The two men shook hands, and Joe motioned him to sit again. "We really appreciate your taking this thing off our hands."

"I'm glad to help, Mr. President," Stone said.

"It's still Joe. I fondly remember our little party in the skybox at the convention," Joe said. "I think I may still have a hangover."

"That was a great evening," Stone replied.

"Stone," Sue said, "are you right- or left-handed?"

"I'm right-handed," Stone replied.

She reached behind her chair and brought out a thick briefcase, then got up, walked around Stone, and snapped a handcuff shut on his left wrist.

Stone had never been handcuffed to anything before, and he was uncomfortable with it.

"Don't worry," Sue said, "Will has the key."

"David, can you stay for a drink?" Joe asked.

It took Stone a moment to realize that he was being addressed.

"I'm afraid I have a date with Will," Stone said, "and if he has the key to the handcuff, I don't want to be late." He stood up and shook hands with both of them.

"You take care of yourself, Tom," Joe called as Stone was escorted out by the agent. Stone gave a little wave and followed the man to his car. It cost him some effort to get the case into the car next to his left leg, but he discovered the chain was long enough to allow him to use his left hand on the wheel. He started the car, turned around, and retraced his route to the main road, then turned right and started the descent to Santa Fe.

He had gone perhaps three miles when suddenly a flying boulder appeared in his path and bounced across the road. Before he could recover from that, his car ran into a field of smaller rocks in his way, and he heard two loud noises and felt heavy jolts. The car came to a stop, and Stone got out.

There was still patchy snow at this elevation, and the moon was reflected off it enough to allow him to see that two of his tires had been destroyed, and the front rim was bent. He got the keys out of the car and opened the trunk. One spare.

Stone got out his iPhone and switched it on: no service, and his battery was low. He considered his options. He could wait around for a car that might not arrive before dawn; he could walk back up the steep road to the Adams house, but he didn't relish carrying the heavy case that far; or he could walk downhill several miles to Santa Fe. It was cold up here, and he chose to wait in the car for someone to pass. He had three-quarters of a tank of fuel, so he started the car and turned up the temperature. He switched on the satellite radio, found some jazz, and made himself as comfortable as he could. Warmth flooded into the car. He checked the time: 10:35 PM. He switched on the emergency flashers, then he nodded and dozed.

He was awakened by the slamming of a vehicle door and a man rapping on the passenger window. "Hello?"

Stone checked the clock: 12:10 AM. He pressed the down button for the window. "Hello, thanks for stopping. I'm afraid I've run into a rock slide and ruined two tires, and I have only one spare."

"Well, my truck spare will be too big for

your car. Can I give you a lift into town?"

"Thank you, yes." Stone got out and got into the passenger side of the heavy pickup. He noticed a National Forest Service sticker on the door. "I'm Stone Barrington," he said.

The man offered his hand. "I'm Tim Heard, the ranger up here. Lucky for you I worked late tonight to finish up my monthly report." He started the truck. "Where can I drop you?"

"Would it be inconvenient for you to leave me at the Santa Fe opera house?"

"I guess I can do that." He nodded at the case in Stone's lap. "What you got there?"

"I'm a jewelry salesman, and I've just made a house call. My boss makes me handcuff myself to it," Stone replied.

The man didn't speak again for the half hour it took them to get to the opera. "There you go," he said finally. "Looks like everybody's gone home."

"There's someone expecting me," Stone said. He thanked the ranger and got out and waved him off. He walked into the parking lot and halfway across it before it dawned on him that it was empty of vehicles. "Shit!" he hollered. He tried his cell phone: dead. He'd have to walk home, but it wasn't much more than a mile. He got started.

■ ■ ■ ■

Forty minutes later he let himself in his front gate and trudged up the driveway to the house. He walked up the front steps and turned toward the front door. Holly was huddled on the doormat, her shawl wrapped around her.

"It's about fucking time," she said, struggling to her feet. "I'm freezing out here, and you didn't give me a key."

"I'm so sorry, Holly. I had an accident on the mountain road and ruined two tires. It was a long time before a forest ranger came by and gave me a lift to the opera, then I had to walk home from there." He got out his key, opened the front door, and they walked into the warm hallway and to the master suite. He poured them both a neat Knob Creek. "This'll warm us up." They both tossed it down. He held up his left hand. "Did Will give you the key for this?"

"Not that I recall," she said. "Hold on, that's an Agency strong case you've got there. It's made out of layers of Kevlar, carbon fiber, lead, and titanium, and it's equipped with a handy incendiary explosive device inside that will detonate if you mess with it. It will blow you to pieces and set

32

fire to whatever's left."

"Swell," Stone said. "Now I'd *really* like to get this cuff off, but we've no key and no bolt cutters."

"Well, there's a quick way out of this," she said. "I can amputate your hand, and it will come right off. Hang on, I'll see if I can find a sharp knife."

5

Stone opened his eyes slowly. Sunlight was streaming through the bedroom window, backlighting an empty Knob Creek bottle. He lifted his head, then let it fall back to the pillow, and his stomach reminded him that he had not eaten last night.

He found the bed's remote control and sat himself up. Holly was sleeping soundly beside him. He found that he was naked from the waist down but still wearing his suit jacket and shirt — because he was still handcuffed to the strong case.

Then he noticed a small envelope leaning against the lamp on his bedside table; his name was written on it. As he opened it he noted the address on the flap: The White House, Washington, D.C. He read the note inside:

Stone,

I don't know what happened to you. We tried calling repeatedly, and the Adamses' Secret Service agent said you had been there and gone. I sent an agent looking for you, and he found your car abandoned on the mountain road with two bad tires. I guess that explains why you didn't turn up. Enclosed is what you need. Hang on to that package, as we discussed. Hope you made it home all right.

If you need to reach me, call the White House switchboard and ask for extension 2002. They won't ask any questions. You'll hear a beep and leave a message.

Will

Stone shook the envelope and a small key fell into his hand. He inserted it into the cuff, and it opened. Relief washed over him. He got up, retrieved his trousers, and went into his bath and dressing room; he hung up his suit, threw the shirt and his underwear into a hamper, brushed his teeth, shaved and showered, then he found a robe and his slippers and went to check on Holly. She still slept soundly. He handcuffed her left wrist to the strong case and put the key into his robe pocket.

35

He went into the kitchen and checked the refrigerator. He took out eggs, bacon, cheese, and a packet of Wolferman's sourdough English muffins. Gala had remembered his favorites.

He made coffee, and while it brewed, he microwaved the bacon, put the sliced muffin into the toaster oven, and turned to the eggs. He melted a chunk of butter and grated some cheese into it as it melted in a small pan, then he whipped the eggs and scrambled them continuously on a low temperature. When they were soft but not runny, he put everything on two small plates, poured the coffee into a thermos carafe, and took everything on a tray into the bedroom.

Holly was awake, but barely. "Who are you and what are you doing in my bedroom?" she asked.

He set the tray on the bed. "Have some breakfast, and it will all come back to you."

Not until she reached for the plate did she notice the handcuff on her wrist. "Ah, I see you found Will's note."

"I did. A pity it wasn't there last night. I might have slept better."

"I somehow forgot to give it to you, and then I didn't want to wake you." She finished breakfast without mentioning the strong case at her side, then accepted a cup of coffee and drank it. "Okay," she said finally, "where's the key?"

"What key?"

"The one in Will's note, the one you used to unlock this." She held up her cuffed hand.

"Oh, *that* key."

"Yes."

"I ate it."

"What?"

"Well, not exactly ate, just swallowed. I'm afraid you'll have to wait a few hours until . . . well, you know."

"I have to pee," she said, standing up and realizing the case would have to go with her. "When I come back I'm going to have a Glock in my free hand."

Stone removed the tray, stretched out on the bed, and switched on the TV, looking for *Morning Joe.* Then he realized that the program would have aired at four AM, local time. He went through the schedule and marked his usual morning programs for recording on the DVR, then switched to CNN.

Holly came back. "I forgot my gun," she said.

"You'd get better results with a laxative."

She got into bed with the case. "Let me

put this as plainly as I can. If you don't unlock this handcuff immediately, I'm going to make it my business to see that your life is entirely miserable for the next two weeks. Oops, make that three — Kate extended my little holiday for a week last night, and she took some pleasure in doing it, so I'm not in the best of moods. You might keep that in mind."

Stone felt his belly. "Excuse me," he said. He went into his bathroom, took the key from his robe pocket, flushed the toilet, and went back into the bedroom. "Success!" he cried, holding up the key.

She held out her hand. "Give."

Instead, he unlocked it for her. "There," he said. "I'm glad you got to see how that felt."

"All right, what happened last night?"

"Rock slide, collision with rocks, two ruined tires. After midnight a forest ranger came along in a truck and took me to the opera house. No one there, of course, and my phone was dead, so I had to walk home." He got up and plugged in his phone to recharge.

"Poor baby," she said, patting his hand.

"You could have given me the key last night."

"I didn't have the key, just an envelope,

which was always where you found it this morning."

"You might have mentioned it."

"I didn't know what was inside."

"You could have guessed."

"I was too cold to guess, after spending two hours huddled on your doormat."

"I hope you understand that I am innocent of all blame."

"You could have given me the house key."

"I'm sorry, I didn't foresee that you would need it. Anyway, you could have asked."

"All right, enough of this," she said. "What are we going to do today?"

"First, I'm going to secure this," he said, picking up the strong case. "Then we'll see." He took the case into the study, where he knew Gala had a safe, and he thought he knew the code. It worked, but the case was too large to fit into it. He went back into the bedroom.

"It wouldn't fit in the safe, right?"

"Right." He tried to get it under the bed, but the base that held the mechanism prevented that.

"Under the bed? That's the best you've got?"

"I'm open to suggestions," he said.

"Freezer?"

"Too obvious and the case is too big."

"Oven?"

"The same."

"Put it in the pool or the hot tub."

"Is it waterproof?"

"I don't know."

"You're an intelligence officer, you're supposed to be more devious than that."

"I really don't know if it's waterproof."

"I mean, devious about where to hide it."

"Oh, why don't we just lock it in the trunk of the car and take it with us until we can buy a bigger safe?"

"That's a thought, except we don't have a car. Will had the Secret Service return it, I suppose."

"Okay, what are we going to do today?"

"We're going to buy a car and a safe." Stone called the American Express concierge and ordered up a car and a driver. He hung up and checked his watch. "You've got forty-five minutes to get beautiful."

6

They put the strong case into the trunk and got into the large SUV.

"Good morning," said the driver. "I'm Dan Rivers. I see you've got me booked for four hours."

"That is correct, Dan," Stone said. "We have some shopping to do. Can you take us to the Porsche dealer?"

"In Albuquerque? Sure, it's an hour's drive."

"No Porsche dealer here?"

"Nope."

"Bentley?"

"Nope."

"Mercedes?"

"That we have."

Fifteen minutes later they pulled up to the showroom. Stone and Holly got out and peered through the glass. Three cars, one C class and two E classes. They walked inside.

A salesman ambled over. "Good morning.

Can I show you something?"

"Do you have anything larger than this?" Stone asked.

"Not in stock, but I can get you just about anything in a matter of days."

"We need something immediately," Stone said. Then he saw something interesting parked outside. "Is that for sale?"

"The Porsche Cayenne Turbo? It certainly is."

"Let's have a look at it." Stone walked outside and around the car; it needed washing.

"This," the salesman said, "is a deal. I took it in trade yesterday for an S550. The guy's wife didn't want an SUV. It's less than a year old and has under three thousand miles on it."

"Let's drive it," Stone said.

"I'll go get the key."

"I've got one of these," Holly said. "It's a sensational car. Zero to sixty in four-point-three seconds — nearly as fast as the 911 sports car."

The salesman returned with the key. "Just put this in your pocket — you don't need the key to start it. Ignition switch is on the left, foot on the brake and turn it."

Stone got in, followed instructions, and the engine leaped to life. Five minutes later they were tearing down a back road, taking corners fast. They returned to the dealership. "I had my heart set on an S550," he said.

"Let's go pick some options, then give me a week or ten days."

"How much for the Cayenne?"

The man mentioned a number.

Stone mentioned a lower one.

"Is this cash or financed?"

"Cash."

The salesman mentioned another number.

"Done. How long to get it cleaned up?"

"Give me an hour," the salesman said.

Stone went into the dealership, was introduced to an accountant, signed the papers, and wrote them a check.

"We'll have to clear this," the man said.

"I'll be back in an hour. Get it cleared."

They went back to their car and driver. "Give me a second," Stone said. He got out his iPhone and Googled safes in Santa Fe, then gave the driver an address.

"Something I should mention," the driver said as he pulled out of the dealership.

"What's that?"

"Do you have some personal security or something?"

"Why do you ask?"

"Because we're being followed — two

cars, changing places every block or two."

"What kind of cars?"

"A black one and a silver one, both Japanese, I think. I can't tell the brands apart."

"Have you had any experience at being followed?"

"I'm a retired police detective, I've had more experience following than being followed."

Stone didn't look back. "Is there a mirror on the passenger sun visor?"

The driver turned it down; the mirror was there.

Stone swapped places with Holly and kept his eyes on the mirror. "They're both Toyotas," he said after a couple of minutes.

"If you say so."

"Think you can lose them before we reach our destination?"

"I believe I might be able to do that." He turned into a parking lot, then into an alley behind a row of stores, then into the next street over. "They caught a light," he said, making another turn, "and we're a block from your destination."

"Drop us there, then drive around for a while, until they figure out we're no longer with you. We'll get a cab."

The driver let them out in an alley next to the safe store. Stone tipped the driver gener-

44

ously and they went in the back way.

"Oh, shit, the strong case!" Holly said, and ran out the door. She came back a moment later with the case. "He remembered."

A salesman approached and started showing them safes. "I like the tall, skinny one," Stone said.

"Good choice. It will take up less than half a closet."

"Stone set the strong case inside it, and it fit, with room to spare. "Can you deliver it to Tesuque this afternoon?"

"We close at five — say, five-thirty, six o'clock?"

Stone gave him the address, directions, and a credit card. "Oh," he said, "can you call a cab for us? Going to the Mercedes dealership."

"Certainly."

The Cayenne sat out front, gleaming, and the salesman came outside. "Here's your paperwork and spare key," he said, "including the original window sticker with the options list. It's loaded to the gills."

Stone went over the list. Umber, with cognac and espresso leather; and, seemingly, every possible option.

"We're giving you a year's subscription to the satellite radio and a tank of gas."

Stone shook the man's hand, then he put the case into the trunk and pulled the cover over it, got into the car and drove away.

"You're going to love it," Holly said.

"Let's get some lunch. Santacafé okay?"

"You're my guide, I'll trust you."

They drove to the restaurant and were given a table in the garden, where Stone could keep an eye on his new car and its contents. They ordered margaritas and some lunch.

"Who do you think was following you?"

"I don't know," Stone said, "but nobody was following me yesterday or the day before or last week, and the only thing that's changed since then is the presence of that strong case."

"Uh-oh," Holly replied.

7

They were about to have a drink when the doorbell rang, and Stone found a van backed up to his front door. The salesman and another man got the safe onto a dolly and wheeled it down to where Stone stood before a double-doored hall closet.

"Right here," Stone said.

"Looks good," the salesman said. The two men rolled the safe into the closet. "Right about here?" The tall, thin safe took up only a quarter of the closet.

"That's fine."

They muscled it off the dolly, and the man tapped in a code and opened the door. "We should fix it to the floor with lug bolts," he said.

Stone left them to drill from inside the safe, then wrench the lug bolts through the flagstone floor and into the concrete pad.

"There you go," the salesman said. "Let me set up the lock for a code." He tapped a long number into the keypad and closed the door. "Here's how it goes," he said. "You tap in a six-digit code, then press pound, then tap in the code again. If you make a mistake you'll get a red light, so you'll have to start over. If you don't make a mistake, you'll get a green light, then just turn the wheel to the left to lock the safe. After that, your code will open it."

Stone followed the man's instructions, then locked the safe, then reopened it with his code. He thanked the men, handed them a fifty for a beer on him, and saw them to the door. He came back, opened the safe, stowed the strong case inside it, closed the door, and turned the wheel. "Safe at last," he said. "Let's have a drink." Holly was nowhere to be seen. He heard a whining noise from the kitchen; he went there and found her mincing something in a Cuisinart.

"What's that?"

"Ginger."

"What for?"

"I'm going to make you a Southern Baptist."

"Too late, I'm already an Episcopalian, nominally."

"A Southern Baptist is also a cocktail — ginger juice, sugar, and rye whiskey."

"Sounds awful."

She poured the ingredients into a cocktail shaker, shook it until it was too cold to hold, then filled two martini glasses and handed one to Stone. "Taste it."

Stone did. "That's wonderful," he said.

Holly brought her own glass to a sofa in front of the fireplace, and Stone lit the fire.

"Why are you an Episcopalian?" Holly asked.

"Two reasons. First, my mother was, and she took me to church. My father, in addition to being a communist, was a confirmed atheist."

"What's the other reason?"

"The Episcopalian motto — 'Almost everything in moderation.' "

She laughed. "It's good to have an out, huh?"

"It's absolutely essential. Do you have a religion?"

"I'm a Southern Baptist."

"The cocktail or the church?"

"I'm an army brat. Everybody was a Southern Baptist. There are no outs in the faith, you just have to make your own."

"This is a little on the spicy side," he said, holding up the golden liquid and inspecting it.

"It's the fresh ginger."

"Ah. I've never had a drink with ginger in it."

"I've never seen you drink anything but Knob Creek and vodka gimlets."

"They have sufficed for lo, these many years," Stone said. "Until now. I think I'll have to add the Southern Baptist to my repertoire."

Stone's cell phone rang. "Hello?"

"I expect you can tell who this is without mentioning any names," Will Lee said.

"I believe I can do that. Sorry about disappearing."

"We understood when they found your car. It's safely back with the rental people. Well, maybe not safely."

"That's the thing about large rocks in the road. I found what's-her-name freezing on my doorstep."

"I'm sorry about that. The agent must have thought she'd have a key."

"She took a while to forgive me, but eventually . . ."

"I'm glad. Listen, I've had some troubling news. This morning, our friend up the mountain was left alone in his back garden for a few minutes, and while he was there, a man approached and the two of them had a conversation. They were spotted by an agent from upstairs, but by the time the man reached our friend, the visitor had departed, and since there were only two men on duty, they didn't have the manpower to organize a search."

"Our friend wasn't harmed, I hope."

"No, not at all. What is troubling is that our friend apparently believed he had been conversing with you."

"I haven't been back up there."

"I figured."

"Does anyone have any idea who the visitor was?"

"No, none at all."

"What did he and our friend discuss?"

"According to him, they discussed your visit last night and what transpired at that time. Where is the item?"

"I bought a large safe, and it's safely locked inside. The safe is bolted to the concrete and stone floor."

"That's good. Have you had any unexpected attention from anyone?"

"This morning we left the house to go into town to buy a car and the safe. Our driver, who was a former cop, picked up on two cars, probably rental Toyotas, following us."

"Do they know where you live?"

"I'm not sure. The phone isn't listed in my name here yet, and we didn't notice the two Toyotas until we were downtown, so I don't think they followed us from the house. Certainly, they didn't follow us back, since our driver had lost them, and we returned home in my new car."

"How long do you intend to remain there?"

"We've no definite plans."

"If you receive any further unwanted attention, I think you should relocate."

"Relocate where?"

"Anywhere but there."

"Is there a number where I can reach you?"

"No, I'm on someone else's cell phone. If you want to get in touch, call the White House switchboard and leave a message, and I'll call your cell number on a secure line."

"All right."

"Are you armed?"

"There's always something in my bag, since I don't have to bother with airport searches."

"Perhaps you should keep it within reach."

"Do you think someone might get rough for the item?"

"I've no idea, since I don't know who's interested. I'm just erring on the cautious side. I wouldn't want anything to happen to you on my account. Neither would the lady of the house."

"I'm grateful for your concern, but remember, I have an ace bodyguard here."

Will laughed. "That's right, you do, don't you? Give her my love and tell her to enjoy her extra week off."

"I'll make a point of it."

Will hung up.

"What's going on?" Holly asked.

"Someone got to Joe for a few minutes' conversation, and Joe apparently thought the man was me."

"And you think that's why we were followed today?"

"Will seems to think so, but he has no idea who they might be."

She kissed him. "Don't worry, I'll protect you."

8

They grilled some steaks for dinner and found a good cabernet in the wine closet. "Gala did a great job of stocking up for us," Stone said, "but we're going to have to eventually do some grocery shopping."

"I won't mind that," Holly said. "It's one of those things I never have time to do in Washington. I usually eat in the White House Mess."

"So, you're going to cook?"

"I love cooking, and I never get the chance."

"Then you've come to the right place."

Holly did the dishes while Stone walked around the house making sure all the doors were locked and that the front gate was closed. "There are a hell of a lot of doors in this house," he said when he returned. "I think I'm going to get Mike Freeman's people from Strategic Services to survey the security system and maybe put in some cameras. I'll call him in the morning."

They turned out all the many lights, then repaired to the master suite, where a large TV rose from the floor when the remote control was used. They got into bed and found a movie, but it didn't last long. Soon they were making love, and when they were exhausted they turned off the TV and fell asleep.

In the wee hours, Stone came half awake. There was a distant rumble coming from somewhere and there was a light on outside that filtered into the bedroom. He got out of bed, found his slippers with his toes, and went to the door that opened onto the master suite portal. He unlocked it and went outside. The hot tub, set into the ground a few feet away, was on, and so were its underwater lights. He found a switch on the instrument panel and turned it off, then pulled the cover over it. He went back to the door and found that it had locked behind him.

"Well, shit!" he muttered to himself. He knocked on the door to summon Holly, but got no response. He found a stone and rapped hard on the glass with that. Finally, a sleepy Holly got the door open.

"What happened?"

"The hot tub came on — it must be on a

55

timer. I went out to turn it off, and the door locked behind me."

"What time is it?"

"Around two o'clock, I think." He secured the door again.

"Who would set a hot tub to come on in the middle of the night?"

"Good question. I'll look into it tomorrow."

They got back to sleep, until they were wakened by bright sunlight streaming into the room. Stone got up and closed the blinds, but they were both awake now.

"It's six o'clock," Holly said. "That makes it eight o'clock where my stomach lives. I'll make breakfast."

She was back in half an hour with breakfast and a *New York Times.*"

"Where'd you get that?" Stone asked.

"It was on the kitchen doorstep. Apparently, you're a subscriber."

Stone turned on his recording of *Morning Joe.* Then, at seven o'clock — nine in New York — he called Mike Freeman.

"Where are you?" Mike asked.

"In Santa Fe, where I've just bought a house, and I need the security system checked out and, if necessary, beefed up."

"Hang on." He came back after a minute or so. "What's your address?"

Stone gave it to him.

"I've got a team in Albuquerque. They'll be there before noon, your time."

"I'll look forward to seeing them."

"What created the urge for more security?"

"Paranoia. See you, Mike." Stone hung up. "There'll be people here later this morning."

Then a strange woman's voice called out, "Hello?"

"Who is it?" Stone shouted.

"It's Maria." Maria was Gala's housekeeper.

"Come in, Maria."

A middle-aged woman wearing an apron came into the bedroom.

"I'm very glad to see you," Stone said.

"Miss Wilde said you might need me."

"I certainly do. You go right ahead and do whatever you think needs doing."

"Yes, Mr. Barrington."

"Oh, and this is Ms. Barker."

Holly gave her a wave.

"You already ate breakfast?"

"I didn't know you were coming," Holly said.

"Tomorrow I'll have your breakfast ready. Seven o'clock?"

"That's fine," Stone said, and she went on

57

her way.

"I wonder what other services we have here," Stone said.

A little after eleven a large green van pulled into Stone's drive and two men knocked on the door.

Stone opened it. "Strategic Services?"

"Mr. Barrington?"

"Come right in."

"Mr. Freeman said you need a survey."

"There it is," Stone said, waving an arm. "Check it out."

An hour later, the men came into the study, where Stone was working on the *Times* crossword. "What did you find?"

"You've got a pretty good system here," the man said. "I can recommend some additions, though."

"Shoot."

"I think you need some cameras around the place, about a dozen."

"Good idea. Go ahead."

"Also, your door locks are already wired, but I can put an app on your iPhone that will let you lock them all at once."

"Another good idea. Can you do the same with the lights?"

"May I see your iPhone?"

Stone handed it to him. He switched it on and began tapping things into it. "You've got a Lutron system installed here. I can download the app, and you can turn all the lights on and off at once. You also have a built-in Sonos sound system. I can set that up for you, too. Give me a password."

Stone gave it to him and went back to his crossword.

Late that afternoon the men found him again. He showed Stone two apps on his iPhone. "One is for the Sonos system and the other for the outside cameras." He sat down and gave Stone a tutorial on both systems. Holly came into the room in time to hear it all.

"You also have an intercom to the gate and to the front door, and a camera at both." He showed them how to answer both and how to operate the gate from the phone. He held up a plastic bag of keys. "I've rekeyed all your locks and made you some spares, too."

"Wonderful, we had only one key."

"Then throw that one away. There, I think you're all fixed," he said. "Anything else I can do?"

"Not a thing," Stone said.

"Oh, I put an alarm on your safe. If anybody messes with it, it will tell you on your phone. And all this stuff will work anywhere in the world where there's Internet access."

Stone thanked him, gave him money for drinks, and the men left.

"You feel safe and secure now?" Holly asked.

"What with all this gear and you here to protect me, I feel just fine," he said. "Here's a key to everything for you."

Holly pocketed the key. "Dinner in an hour." She kissed him and went back to the kitchen.

Stone got out his iPhone, turned on the sound system, found some jazz, and went back to his crossword.

9

In the dead of night, when they were sound asleep, Stone was wakened by a noise. He couldn't figure out what he'd heard, then it came again: a chime. Then he noticed that his iPhone was lit up and the word "Safe" was flashing on the screen.

Stone picked up the phone, went to the Lutron app, and hit the switch for "all on." Lights in every room came on. He opened his bedside drawer and took out his little custom .45, racked the slide, put the safety on, and got out of bed.

He found his slippers and padded out of the bedroom into the bigger rooms and down the hall where the safe was in a closet. One of the double doors was open. He looked inside and found the safe intact, then he began a search of the house, ending up back at the safe closet. He used his code to open the safe and found the strong case where he'd left it, undisturbed. He closed the safe and then, as he was closing the closet doors, he felt a cool breeze on his cheek.

He followed it back to its source: a circle had been cut out of a windowpane, and that window was now unlocked. He looked through the hole and saw the circle of glass lying on the ground near the bottom of the window. Then he checked the alarm system on his iPhone and found he had forgotten to turn it on.

He went back to the bedroom and found Holly sitting up in bed, wide-eyed. "What's wrong?" she asked.

"You distracted me last night and I forgot to set the alarm system. Somebody got in and had a go at the safe, but he didn't get anywhere because the safe alarm went off and I went to check on it. I found a window-pane cut out and the window unlocked. I'll replace the pane in the morning."

"And you're blaming me for this?"

"Certainly — you distracted me." He got into bed. "Would you like to distract me again?"

"Is the alarm system set now?"

"It is."

"So we can expect not to be interrupted?"

"We can."

She shucked off her nightgown. "Then

what are you waiting for?"

Stone did not wait.

Sometime after dawn the doorbell rang, and Stone picked up the phone to answer it. Who the hell would be calling at six AM? "Hello, who's there?"

"It's Maria," she said. "My key doesn't work."

Stone got up, let her in, and gave her a new key. "I'm sorry about that, Maria, all the locks were rekeyed yesterday." He gave her the new alarm code. "Now you're all set." He went back to bed, then, at the stroke of seven, Maria came in with breakfast and left them to it.

They were on coffee when Holly said, "What do you think is in the strong case?"

"I don't know," Stone said. "It all has something to do with Ed Rawls. Remember him?"

"How could I forget? We saw him at Dark Harbor a while back. I got kidnapped that summer, remember?"

"That's right, I'd forgotten you were there."

"Thanks a lot."

"I mean, I'd forgotten you met Rawls."

"Him and his bunch of Old Farts, as I recall they named themselves. All old

Agency hands, retired. What would Rawls have to do with the strong case?"

"Will thinks it's some sort of dirt that might hurt Kate's run for reelection, and it may have come from Rawls."

"How could a disgraced CIA officer have something on Kate?"

"I don't think he has anything against Kate; he was her mentor when she was at the Agency."

"And she got him sent to prison. That could have annoyed him and made him less protective of her."

"If he'd wanted to hurt her he could have done it when she ran the first time."

"Well, there is that."

"Also, Will pardoned him."

"I'd heard that, but I didn't believe it. Why would Will do that?"

"Ed was very helpful to Will when he ran the first time. He kept coming up with stories of planned attacks on his campaign, and Will was able to head off some of them."

"Wasn't Rawls in a federal prison at the time?"

"He was, which made his help very surprising. Ed seemed to know everybody of any importance — politicians, journalists, et cetera."

"Other Agency officers, too," Holly offered.

"Were there people at the Agency who would hold grudges against Kate?"

"She was a very popular director, when she got the job, but then there were the people who wanted the job and didn't get it. They and the people they might have promoted didn't like her much."

"Who would have been the most important one on that list?"

"Hugh English. He was director of operations, ran the clandestine side. Everybody expected him to get the job."

"But he reckoned without Will Lee."

"Right, he wouldn't have expected Will to appoint his wife. I mean, he needed the acquiescence of Congress to get that done."

"Must have been a real shock to her competitors."

"You bet your sweet ass. I expect they voted Republican that year, to a man."

"Where is this Hugh English now? Do you know?"

"He's teaching at a small liberal arts college somewhere in New England — Connecticut, maybe."

"Would he be in touch with people in his old circle at the Agency?"

"Of course. The Agency is a very select

club, and when you leave it you find yourself among people who don't know as much as you do. The people who know are your old colleagues, and they tend to stick together. Look at Ed and his Old Farts."

"Would English and his old crowd tend to cluster, like Ed and his bunch?"

"They tend to find each other jobs — teaching at colleges or corporate consulting — often with defense contractors."

"Is that considered ethical?"

"Sure, as long as they aren't using their knowledge of the Agency's workings to make money."

"Then what do they do for defense contractors?"

"They use their knowledge of the Agency's workings to make money."

"Oh, well, I guess that's all right then."

"There's a fine line between giving advice based on what you know about the Agency and giving away operational secrets."

Stone picked up his iPhone and looked up a number and dialed it.

"Who are you calling?"

"Ed Rawls."

10

Stone put the phone on speaker so Holly could hear the conversation. The phone rang once, then went straight to voice mail.

"You have reached the person you were calling," Ed Rawls's gruff voice said. "At the tone, don't bother leaving a message because he's not going to call you back." The beep came. "Ed, it's Stone Barrington. Break your rule and call me." He left his cell number and hung up.

"Sounds like Ed's gotten a little antisocial," Holly said.

"I wonder why? I always thought of him as being on the gregarious side."

Stone looked up another number.

"Who are you calling now?"

"Jimmy Hotchkiss, who runs the Dark Harbor Store. Jimmy knows everything about everybody on the island."

Stone pressed the speaker button again. This time the phone was answered on the first ring.

"Dark Harbor Store, this is Jimmy."

"Hey, Jimmy, it's Stone Barrington. How you doing?"

"Well, we had quite a winter — ninety inches of snow on the island, first one of those in a long time. How 'bout you, Stone?"

"I can't complain," Stone replied. "Well, I guess I could complain, but it wouldn't do any good."

"I know the feeling. What can I do you for?"

"Jimmy, I just tried to call Ed Rawls, and his voice mail message was not what you would call responsive."

Jimmy laughed. "It pretty much tells everybody to go to hell, doesn't it?"

"Pretty much. What's up with Ed?"

"Well, these days, he greets callers with a shotgun in his hand, that's what."

"How come?"

"Nobody knows for sure. He used to do his grocery shopping here. Now he calls in his order and we leave that and his newspapers in a plywood box he's built at his gate. The kid who delivers it has never seen him."

"Is he ill?"

"He hasn't had the doctor in, far as we know."

"Have you talked with anyone who's actually had a conversation with him?"

"Nope. I don't think anybody has. When you coming back to the island, Stone?"

"Maybe sooner than I'd planned."

"You better be careful with Ed. He hasn't fired at anybody yet, but he's waved that shotgun around a couple of times when people turned up at his gate by mistake."

"I'll keep that in mind. What about the Old Farts? Are they still around?"

"Ed's the last man standing. The others kicked off — one, two, three. Heart attacks, strokes, you know. Of course, the first one was murdered."

"I remember."

"Come see us when you get in."

"Thanks, Jimmy." They said goodbye and hung up.

"Sounds like old age and loneliness have made Ed become a little unhinged," Holly said.

"Possibly. Sounds to me like Ed is feeling threatened."

"Paranoia?"

"It's not paranoia if somebody's after you."

"So, are we going to abandon Santa Fe

for Maine?"

"Santa Fe is looking a little less hospitable than when we got here," Stone said. "That strong case is attracting too much attention."

"Are you sure it's not just paranoia?"

"We've been followed, and someone broke into the house last night. What else has to happen before *you* start to feel a little paranoia?"

"I guess that's enough," Holly said. "When do we leave?"

"Get packed," Stone said. "I have to repair that window, then we're out of here. You know what I wish we'd done?"

"What?"

"Brought Bob with us."

"You mean the killer Labrador retriever?"

"I mean the noisy dog."

Stone called Joan and informed her of his change of location.

"You sick of Santa Fe already?"

"No, I just have a hankering for Maine. Pack up Bob's things and ask Fred to meet me with him at the airport in Oxford, Connecticut." He looked at his wristwatch. "In about six hours. Also, please call Seth and Mary and tell them we'll be two for dinner this evening, then staying on for a while.

Ask Seth to call the airport in Rockland and get me a ride to Islesboro and ask them if they have hangar space for the Citation for a week or so." They went over some business for a few minutes, then he hung up. "I'd better go fix the window," he said.

They took off from Santa Fe with a stiff tailwind and made it to Oxford, Connecticut, in a little over three hours.

"Why here?" Holly asked as they taxied in to the FBO.

"Less hassle than in Teterboro, quicker in and out. Also, whoever has been interested in us could be tracking our flight on the Internet, so from here, we'll fly VFR and set the transponder to twelve hundred. If they're watching, they won't be able to distinguish us from a lot of smaller airplanes."

"But we'll have to stay under eighteen thousand feet."

"Right, but it's less than an hour to Rockland."

As they approached the ramp, Fred came out of the building with Bob on a leash. Bob went nuts when he saw the airplane.

Stone greeted them both and ordered enough fuel to get them to Rockland with reserves. They stowed Bob's bag with his food and toys, then took off for Rockland under Visual Flight Rules without filing a flight plan.

At Rockland, they put Stone's airplane into a hangar and, at his insistence, locked it. "If anybody should ask, I'm not here, and you haven't heard from me," he told them.

The three of them piled into a Cessna 182 and made the flight to the island of Islesboro in fifteen minutes, setting down on the fairly short landing strip. Seth was there to greet them in the 1938 Ford station wagon that belonged to the house.

"Can't say I'm surprised to see you," Seth said, shaking their hands. "Nothing you'd do could surprise me."

Another fifteen minutes and they were at the house. Seth took their bags upstairs.

"Anyone asking for me?" Stone asked when he came down.

"Yup, Jimmy did, when I went to the store."

"So by suppertime everybody will know I'm here."

"I expect so," Seth said. "That okay with you?"

"Oh, sure. There are no secrets around here. Any phone calls?"

"One. They hung up when I answered."

"Maybe that was Ed," Stone said to Holly.

"Or somebody else," she said darkly.

11

Dinner was the usual first-nighter: lobster bisque followed by lobster, shelled and tossed in butter.

"You wouldn't get this in Santa Fe," Stone said to Holly. "I'm sorry to have yanked you out of the town so quickly."

"Don't worry, I'm happy to be here."

Seth came in with the strong case. "This yours?" he asked, holding it up by the handcuff. "I found it in the car."

"Yes, I forgot that. Just leave it here by me," Stone said.

Seth, being a Mainer, liked to mind his own business and didn't ask about the handcuff, just set the thing down where he was asked to and left.

"What do you suppose Seth thinks about that?" Holly asked.

"He can think whatever he wants to," Stone said. "After all, nothing I do surprises him. He said so himself."

After dinner he went to the secret room maintained by his cousin Dick Stone, after whose murder Stone had come into his house. He unlocked it, revealing the small office. "The Agency computer is gone," Stone said.

"The Internet setup, too. Now you're just an ordinary civilian who has to supply his own Wi-Fi."

"Already supplied," Stone said. He opened Dick's safe and tucked the strong case inside, then he closed it and unlocked the compartment that held Dick's weapons. Gone were the fully automatic machine gun and the assault rifle. The riot gun and a couple of handguns were still there.

"They took whatever was on the Agency's inventory list," Holly said.

Stone handed her a 9mm semiautomatic pistol and a couple of loaded magazines. "So you won't feel naked," he said.

"Thank you."

"Nobody is coming in here," Stone said. "This house was built to Agency specs, remember?"

"I remember, and it gives me a warm feeling all over."

"I believe you said something about getting naked," Stone said, locking the secret room and straightening the picture that hung on the door.

"I believe it was you who mentioned naked, in reference to sidearms, but now that I think of it, I'm ready to get naked."

"Then let's get upstairs," Stone said, and on the way he armed the alarm system and checked the panel to be sure all the windows were secure.

The following morning, as they were finishing breakfast in bed, Stone's cell phone rang. The caller's number was blocked.

"You said to call you," Ed Rawls said. "What's up? Don't waste my time."

"I'm coming to see you this morning, Ed, and Holly Barker is coming with me, and I don't want a shotgun pointed at us. That concise enough for you?"

"Yep." Ed hung up.

"You think he's gone completely nuts?" Holly asked.

"Jimmy Hotchkiss said they had ninety inches of snow up here this winter. What sort of effect would that have on you if you were alone and couldn't see out the window for four or five months?"

"It would make me glad to see people," Holly said, "just like any normal human being."

"Ed was never that normal," Stone said.

"He was always a little tetchy about callers at his place."

"I'll grant you that, but he knows us. Who can he trust if not you and me?"

"Why don't we stop arguing and go find out?"

When they got to Ed Rawls's gate, it swung open and the big log across the road swung back on its rollers, too. Once they were through, both returned to their original positions.

"Did you see the camera?" Holly asked.

"Yes. It wasn't there last year." As they came around a curve the cottage was revealed. Ed Rawls was standing on the front porch, a shotgun in his hand. They got out of the car.

"Ed, I warned you about that shotgun," Stone said.

"It ain't pointed at you, is it? Get your ass inside so I can lock everything down." He opened the door for them and followed them in, then spent a long moment working several locks. The room looked as cozy and comfortable as ever, but the windows all had blackout curtains. "Siddown," Ed said. "I've got lunch on the stove."

They sat down and waited while he rummaged in the kitchen, then came out pushing a cart that held three grilled ham and cheese sandwiches, a bottle of red wine, and a bottle of bourbon. "Help yourself," he said. "Wine or whiskey?"

"I guess a glass of wine," Stone said.

"Me too," Holly echoed.

Ed poured them all a glass, switched on the TV and Fox News came up, but he immediately changed to MSNBC, looking embarrassed. He watched the headlines in silence until they had finished eating, then he wheeled the cart back into the kitchen, refreshed their glasses, and sat down.

"Okay," he said, "what do you want?"

Stone and Holly exchanged a glance.

"Are you on some kind of medication, Ed?" Stone asked.

"None of your business, but no."

"Then why are you so fucking hostile?"

"You think this is hostile? This is my sunny disposition face." He pointed at his chin.

Holly burst out laughing, and Ed managed a small smile.

"I guess you think I'm paranoid, or something."

"Or something," Stone replied. "Is somebody out to get you?"

"I think that's a reasonable assumption, given the circumstances."

"What are the circumstances?"

"Two pros with weapons arrived here a couple of weeks ago."

"And you're still here. Where did they go?"

"Into Penobscot Bay," Ed replied. "Though the tides probably took 'em out into the Atlantic."

Stone sighed. "Who sent them to see you?"

"I didn't have time to ask."

"Domestic or foreign?" Holly asked.

"One of 'em sounded like a Texan," Ed replied. "The other one never had the opportunity to speak."

"Political or criminal?"

"Most of the politicians I've known have been criminals."

"You owe your liberty to a politician," Stone said.

"One of two or three I've come across who are decent human beings."

"Are you including Joe Adams in that crowd?" Stone asked.

"Yes, I am. And Kate, too. I've never blamed her for turning me in. I deserved it. That's why I helped her — and Will, too." He looked curious for a moment. "Why do you bring up Joe Adams?"

"I spoke with him a few days ago," Stone said.

"Did he speak to you? I mean, did he

make any sense?"

"He made more sense than I expected him to."

"I'm glad to hear it."

"When did you last see Joe?"

Ed looked at him sharply. "That's a loaded question."

"Then unload it for me."

"A while back," he said.

"How did that come about?"

"He and Sue spend their summers in Maine, you know."

"I didn't know," Stone said. "Where?"

"On Mount Desert Island, 'bout an hour's drive from here, if you make the ferry."

"Did they invite you, or did you just show up?"

"I made an appointment."

"What did you and Joe talk about?"

"This and that. It was a short conversation."

"Did you leave something with Joe?"

"Maybe."

"I'm sorry, Ed, but maybe doesn't cut it. I need some answers."

"All right," Ed said, "I've answered your questions, now it's my turn."

"Okay, shoot — but I don't mean that literally."

"What the fuck are you doing here, Stone?"

"I live here, sometimes."

"Why this time?"

"Because I need to know what you left with Joe."

"I left a case with him."

"I know that already. What was in the case?"

"How the hell do you know that?"

"You just told me."

"Don't fuck with me, Stone. What do you know?"

"Not as much as I want to know. What was in the case?"

"Among other things, a manuscript."

"Fiction or nonfiction?"

"Reality. Every word of it true."

"Anything in it that would cause somebody to send a pair of hit men to see you?"

"I think you can assume that."

"Who's involved in this?"

"People in high places, with a great deal to lose."

"Are you talking about a conspiracy theory?"

"I'm talking about a conspiracy — no theory involved."

"Does this have some effect on Kate's reelection campaign?"

81

"Not if I can help it."

"But it could?"

"Only if I'm dead. Not even then."

"Well, Joe gave it to me."

Rawls stared at him, agape.

12

Rawls closed his mouth. "I don't fucking believe you."

Stone shrugged. "It's an Agency strong case, thick and heavy."

"It's heavy because it's wrapped in lead sheeting inside, so it can't be X-rayed. You'd never get it through airport security."

"I brought it in my airplane. You don't get X-rayed in an FBO."

"Why did Joe give it to you?"

"I think because he's known since he first got sick that he's fading. Sue may have had something to do with his decision, too. Will asked me to go and get it from him and hang on to it."

"Where is it now?"

"Locked in a safe at my house."

"Have you looked at what's inside?"

"Joe didn't give me the key. I suppose you have it."

Rawls didn't answer that.

"Come on, Ed," Holly said. "There will only be two keys, and normally the Agency would have one."

"This ain't normal times," Ed said.

"All right," Stone said, "suppose you get visited again, and your luck doesn't hold. Who gets the case then?"

Rawls looked away. "I guess you're as good a bet as anybody, if Will wants you to have it."

"He gave me the key to the handcuff, but not the case."

"Then ask him for the other key."

"He doesn't want to be contacted, unless it's absolutely necessary. He has to go through third parties, and I think that makes him uncomfortable."

"He's right to be uncomfortable," Rawls said.

"What do you mean by that?"

"Do I have to draw you a picture?"

"*Please* draw me a picture, Ed. I need to know what I'm dealing with. And who."

"I need to think about that."

"It seems that Will and Joe have already done the thinking for you, otherwise the case wouldn't be in my safe."

"Who knows you're here?"

"The short answer to that is Jimmy Hotchkiss."

"Hah! You mean everybody knows."

"Everybody on the island."

"Who *off* the island knows you're here?"

Stone shrugged. "I took some steps to avoid being seen headed here. The trail of bread crumbs stopped in Oxford, Connecticut."

"You mean you turned off your transponder there."

"I mean I stopped for fuel and left without filing a flight plan and squawking twelve hundred."

"That was a good idea, Stone," Ed said with something that sounded nearly like admiration.

"And he never even went to the Farm," Holly said, referring to the Agency training school in Virginia. "If he had, maybe nobody would know he has the case."

"Who knows?" Rawls asked.

"We were followed once in Santa Fe," Stone said. "And that night, somebody broke into my house and tried to get into my safe. I spoke to Will after that, and he told me that someone had visited Joe when he was taking the sun in his garden, and Joe had thought he was speaking to me. Apparently, they discussed the case."

"Oh, shit," Rawls said.

"When I heard that, we decamped for here."

"Did you fly nonstop from Santa Fe to Oxford?"

"Yes, and I filed a flight plan."

"They're going to look here," Ed said. "They'll know you have a house on the island."

"Maybe," Stone replied. "I expect they'll be more careful next time, given what happened to the last people they sent."

"Where's your airplane?"

"Locked in a hangar at Rockland Airport. We were flown here in a little Cessna."

"That's good. You'd better have another word with Jimmy and tell him to keep his mouth shut."

"Good idea."

"I want to show you something," Ed said. "Something that only I know about."

"All right."

Ed went to a window facing the rear of the house and drew back the curtain. Stone followed him. "You see that rose garden there, with the concrete edge around it?"

"Yes."

"When I bought this property there was another house on it, old and in disrepair. I tore it down. Where that rose garden is was a small swimming pool. I built a new bottom in it, two feet down and filled it in with dirt." He paused and waited for Stone to catch up. "Get it?"

"So, below the new bottom, the old pool is still there?"

"Correct." He walked over to a sideboard next to the window. "Holly, you may as well see this, too." He removed two books from the near side of the bookcase atop the sideboard, reached into the shelf, pressed a board at the back, and a small door popped open. He showed them a bolt inside, then slid it back and pulled on the bookcase. The whole thing, sideboard included, swung into the room, revealing an opening. Ed reached inside and flipped on a light switch, il-luminating a fairly short tunnel, lined with concrete blocks, then he led the way, beck-oning them to follow.

The tunnel ended in another wall, and Ed swung open a concrete block, slid back another bolt, and flipped another light switch. "Watch your head, it's a low ceil-ing."

Stone followed him into a room that was, obviously, the lower six feet of the old swim-ming pool. There were half a dozen filing cabinets along a wall, each column of draw-ers secured by a steel bar and a heavy padlock, and a large safe sat opposite them.

A computer sat on the desk and next to it, a large printer. They were much like the Agency equipment in Dick Stone's little office. "I built all this myself, with the help of the Old Farts," Rawls said. "Took us a whole winter. Everything is here."

"Everything? Like what?" Stone asked.

"Everything that backs up what's in my manuscript — files, photographs, documents, a lot of it taken from the main library at the Agency. I got into the computer using a phony password I set up, and downloaded and printed everything."

"And nobody knows about this?"

"Just you two. Everybody else is dead. You're going to need to know this later, but for Christ's sake, be careful who you tell."

"Does Will know about this?"

"Nope. He'd be the best person to tell, though. When the time comes."

"And when would that be?"

"When this whole business blows. If I'm not here at the time, this is your insurance."

"Insurance against what?"

"Against the wrong people getting ahold of the strong case. Everything here is on thumb drives in the case, along with the manuscript. If somebody tries to force open the case, it will explode and destroy the contents."

"Jesus, Ed, you're saddling me with *this.*"

"You see, it's what happens when you get too curious. You find out things you didn't want to know."

13

Stone and Holly were escorted to their car by Ed Rawls, still carrying his shotgun. "Try not to get seen leaving here," Ed said. "Take a circuitous route home."

"Are you going to give me the key to the strong case?" Stone asked as he got into the car.

"Eventually," Ed said, closing his door for him. The log and the gate were both open when they got there, and both closed after they had passed through.

"I don't like this," Stone said.

"What are you referring to? There's so much not to like."

They turned right instead of left and began a circuit around the island.

"I'm bothered by Ed being holed up like that."

"He seems pretty comfortable."

"If these people, whoever they are, want him out of the way, they're eventually going to win."

"Not before Ed kills a few of them," Holly said. "We know that he's prepared to do that. I think these people know they have to be careful, that they can't murder someone on a Maine island in Penobscot Bay and expect it to go unnoticed."

"It sounds like Ed hasn't spoken to anybody but Jimmy Hotchkiss since last fall, so it's not like he'd be missed on the island."

"He'd be missed by Jimmy Hotchkiss, who, as you've pointed out, seems to have the ear and attention of everyone here."

"That's a good point. I'll stop worrying until something happens to Jimmy."

Holly laughed. "You do that."

When they got back to the house there was an envelope stuck in the front screen door. Stone retrieved it; it was made of thick cream-colored paper, and engraved on the rear flap was the legend "United States Senate, Washington, D.C."

"What's that?" Holly said.

"Let's go find out," Stone said, unlocking the front door and letting them in, then re-locking it. They went into the living room and sat down on the leather sofa. He held out the envelope to Holly. "You want to inspect this for explosives before I open it?"

Holly backed away a few steps. "You go right ahead," she said.

Stone took a silver letter opener from the coffee table and slit the flap. "Apparently, it's safe," he said, and Holly came and sat beside him. He removed a single sheet of notepaper on which was engraved *Whitney Saltonstall, United States Senator from New York.*

"Do you know Senator Saltonstall?" Holly asked.

"Yes, I've had lunch with him a couple of times at a club we both belong to."

"Which club?"

"It doesn't have a name. Members just call it 'the Club.' "

"How idiotically classy," Holly said, moving in close and reading the note along with him.

My Dear Stone,

I am aboard the motor yacht Breeze, anchored off the Tarratine Yacht Club, as a guest of my friend Christian St. Clair. If you are resident on Islesboro at this time, we would both be very pleased if you and your companion (if you have one, as you usually do) would join us this evening for drinks and dinner. Dress will be black tie, or nautical uniform. If you receive this, you may text a reply to the number below. A launch will collect you from the Tarratine's dock at 6:30 PM.

With kindest regards,
Whit

"Whew," Holly said. "You keep fancy company."

"I don't know St. Clair," Stone said, "do you?"

"All I know about him is what I read in the papers, the business press, and the occasional Secret Service report, if he's dining at the White House."

"I should think that the latter would contain just about everything known about the man except his vaccination list."

"It depends on what the President wants to know," she said. "It could be as simple as 'The subject has no arrest record and has never threatened the life of the President of the United States,' all the way up to, and including, a copy of his most recent financial statement, tax return, cardio workup, and proctological exam."

"Which have you read?"

"The short one. I know that the gentleman is fifty-one years old and the fourth or fifth richest man in the United States, and that his fortune is based on oil, natural gas, renewable energy, and various high technologies."

"What are his politics?"

"He's a Democrat who is on, a little left of, the political centerline, depending on whom you talk to."

"Will you eat his food and drink his wine?"

"If you insist."

"Okay, you'd better start thinking about what you're going to wear."

"That would be an LBD with my best jewelry and flat shoes, since we'll be aboard a vessel that might move under our feet, and our host is fairly short. What about you?"

"I actually possess a nautical dress uniform," Stone said.

"And what, pray, does that consist of?"

"You'll find out." He texted Saltonstall: *Stone Barrington and Holly Barker are pleased to accept.*

At close enough to six-thirty they left the house by the back door, having first armed the security system, and walked the few yards to the yacht club, next door. As they passed the front porch, where people were gathered for drinks, they were greeted by sporadic applause. Stone gave them a salute.

94

"Well, if anybody didn't know we were here, they know now."

They walked out onto the dock, where an exquisitely varnished launch awaited them, with a uniformed crew of three. One held the lines, one assisted them aboard, and the third attended to the helm. A moment later they were slowly under way, mindful of the dozens of boats moored in the little harbor.

"I believe that must be *Breeze,*" Stone said, nodding toward a very traditional yacht moored in the outer harbor.

"Yes, sir, it is," a nearby crewman said.

"What's her length?"

"A hundred and twenty feet."

"When was she built?"

"Launched this spring, finished her sea trials three weeks ago."

"I would have put her at about 1935."

"Mr. St. Clair is a traditionalist," the man replied. "Although she has the grace of that era, everything else about her is either up to date or ahead of her time."

"I was expecting more of a superyacht," Stone said quietly to Holly.

"You mean a giant, plastic bathtub with a helicopter strapped to its back?"

"Something like that."

"It seems Mr. St. Clair prefers the understated."

14

The launch pulled up to a gangway hung on the yacht's starboard side, and they were greeted at the top by the captain, who escorted them to the afterdeck, where several couples were arrayed on comfortable furniture. Piano music wafted from an invisible sound system.

"Mr. Barrington and Ms. Barker," the captain announced. A rather short but well-proportioned man dressed in what Stone recognized as a New York Yacht Club mess kit turned to greet them. "Mr. Barrington, Ms. Barker, welcome aboard *Breeze.* I'm Christian St. Clair, and this is my wife, Emma." He indicated the woman beside him, who was somewhat taller than him. "I believe you know Senator Saltonstall."

"It's Stone and Holly, please," Stone replied, and hands were shaken. Senator Saltonstall got up from his chair and greeted them, introducing his wife, Allison. The other guests and wives were introduced as well, the men in dinner suits, and Stone recognized some of their names: a magazine publisher, a philanthropist, and the executive editor of the *New York Times.*

"And I'm Christian," St. Clair said. "May we get you some refreshment?" He indicated a bar trolley nearby, crowded with bottles, and Stone looked at Holly.

"The usual," she said.

"Two Knob Creeks," Stone said, "on the rocks." The drinks were placed on a small silver tray then transported the six feet to where they stood.

"What a beautiful yacht," Stone said. "I was surprised to learn that she's new."

"Thank you," St. Clair replied. "I prefer the old to the new in most things, but not in yachts or airplanes."

"I don't blame you."

"I see you are a member of the Royal Yacht Squadron," St. Clair said, indicating his mess kit. "Somehow I hadn't expected to find one in Islesboro."

"I have a house in England, across the Solent from the Squadron. My membership is quite new."

"Ms. Barker, I believe you are the national security advisor to the President, are you not?"

"I am, for my sins," Holly replied.

"I didn't know Kate Lee's staff were allowed to leave the premises, at least not as far as Maine."

"Sometimes she insists," Holly said. "She felt I had too much unused vacation time."

"I'm glad we found you here, Stone," the senator said. "When did you arrive?"

"Only yesterday. Your timing was perfect."

"Are you staying the summer?"

"I wish we were — work will catch up with both of us sooner than I'd like."

"Did you manage to land your airplane on the island?"

"It would have been fun to try, but unwise, given the runway length. We landed at Rockland and were brought over in something smaller."

"How did you come to choose Islesboro?" Emma St. Clair asked.

"It was chosen for me," Stone said, "by my cousin Dick Stone, who died a few years ago. He left the house to a trust and lifetime occupancy to me. I subsequently bought it from the trust."

"Such a lovely place to be," she said.

"It certainly is."

Everyone chatted companionably for another hour before dinner was announced, and the hosts led them through a comfortable saloon to the dining room, where place cards had been set out on a gleaming dining table, set with beautiful china, silverware, and crystal. Stone found himself between Emma St. Clair and the *Times* editor's wife. Their husbands were on opposite sides of the table.

"Tell me, Christian," the editor said, while a first course of foie gras was being served, "anything to the rumblings that have reached me about your considering a run for the presidency next time?"

"You may have heard rumblings," St. Clair responded, "but there is no quake, nor will there be. I lead far too nice a life to exchange it for a political hell."

"Is that what you think Washington is these days?"

"I suppose it's no hotter than usual, but it would be hell for me. There isn't even a presidential yacht anymore."

"Wouldn't this suffice?" He waved an arm.

"As long as it stays out of the Potomac, yes."

"Stone," Saltonstall said from the other end of the table, "I hear you've bought a place in Santa Fe."

"A friend was leaving town and offered it

to me, pretty much furnished. I couldn't resist."

"Do you ever practice law anymore?"

"Occasionally, but I try not to be caught at it. Anyway, an iPhone and a laptop make an office these days."

"You are a wise man, Stone," St. Clair said. "I operate much the same way, to the extent I can."

"He's spent more time on the design and building of this yacht the past two years," his wife said, "than on any sort of productive work."

"Darling, I'm surprised you find all this unproductive, and anyway, you spent just as much time on the interiors as I spent on the rest."

"Where did you have her built?" Stone asked.

"I bought a little boatyard on the bay," he replied, "built a larger shed, and hired a yacht designer, a manager, and a workforce of thirty craftsmen. I find you get more attention from the builders if you're not competing with other people's yachts. We built *Breeze* and the two launches in less than two years — record time."

"Will you keep the yard?" the editor asked.

"I will, along with a staff to maintain the yacht. I sent the others off with a nice bonus, and they have all already found work in other yards. *Breeze* looks good on their résumés."

"That's a brilliant way to build a yacht," Stone said.

"Especially if you consider that I paid about the same as if I'd hired a top yard to do it. As it was, the company I set up made a very nice profit, and we may take on other yachts to maintain. Of course, if I'd built a larger vessel, I'd have had to go to Abeking & Rasmussen in Germany or Palmer Johnson in Wisconsin or some other brilliant builder thousands of miles away. Just think what I saved on jet fuel by doing it in-house, as it were."

Everybody laughed.

A steward came into the room with a sheet of paper on a silver tray and offered it to St. Clair. "Excuse me, sir, but I thought you'd like to know."

St. Clair picked up the paper and read it, while the others chatted. He tapped on a wineglass with a fingernail, and everybody got quiet.

"Ladies and gentlemen," he said, "I'm sorry to interrupt your dinner, but it's my sad duty to inform you that former President Joseph Adams died suddenly this afternoon at his home in Santa Fe. He and

101

Sue were due at their home on Mount Desert Island later this week for the summer. We had planned to call in and see them."

Everyone seemed locked in a stunned silence.

St. Clair raised his glass: "I give you a great man — Joe Adams."

Everyone raised his glass and drank.

"I knew him well," St. Clair said, "and I've never known a better human being."

The others exchanged reminiscences, then St. Clair turned toward Stone.

"You're very quiet, Stone. Did you know Joe Adams in Santa Fe?"

"We met at the Democratic Convention in Los Angeles some years back and spent a riotous evening together in a skybox belonging to a mutual friend. I think we had more fun than any of the delegates."

"It's a pity he got to serve only a few months as President, after his predecessor died," Saltonstall said.

"He and Sue came to Maine every summer," St. Clair said. "Joe loved it here."

The rest of the evening was quieter.

15

After dinner they adjourned to the yacht's saloon for brandy and coffee and watched the TV coverage of Joe Adams's death for a while. It was nearly midnight before the group showed signs of breaking up. Stone and Holly thanked their hosts profusely and rose to go.

"If you hang around Islesboro a little longer, perhaps we'll see you again," St. Clair said. "We'll be cruising for a couple of weeks. Perhaps you could join us for a few days. We're not fully occupied aboard."

"That would be delightful," Stone said, "if we're able to stay longer." They exchanged cards, and Stone and Holly boarded the launch for the return trip to the dock.

"What did you think of Christian St. Clair?" Holly asked as they were walking back to the house.

"I liked him," Stone replied. "He's smart, unpretentious, and he didn't talk about business or, very much, about politics. He'd rather talk about his boat, and I liked that about him. How about you?"

"He was all right, I suppose. I'm uncomfortable in the presence of that kind of money."

"Why?"

"I don't know, I suppose it's because a lot of the wealthiest people seem to use it badly, or to promote self-serving political causes, or they're greedy for even more."

"Christian seemed very relaxed and comfortable in his skin, and I like it that the man, at the most productive time of his life, would spend two years building his dream yacht, overseeing it himself. He could have just written a huge check to a big yard, but he didn't."

"Maybe he's just obsessive-compulsive," Holly said.

"But, unlike you, not about his work."

As they arrived at the back porch of the house, Stone suddenly realized that someone was sitting in a rocker on the porch.

"Evening," Ed Rawls said, rising.

"Why, Ed," Stone said. "I'm sorry I didn't know you were coming. We were out to dinner."

"So I saw."

"Come in and have a drink."

Rawls followed them into the house and accepted a brandy. "Have you heard about Joe Adams?"

"Yes, we watched some of the coverage on TV after dinner."

"This means we have a whole new timetable."

"Funny, I didn't know we had an old timetable."

"Joe doesn't have to be protected anymore, though Sue might need to be. After all, she knows about the strong case."

"As a former first lady, Sue will continue to be protected by the Secret Service," Holly said.

"As Joe was? Remember, somebody walked up to him in his own garden in Santa Fe. If the Secret Service had protected him, we might not be where we are today."

"And where the hell are we, Ed?" Stone asked, trying not to sound exasperated.

"In trouble," Rawls replied. "While you were supping with Christian St. Clair, two men examined your house rather slowly. I kept in the shadows, so they didn't see me, which was good because I wouldn't have wanted to leave a couple of corpses on your back porch."

"What did they look like?" Stone asked.

"Respectable, but out of place. They were

wearing suits and ties."

"You make that sound sinister, Ed."

"Don't you find it so? On Islesboro? They would have been the only people dressed that way on the entire island — except for you, of course, in your monkey suit."

"My dinner host specified the dress for the evening," Stone pointed out.

"Ah, your dinner host, Mr. St. Clair."

"How did you know about him?"

"Well, he's been building that yacht around here for the last couple of years. Folks couldn't wait to see it."

"What do you have against Christian St. Clair?" Stone asked.

"I'm suspicious of men who have their own police forces."

"What do you mean?"

"I mean, he has more security people working for him than any police force between here and Portland — maybe between here and Boston."

"Perhaps he just has a lot to protect — he owns a lot of things."

"Tell, me, Stone, how did he react to the news of Joe Adams's death?"

"Sadly. We all did."

"And who were your dinner companions?"

"Whitney Saltonstall and the publisher of

Vanity Fair and an editor of the *New York Times.*"

"Covering all his bases, wasn't he?"

"Ed, you're becoming tiresome. Either tell me what you're talking about, or just stick to your brandy."

"Just think about how much influence was gathered aboard St. Clair's yacht," Ed said. "*Vanity Fair,* for social coverage; the *Times,* for news and influence; and Whit Salton-stall, for power in Washington."

"I forgot to mention the national security advisor."

"Thank you, kind sir," Holly said.

"And then there's you," Ed said to Stone.

"What could he possibly want from me?"

"Your goodwill, Stone."

"Well, then, he bought that cheaply, for the price of a fine dinner and good company."

"He'll be offering you more soon."

"Why?"

"Because he's the sort of fellow who prefers having friends rather than enemies. He collects friends, like pearls on a string, and believe you me, he has a very long string."

"Who doesn't prefer friends to enemies?" Stone asked.

"Some of us don't have the choice — the

choice is made for us."

"And where do you think I fall on the friends-to-enemies arc?"

"St. Clair hasn't decided yet," Rawls said. "He's still sizing you up. He doesn't know yet how much you know."

"Well, I can tell him, not very much."

Rawls reached into a pocket and came up with an object. "Catch," he said, and tossed it to Stone.

Stone caught it and looked at it; it appeared to be an oddly shaped piece of titanium. "What is it?"

Holly spoke up. "It's the key to the strong case," she said.

16

Rawls stood up, tossed off his brandy, and set down the glass. "I'm outa here."

Stone walked him to the door and watched as Ed turned off the outside light, allowed his eyes to become accustomed to the darkness, then made his way to a jeep and drove away, turning the wrong way on the road.

Stone went back inside. "I'm beat," he said, pulling his bow tie loose and unbuttoning his collar. "Let's go to bed."

"Don't you want to open the strong case?" Holly asked.

"No, I don't want to even think about it. Coming?"

"Soon, I hope," she said, joining him on the stairs.

"I'm not sure I have it in me," Stone said. "We'll see."

They slept well, had breakfast in bed, then dozed off again. The doorbell rang. Stone looked at the bedside clock. Ten minutes past eight. He picked up the phone, which automatically connected him to the intercom. "Yes?"

"Stone Barrington?"

"Yes."

"FBI."

"You must have the wrong house."

"Are you Stone Barrington?"

"Yes."

"We've got the right house. Are you going to let us in?"

"Wait right there." Stone put on his nightshirt and a robe over that, then got into his slippers and walked downstairs. He had a good look at the two men through the armored glass before opening the door on its chain. "Let me see some ID."

The two men held up badges, close enough that Stone could read their names on the IDs, Smithson and Peters. He opened the door. "Come in."

He led them into the living room and pointed at chairs. "All right, what is it?"

"Are you alone in the house?" Smithson asked.

"None of your business," Stone replied.

"Mr. Barrington, I caution you that it's a crime to lie to a federal agent."

"I'm not lying, it's none of your business."

"It's going to be like that, is it?"

"Probably, unless you give me a good reason to talk to you. Your curiosity is not enough."

"We're investigating the theft of a . . . piece of luggage."

"Thank you, but all my luggage is present and accounted for."

"Not your luggage."

"Then why are you in my house at this hour of the day?"

"That was dictated by the ferry schedule."

"Doesn't the Bureau have helicopters anymore?"

"We do, but that seemed like overkill for this errand."

"Is there anything else?"

"I told you, we're investigating the theft of a piece of luggage."

"We've already been through that — let's not start again."

"Did you visit the home of former-President Joseph Adams in Santa Fe a few days ago?"

"Yes, but I didn't steal any of his luggage."

"What did you and President Adams talk about?"

"We reminisced about old times. Mr. Adams appeared to confuse me with someone else."

"With whom did he confuse you?"

"Someone named Tom. I didn't get the last name."

"Why did you visit President Adams?"

"To reminisce about old times."

"Mr. Barrington, are you hiding something from us?"

"I'm sorry, my attorney has just advised me that I don't have to answer that question — or any other question."

The two men looked around. "I don't see an attorney," Smithson said.

"You're looking at him."

"You're an attorney?" Smithson asked.

"I'm surprised you don't know more about the people you question."

"He's an attorney," Peters said to his partner.

"Well, at least one of you Googled me," Stone said.

"Mr. Barrington, if we searched your house, would we find a piece of luggage that doesn't belong to you?"

"I haven't invited you to search my house, and you haven't shown me a search warrant."

"We can get one."

"And where would you do that?" Stone asked.

"From the nearest United States attorney."

"You'd go all the way to Boston to have the fun of searching my house?"

The two men looked at each other. "Where's the nearest U.S. attorney?" Smithson asked.

"I don't know," Peters replied.

"Well, I'm not going to tell you," Stone said. "Anyway, if you located one you'd be obliged to show him some probable cause. Have you got any of that handy? If you can show me some, I might save you a trip to the U.S. attorney."

The two men said nothing.

"That's what I thought," Stone said. "Gentlemen, if you hurry, you can still catch the ferry, otherwise it's a two-hour wait, if it's not refueling day, and then it's a six-hour wait. And there's not much fun to be had on the island dressed as you are."

Smithson looked at his watch. "Let's get out of here," he said to his partner. Then, to Stone: "We'll be back."

"Promise?"

"Believe me."

"Don't forget your search warrant — or your probable cause."

He locked the door behind them.

Holly came down the stairs. "I heard some

of it from above. What the hell did they want?"

"A missing piece of luggage. Sound familiar?"

"Uh-oh."

"Do you think everybody on the planet has come to know about this?"

"A good many of them, apparently."

"I don't get why the FBI is interested."

"Neither do I, but has it occurred to you that it might have been the FBI who visited Joe Adams in his garden? Or followed us around that day? Or prowled around this house the other night?"

"Well, they were wearing suits and ties, weren't they? The FBI is just about the last holdout for that particular fashion statement."

"You know, if I were in my office I could look into this."

"And what scientific equipment would you have there that would allow you to look into it that you don't have here?"

"You have a point," Holly admitted.

"Then why aren't you looking into it?"

"Frankly, I don't know where to start."

"Well, I do," Stone said. "Where's my cell phone?"

"Upstairs, I guess."

Stone started up the stairs. "I'll be right

back." Stone found his phone and called the White House operator. "I'd like to leave a message for President Will Lee," he said.

"Who's calling?"

"My name is Stone Barrington."

"Would you like me to connect you?"

"No, I'd just like to leave a message for him to phone me. He has the number."

"Thank you, sir."

Stone hung up and went downstairs. "Now we wait," he said to Holly.

17

They had just finished lunch when Stone's phone rang. The calling number was blocked.

Stone turned on the speaker so Holly could hear. "Hello?"

"It's me. You called?" Will Lee said.

"I did. The kettle is coming to a boil around here."

"Are you in the north?"

"Yes. Last night two men in suits and ties were observed taking a close interest in my house, and this morning, two such men rang my doorbell and introduced themselves as FBI agents. Do you know why the FBI would have any interest in me?"

"No. What did they want?"

"They said they were investigating a report of the theft of a piece of luggage, and they mentioned our friend on the mountainside and asked about our conversation."

"Who have you been talking to around there?"

"Here's a complete list — a female person of your acquaintance, a former government employee who lives here, Whit Saltonstall, the editor of the *New York Times,* and the publisher of *Vanity Fair,* all of whom I saw at dinner last evening on the yacht belonging to Christian St. Clair."

"What an interesting group."

"Yes, they were."

"At the dinner, did anyone inquire about the luggage?"

"No."

"Did our friend's name come up?"

"Only when we learned of his death."

"Yes, we're very sad here about that."

"Was there anything unusual about his death?"

"He collapsed in his garden after breakfast yesterday. The local medical examiner said the cause of death was neurological damage associated with Alzheimer's."

"Do you know if that is a typical cause of death in someone at his stage of the disease?"

"I know it's a neurological illness, and that eventually some, perhaps many, Alzheimer's victims die of it."

"Can you think of anyone to whom our

friend's existence might have been a threat?"

"Among politicians he had fewer enemies than most. Still . . ."

"Does a name come to mind?"

"Anyone, I suppose, who fears that the contents of the package might become known. Is it secure?"

"Yes. I have obtained the means to open it. Should I?"

"I suggest not. Your situation might become more dangerous if it were thought that you were familiar with the contents."

"Why didn't you mention that at the outset?"

"I'm very sorry, this was to have been a simple matter, and I did not anticipate the ensuing complications."

"Can I send it to you?"

"Absolutely not. It would have to pass through too many layers of inspection. Also, it should not be mailed or sent by commercial shipper."

"Can you send someone to relieve me of it?"

"I have no such person at my disposal."

"So I'm stuck with it?"

"I'm sorry, but yes, for the time being."

"How about if I just dump it in Penobscot Bay?"

"It would send out a signal that would

trigger alarms."

"Swell."

"If you will be patient, I will try to find another means of securing it. In the meantime, do not, repeat, *not* give it to your neighbor. Is that clear?"

"Yes, I understand."

"I know this is inconvenient, and I apologize for that. Goodbye." Will hung up.

Holly looked at him with curiosity. "I'm surprised you didn't tell him that Ed Rawls has cached all the source materials of what's in the strong case."

"At the moment, if what Ed has told us is true, you and I are the only people besides him who are aware of that."

"And you're afraid Will might tell somebody else?"

"We don't know who else Will has talked to about this. Kate? Members of his staff? He may be taking advice from some source we're not aware of, and anyway, I don't see how it's in anybody's legitimate interest to know what Ed has in that former swimming pool."

"Well, it sure doesn't seem that it's in *our* interest to know about it. I wish Ed had never told us."

"I'd rather know it than not know it. That way, if I come to lose the strong case, at

119

least I know there's a backup."

An hour later, as Stone was reading the *Times,* his phone rang again. "Hello?"

"I've done some checking," Will said, "and I am reliably informed that yesterday and today there is a regional meeting of some northeastern FBI personnel taking place in Boston and that, at this moment, there is not a single FBI agent present in the state of Maine. That's all I can tell you at the moment."

"Thank you."

"Goodbye." They both hung up.

"What was that?" Holly said.

"The voice of doom." He told her what Will had said.

"Oh, shit," she replied. "Maybe we should get out of here."

"I'm not opposed to that, I just don't know where to go."

"New York?"

"An obvious place to look for me."

"Your place in England or Paris?"

"Do you have your passport?" Stone asked.

"No."

"Neither do I, and I don't particularly want to wait for it to be sent."

She thought for a moment. "I can think of

one place we can go — it's comfortable and, I expect, secure."

Stone brightened. "Christian St. Clair's yacht?"

"Exactly."

Stone found the card that St. Clair had given him and called the number.

"Stone? What a nice surprise to hear from you."

"Thank you, Christian. Holly and I wanted to thank you for your wonderful hospitality last evening. We had a fine time."

"We were all delighted to see you. Have you looked into the possibility of joining our cruise?"

"We have, and we'd be delighted to."

"Are you still in Islesboro?"

"We are."

"We're anchored in North Haven. I'll send a launch for you."

"That's fine. They can come to my dock — it's one down from the yacht club's jetty."

"I should think they could be there in, say, two hours?"

"That's good. You can have them call me when they're a few minutes out, and we'll meet them on the dock."

"I'll do that. Bring your mess kit and whatever else you may need."

"We'll do that."

"See you for dinner, then."

"Good." They hung up. "The launch will be here in two hours," he said to Holly.

"Great. Have you thought about what to do with the strong case?"

"Yes, I'm going to leave it in the safe here. Certainly I'm not going to carry it around."

"What about Bob?" Bob's tail began beating against the floor at the mention of his name.

"Seth and Mary will take care of him. They're already in love."

"I'd better go pack." She ran upstairs.

Stone called Ed Rawls's number and got the usual recorded message. At the beep he said, "Ed, we're going away for a few days. You can reach me on my cell phone, if you need to." Then he went upstairs to pack.

18

Stone saw the *breeze* launch coming from his back window. He checked the security system, armed it, and he and Holly left the house, locking the door behind them, and walked down to his dock. They were taken aboard with the crew's usual dispatch, and as they settled into seats in the cabin, Stone felt his cell phone vibrate and heard a chime. That meant a text.

He checked his messages and found one with a blocked name. It read: BAD TIME TO LEAVE THE ISLAND. He showed it to Holly. "Response from Ed."

"What do you think he means by that?" Holly asked.

"I haven't the foggiest notion." He texted back: TOO LATE, WE'VE DEPARTED. I'LL PROBABLY BE REACHABLE MOST OF THE TIME.

"We'll be about an hour to North Haven," the helmsman said. "There's a *Times* and a

Wall Street Journal on the table behind you."

Stone picked up the *Times,* and a story in the upper-right-hand corner of the business section caught his eye. "Listen to this," he said to Holly, and read it aloud. *"Nelson Knott, the online entrepreneur and Internet marketer of vitamin supplements, placed an announcement on his Facebook front page last night saying that he is forming an exploratory committee to consider a run for President of the United States as an independent candidate in the next election. Knott, who has at one time or another been registered to vote as a Republican, a Democrat, and a Libertarian, said, in part, 'Like most Americans, I have lost faith in all our political parties to change the way we're doing things, which is just awful. I will come to this race without any political baggage or ideology, pledged simply to do the right thing and to do it right. Let's take our country back!' "*

"Oh, that's just wonderful," Holly said wryly. "And look, there's a photograph of him with his lantern jaw and that horrible black wig he wears, while swearing it isn't a wig. He's what, about six feet six?"

"Likely the tallest presidential candidate in American history," Stone said, "according to the article."

"I expect he'll run on that. It's about all

he's got going for him."

"Do you think he'll attract voters away from Kate?"

"My guess is that he'll get a lot more Republican votes than Democratic ones."

Stone turned to the inside page where the article was continued. "It says that the FDA has banned half a dozen of his supplements from sale, saying they contain little that's beneficial except sugar and salt."

"They're constantly after him, but he still manages to flog tons of that stuff on late-night infomercials."

"I don't get it — who does he think is going to vote for him?"

"Maybe the people who buy his self-help books. There are more than a dozen of those tomes, and they're hot sellers on the Internet. He claims to have put all the profits into investments that have made him rich."

"Ah, yes, he claims to be worth five billion dollars, according to this article."

"If anybody believes that, I've got a very nice, very tall monument, beautifully located on the Mall in Washington, that I'd like to sell them."

Stone turned the page and found something else to read. He was on the crossword when the launch slowed and pulled up to the *Breeze*'s stairs.

"Just leave your luggage and I'll have it put into your cabin," the helmsman said, and they climbed the stairs, this time to be met by their host.

"Stone, Holly, welcome aboard again," Christian St. Clair said. "Would you like to freshen up, or would you like a cocktail?"

"I'm pretty fresh," Holly said. "I vote for the cocktail."

St. Clair led them aft, where the others were seated, with one new addition: a man in a double-breasted blazer with shiny brass buttons stood, towering over everyone, especially his host. "Stone," St. Clair said, "allow me to introduce you and Holly to Nelson Knott and his wife, Clarice, who joined us this morning for this leg of our cruise." Knott's hair did not appear to be a wig, and it was no longer black but a chestnut color with a good deal of gray. The woman was more than a foot shorter than her husband, and much cleavage was in view.

Knott offered a huge hand that enveloped Stone's, as if it belonged to a child.

"How do you do?" Stone said, stunned. He looked around. "Where's Whit Saltonstall?"

"Right here, Stone," a voice behind him said. "Walk with me, Stone." He turned and followed his wife toward the launch.

"Are you leaving us, Whit?" Stone asked, catching up.

Saltonstall smiled and lowered his voice. "I won't spend another minute in the company of that ass. He got on at Rockland this morning, when we were still asleep. I can't imagine what he's doing here, and I don't want to find out. Have a pleasant sail." He went down the stairway to the launch, and it pulled away.

Stone went back to the other guests and was handed a Knob Creek on the rocks. Holly already had one.

Now he noticed that the magazine publisher and newspaper editor with whom they had dined the evening before had been replaced by two other couples, who were introduced. One of them was a casino owner from New Orleans who was often on the news at election time; the other was an elderly man with thick white hair who Stone did not recognize.

"I'm sure you know Harold and Cassandra Ozick," St. Clair said, indicating the casino owner, "and this is Clint and Lily Holder." Now Stone had it: Clint Holder was a Texas oilman with widespread interests, including, if the rumors were true, about forty acres of downtown Dallas. He was sometimes known in the papers as "Clint Holdup." Both men were huge contributors to political action committees that backed Republican candidates.

"How do you do?" Stone said, shaking everybody's hand. He could understand why the other guests had abandoned ship, but, since he didn't have that opportunity at the moment, he decided to make the best of it.

The group exchanged small talk for a while, then Stone excused himself and Holly. "We'd better change for dinner," he said. Everybody made moves in that direction. They followed a crewman below and forward to a cabin with a carved rose on the door. Inside, their clothes had been put away, and their luggage had disappeared. The cabin was large, sporting a plush sofa before a fireplace and a king-sized bed. There were fine oil paintings of yachts and yacht clubs on the wall.

Holly leaped onto the bed. "Perfect!" she said.

"We'll see," Stone replied. "What do you think of our fellow guests on the cruise?"

"Oh, I think this is going to be such fun!" Holly said, bouncing up and down on the bed.

19

Dinner started with about half a cup each of the first beluga caviar Stone had seen in years. It was almost impossible to find, legally, just about anywhere but in Iran or Russia, and nobody was leaving any on his plate.

They proceeded to an enormous porter-house steak, about four inches thick, carved at tableside, and the wine was a 1978 Château Lafite-Rothschild, decanted and waiting.

"We are indebted to Clint and Lily Holder for our food and wine this evening," St. Clair said, "and a good thing, since I was going to give you pizza and wine from a screw-top bottle."

They all toasted the Holders.

Stone couldn't help noticing that the casino man, Ozick, was wearing diamond studs and cuff links of about three carats each with his dinner suit, which sported little threads of gold woven into the fabric. His wife, Cassandra, who was forty years younger than he, was wearing a skin-tight dress sewn with rhinestones, if they weren't actually diamonds. Just the thing for a cruise of the Maine islands.

The Holders, however, were dressed elegantly and with more reserve, though Lily's diamond necklace attracted attention, and Clint's studs were tiny oil derricks, encrusted with pavé diamonds.

"Barrington," Clint Holder said, around a chunk of steak, "I've never heard of you. What do you do?"

"I'm a partner in the New York law firm of Woodman & Weld," Stone replied, "and I serve on a couple of boards."

"I know your firm," Holder said. "A hothouse of flaming liberals."

"I don't think the partners would take too much exception to that, except for the 'flaming' part, but the practice of law is pretty conservative, though some of our clients are not."

"What boards are you on?" Holder demanded, as if this were a job interview.

"The Steele Insurance Group and Strategic Services. I also serve on the board of the Arrington Hotel Group, of which I am a principal."

"Ah!" Holder said. "We stayed at your L.A. hotel a few months back, and it was damned fine!"

"I'm glad you had a good experience," Stone replied.

Ozick spoke up. "I'm in the hotel business, myself," he said, "as housing the gamblers at our casinos."

"Yeah," Holder said, "I'm in the cattle business, too." Everybody laughed, except Ozick.

"Nelson," St. Clair said to Knott, "I was interested to read of your interest in the presidency."

"Thank you," Knott replied in a deep, beautifully modulated voice. "I'm grateful for your interest, Christian."

"What sort of planning are you doing?"

"Well, we're forming a new party, to be called the Independent Patriot Party, and we've started work on getting on the ballot in all fifty states."

"And how's that going?"

"We've just gotten started, really, but it's going to be more expensive than I had first thought."

"And how are you going to finance your campaign?"

"I've already loaned it fifty million dollars. That's a start."

"A properly run presidential campaign is going to cost north of a billion dollars," St. Clair said. "Are you going to self-finance all the way?"

Knott laughed, revealing the best teeth Stone had ever seen, or the best dentistry. "I certainly hope not."

"Well, the Republican Party is in pretty bad shape, after the last election, but Kate Lee is going to be very well financed, don't you think so, Stone?"

"I expect so," Stone replied.

"I think Kate has done a creditable job as President," St. Clair said, by way of needling Knott, Stone thought. He also thought that St. Clair knew all of what he'd just asked Knott about, and he was just getting the recital for the benefit of his guests.

"The last presidential candidates in either party that I had any respect for were Joe Adams and John McCain," Knott responded.

"Nelson, I don't know if I mentioned that Holly, here, is Kate's national security advisor."

Knott beamed at Holly. "So, it's *your* fault," he said, laughing, and the others laughed with him.

"I'll take all the credit I can get," Holly replied, beaming back at him, "whether I deserve it or not."

Knott loved that, though his wife was looking at Holly as though she were about to throw a steak knife at her.

"What are your politics, Mr. Knott?" Holly asked.

"I'm for what's right and what works," he replied. "And please call me Nelson. May I call you Holly?"

"Of course," Holly said. "You're a pragmatist. How refreshing."

A steward refreshed everyone's wineglass.

"Ideology doesn't interest me," Knott replied, "not any party's. I'm for American rights."

"Does that include a woman's right to choose?" Holly asked, and everybody froze.

"Of course," Knott said. "It's not my way, but it's the law, and I'm not going to stand in the way of the law."

"How very nice to hear it put that way."

"Excuse me, if I disagree," Ozick said, and his face had gone pink.

"We'll excuse you for disagreeing, Hal," St. Clair said, "as long as you're not disagreeable at my table."

"Then I'd better keep my mouth shut," Ozick said.

"As you wish."

The plates were taken away and a Stilton

appeared on the table, along with a decanter of port. They were shown the label: a Quinta do Noval, 1966.

"And whom do we thank for this?" Stone asked.

"That is from your host," Holder said. "I don't know a damn thing about port."

They all raised their glasses to their host and drank, and the cheese was passed around.

"And where, Christian, do you find such superb Stilton in Maine?"

"From Paxton & Whitfield, Jermyn Street, London. Just around the corner."

After they had made love and were catching their breath, Stone said, "What did you think of Nelson Knott?"

Holly sat straight up in bed. "I think he's a very dangerous man."

"Why so?"

"He's smart as a rattlesnake, but with a lot of charm when he wants to use it."

"And how did you learn this?"

"Don't you ever have trouble sleeping?"

"Never."

"Well, I do, and at three in the morning, Nelson Knott is about all the company you can find on TV. That man is the slickest thing you ever saw, and if he's as rich as

Forbes said he is, and if he's doing what he says he's doing in all fifty states, he's going to be a handful."

"Really?"

"You just watch — the press are going to love him."

20

Stone and Holly got dressed the following morning and went up for breakfast. A hot buffet had been set out under the afterdeck awning. Harold and Cassandra Ozick were already seated at the table.

Stone and Holly helped themselves and sat down. "Good morning," Stone said to the Ozicks.

Ozick muttered something unintelligible, but it didn't sound welcoming.

"That was a great dinner last night, wasn't it?"

"It was," Ozick admitted. "So, you're a member of the Democrat Party, are you?"

"No, I'm a member of the *Democratic* Party."

"Whatever."

"And you're a very big contributor to the Republican Party, aren't you?"

"I buy men, not parties," Ozick said. He caught himself: "That is, I invest in them."

"Interesting," Stone said. "I read somewhere what you did in the last election, but it slips my mind. How much did you invest?"

"Higher than you can count," Ozick said. "And I'll keep doing it as long as there's a Democrat in the White House."

"Tell me," Stone said, "are you happy with your return on investment?"

"We've still got the House."

"But that's not enough, is it?"

"No, it isn't."

"Who are you going to . . . invest . . . in next time?"

"I may have to give it a fresh look. That fellow Knott has already asked me for a hundred million."

"What do you like about Nelson?"

"I like it that he's already a celebrity," Ozick said. "I don't have to invest in making him one."

"And, if he's elected, what do you want from him?"

Ozick looked him in the eye. "Favorable consideration," he said.

"Can you really get a hundred million dollars' worth of 'favorable consideration' out of a President?"

"I'm not just in the casino business, you know, I've got money everywhere, some of it in defense industries."

"Ah, now I get the picture."

"Do you really, Barrington?"

"I think so. You invest, then when, say, a new fighter jet is up for bids, you get the nod."

"A contractor always wants the nod."

"But, because you've invested, you *expect* to get the nod."

"I hope for an improvement in my chances."

"So, there are no guarantees. It's like at your gaming tables — you put down your money, and you take your chances."

"I expect to improve on the margins I get at the casino."

"Because, by your investment, you've stacked the odds in your favor."

"Barrington, you're a lawyer, do you expect me to answer that out loud?"

"If I were *your* lawyer, I'd advise you to stand on your rights under the Fifth Amendment."

"Consider that done."

"How long have you been a big political contributor, Hal?"

"Oh, the last half-dozen elections, I guess."

"But you've lost the popular vote in five of those."

Ozick just glared at him. Before he could speak, Nelson and Clarice Knott joined the table.

Stone looked at the single poached egg on Knott's plate. "I see you're in training," he said.

Knott smiled. "Always. After all, I'm on television every night."

"Good point," Stone said.

"How do you keep your weight down, Stone?" Knott asked, pointing his fork at Stone's eggs Benedict.

"I chose my parents carefully," Stone replied. "They were both as skinny as rails. Oh, and I work out three or four days a week."

"I hate exercise," Knott said.

"Who doesn't?"

Holly broke in. "Last night you said that your political philosophy is to do the right thing."

"That's right."

"Tell me, how do you decide what is the right thing?"

"My folks brought me up to know the difference between right and wrong. I don't have any trouble making that decision."

"When you make a decision, how many people do you have to please?"

"Just one," Knott replied with a grin.

"When I'm at work, not in Maine, cruising, I go to the President just about every day for decisions on one thing or another."

"I expect you do."

"The thing is, she has to please not just herself, but her party, the Congress, the nation at large, and, occasionally," she said, looking at Ozick, "a contributor. How are you going to handle that as President?"

"Don't you worry," Knott said. "I'll handle it. I'm good at handling it."

"Do you think it will be that easy when American lives depend on your decision?"

"I take your point," Knott said.

"My President has one thing going for her that you don't have."

"What's that?"

"When she makes a decision, most of those people I mentioned can predict what she'll do. That's because she has a history, a record of making good decisions. But you don't have that history, that record. How will the people who vote for you know which way you'll jump?"

"They'll trust me," Knott said. "I'm a wealthy man because I know how to get people to trust me."

The St. Clairs appeared from below, served themselves, and joined the table. "Good morning," he said, "I hope I haven't interrupted an interesting conversation."

"Just in the nick of time," Holly said. "I was, I think, about to get a straight answer from a political candidate."

Everyone laughed, even Nelson Knott.

"Holly," he said, "if you want straight answers from me, you're going to have to stay up late at night."

"Is that when you're going to hold your campaign press conferences?" she asked.

"Now, that's an interesting idea," Knott said. "The press would be exhausted, and I'd be fresh as a daisy. I'd like those odds, wouldn't you, Hal?"

"That would give you an edge," Ozick admitted.

"Well, after breakfast," Holly said, "I'm going to want to know how you formulate policy."

"Oh, I'll tell you that now," Knott said. "I have a policy advisory committee at work right now, analyzing. There are experts in every field participating, and when I make a policy statement, it will be followed immediately by a written account."

"Well," said Holly, "that would be a refreshing change in our opposition."

St. Clair artfully changed the subject.

21

Stone sat on the afterdeck late in the morning and read the day's *Times,* which a crewman had brought from ashore. They were motoring quietly, at about ten knots, southeast, toward an eventual destination of Monhegan Island. The captain had told him there was no docking there, but when the wind and tide were right, they could put a launch ashore. The skies were low, but the visibility was good ahead.

Christian St. Clair and Nelson Knott were inside, at the far end of the saloon, talking earnestly. The other two couples and Clarice Knott were on the top deck, taking the breeze. Shortly, the two men in the saloon stood, and Knott went forward and up the stairs to the higher deck. Christian St. Clair walked aft, poured himself a cup of tea from an urn, and sat down with Stone.

"How is your cruise going?" he asked Stone.

"Just the way a cruise is supposed to," Stone said, "though in greater comfort than I'm accustomed to."

"What do you think of your shipmates?"

"I'm very impressed with my hosts and their yacht."

St. Clair smiled. "And the others?"

"I'm enjoying annoying Hal Ozick, and Holly is having fun needling Nelson Knott."

St. Clair laughed. "And what do you think of Nelson?"

"I think he's a pretty slick article. How about you?"

"He's brighter than I expected him to be, and more articulate."

"Are you sure he's not just glib?"

"Fairly. He's not kidding about his advisors, and he reads their reports constantly. I think he's fueling up on policy for his run."

"He's already decided to do it, then?"

"Oh, yes, I think he decided years ago. He seems to have learned a lot by watching the last Republican candidate do it badly, and he's determined to do it well."

"His chief talent seems to be the ability to tell people what they want to hear."

"That's a very great political gift," St. Clair said.

"It is, if there's an ethical basis beneath the philosophy."

"I think he will form that eventually. In the meantime, while he's exploring his options, he seems to be quite malleable."

"I think that would interest both Hal Ozick and Clint Holder," Stone said.

"I'm sure you're right."

"Does it interest you, Christian?"

"I'm always interested in furthering the national discourse."

"And in shaping it?"

"It's only worth furthering after it's been shaped."

"I thought as a Democrat you were committed to Kate Lee."

"I think it would be a healthy thing for Kate to have an opponent who stretches her a bit."

"Stretches?"

"Challenges, makes her think harder. Does Nelson interest you?"

"In the way that a lab specimen interests a scientist," Stone replied. "I think the man has it in him to be dangerous."

"In what way?"

"Once he's digested his position papers and decided how he's going to go about getting what he wants, he could be a danger to Kate. If he should be elected, he might be a danger to himself and others."

"All the more reason to take him in hand,"

St. Clair said.

"You mean, control him?"

Christian didn't answer directly; he just gazed thoughtfully out across the gray-blue water.

"Would it be like building this yacht?" Stone asked. "Starting with a vision and overseeing every detail of its design and construction?"

"That's an apt metaphor," St. Clair replied dreamily, still keeping his attention on the water. Suddenly, he stood and pointed: "Porpoises," he said, smiling.

Stone swung around and saw a pod of half a dozen skimming along the surface, diving and coming up for a breath. They moved closer to the yacht and Christian and Stone got up and went to the rail for a better view. The animals were playing around the bow, now, so clearly enjoying themselves.

"Such lovely creatures," St. Clair said. "They have the knack of coming within inches of the bow, and yet they never get run down by what they're chasing."

"They just ride the bow wave," Stone said. "There's an art to that, and, maybe, a life lesson."

"I've been doing that all my life," Christian said. "Flirting with danger but keeping just far enough away to keep from being hurt."

"What sort of danger?"

Christian shrugged. "Land values, building costs, rates for borrowing and lending, pursuit of and by the competition, those sorts of things."

"Are you considering adding politics to the list?" Stone asked.

"It might be fun," Christian said, smiling a little, "but it's the most dangerous game of all, so much at stake, so much to go wrong, so many ways that things can happen, so many variables."

Stone wondered what he was thinking. Then his phone rang. He glanced at it: caller's name blocked; one of two people. "Excuse me," he said to Christian. He walked into the saloon and answered it.

"Good morning," Will Lee said. "Can you talk?"

"I can listen," Stone said.

"I hope you're aboard a yacht."

"I am."

"In Penobscot Bay?"

"Yes."

"Somebody else's yacht?"

"Yes."

"Whose?"

"Christian St. Clair's."

146

"Well, that's interesting. I'm going to want to pump you about that experience. Who else is aboard?"

"Harold Ozick, Clint Holder, and Nelson Knott. And their wives."

"Have they mugged you yet?"

"Not yet. They've been cordial, for the most part. Except Ozick, maybe."

"He's not a cordial sort."

"Are you tracking me?"

"I'm tracking Holly," Will said. "It's easier."

"Yes, she's using one of your cell phones, isn't she?"

"She is."

"Do you have a message for her?"

"No, and I don't want her to know I called. It would just make her think of work. I wanted to talk to you."

"Here I am."

"I was going to tell you that you might run into Christian St. Clair," Will said, "and, if you did, to watch your ass."

"I'll do that. The junior senator from my home state was here, but he jumped ship when he saw who his companions were going to be."

"He's a smart man, and you'd be smart to do the same."

"You're going to have to tell me what you mean."

"Later," Will said. "Right now I'm needed." He hung up.

Stone's phone was ringing again, from the other blocked number.

22

Stone pressed the button. "Hello, Ed."

"Stone, we need to talk."

"So talk."

"Not on the phone — face-to-face."

"I'd have a long swim," Stone said.

"Start now."

"Is it really that important?"

"I believe so."

"I'll see what I can do."

Stone went forward to the wheelhouse, where the captain was watching the autopilot steer the boat.

"Good morning, Mr. Barrington."

"Good morning, Captain, where are we?"

The captain looked down from his stool and pointed at the large screen in front of them. "Right there," he said, "where the little boat is."

"And we're how far from Islesboro?"

"About fifteen miles."

"I'm going to need a launch to take us there."

"You should speak to Mr. St. Clair," the captain said. "I'll need his permission."

Stone went back to the afterdeck, where St. Clair had finished his tea. "Christian, I'm sorry, but we need to leave the yacht and return to Islesboro."

"Sounds urgent."

"Some personal business I have to take care of personally." Stone wondered what that could be. "The captain says we're only fifteen miles out from Islesboro."

Christian picked up a nearby phone and pressed a button. "Captain," he said, "please alter course for Islesboro and prepare a launch to take Mr. Barrington and Ms. Barker to his dock." He hung up. "That's done."

"I'd better pack," Stone said, and went below. Holly had fallen back asleep.

"Up and at 'em," Stone said, kissing her on the ear with a loud smack.

"Are we sinking?" she asked sleepily.

"Ed Rawls seems to think so — so does Will Lee. They've both advised us to get back on dry land."

"Oh, all right," she said, sitting up. "Do I have time to shower and pack?"

"Both, if you hurry." Stone could feel the

150

yacht making its turn.

They were dropped at Stone's dock, and they went to the house. Stone unlocked the door and looked around. "Everything seems shipshape," he said. He unlocked the door to Dick's little office, then opened the safe. It was there, unmolested. He returned to Holly. "All seems to be well."

His phone rang.

"Yes?"

"Can you get over here, please?" Rawls asked.

"Give us a few minutes."

"As few as possible."

"Are you all right?"

"Not really."

"We're on our way."

They stopped at the gate and waited for it to open; it took a moment, then they had to wait another moment for the log to roll out of the way before driving through.

The front door was open. "Ed?"

"Come in," Rawls said.

They found him sitting in his reclining chair. CNN was on. "What's going on?"

"Look around you," Ed said.

Stone looked around and saw nothing. "What am I looking for?"

"Someone's been in the house."

"How can you tell?"

"Things have been changed, things only I would notice."

"What about the bookcase?" Stone asked, referring to the entrance to the former swimming pool.

"Books have been taken down and replaced, but in the wrong order."

"Did they breach your archive?"

"I don't know — maybe, maybe not."

"Was anything disturbed there?"

"If they got in, they were more careful than they were in the house."

"Where were you when this happened?"

"Sleeping. I took a pill last night, an Ambien."

"Would that make you sleep soundly enough for them to get in without waking you?"

"I checked the pill bottle. My dosage is five milligrams. The pills had been changed to ten milligrams. That would be enough to keep me down. Plus, I had a few drinks last evening. I'm still woozy."

"Well, at least you gave us an excuse to get off the yacht. I think we'd worn out our welcome with our fellow passengers."

"The same ones as before?"

"Nope." Stone told him about Ozick and

Holder. "Whit Saltonstall jumped ship as we were arriving, as soon as he got out of bed and saw who was joining."

"Did you make any friends?" Ed asked.

"I don't think so."

"Not a chance," Holly said. "We asked too many uncomfortable questions."

"Will Lee called, too, just before you did, and voiced the opinion that we should get off."

"Maybe Kate has sent a submarine to torpedo it," Holly said.

"What a great idea!" Ed replied. "Stone, would you mind making me a cup of coffee? I can't seem to get out of this chair."

"I'll do it," Holly said. "Stone hasn't made a cup of coffee for at least a decade."

"I can't argue with that," Stone said, taking a chair. "Make me one, too, will you? And yourself?"

When Holly came back with the coffee, she had to wake up Ed. "It's very strong."

"That's how I like it," Ed said, pressing the button on his chair that returned it to a sitting position. "Now that I think of it," Ed said, "they probably didn't get into the archive. If they had, I doubt if I'd be alive."

"Oh," Stone said, "I forgot to mention that one Nelson Knott was aboard."

"Now *that* is interesting," Rawls said. "I

saw the news on TV about his announcement."

"Ozick told me that Knott had already asked him for a hundred-million-dollar donation to his PAC."

"Did he get it?"

"I don't think so, but Ozick is mulling it over, and I think he'll come up with it. I mean, if he doesn't want Kate to be re-elected, what are his choices? Barry Goldwater is dead, and Pat Buchanan isn't running. Knott told us he'd already loaned his campaign fifty million."

"He could write that check," Rawls said. "*Forbes* says he's worth fifteen billion."

"Holly is worried," Stone said.

"I am," Holly agreed. "He's richer and smarter than the last guy, and he's great on TV."

"That's half the ball game," Ed said.

"Yeah, but the other half is going to be a lot tougher," she said.

"Ed," Stone said, "I think you'd better come home with us — pack a few things."

"I don't want to leave here."

"Ed, if you didn't believe you were in danger here, you wouldn't have insisted we come ashore. My place is much more secure than yours, so kindly get your ass in gear. And leave your car here and ride with us."

"Oh, all right," Rawls said, struggling out of his chair. "Gimme a minute."

23

Stone and Holly drove Ed back to Stone's house, and they pulled the old station wagon into the garage, so nobody would see them enter the house. Bob greeted them as they came in the door.

"Who's this?" Rawls asked.

"This is Bob."

"I used to have a Lab. Great dogs."

Bob allowed himself to be scratched behind the ears.

Stone grabbed Ed's bag and led the way upstairs to a bedroom. He left Ed to get settled and went back downstairs.

"I feel better with Ed here," Holly said.

"So do I. I keep thinking we're going to find him dead at his house."

Ed came back downstairs. "Did you open the strong case yet?"

"No," Stone replied.

"That's good. You don't want to know too much at this point. As it is, they probably think I've told you everything."

"They?" Holly asked.

"For want of a better name."

Stone fixed them all a drink, called Seth and Mary and told them they'd be three for dinner, then they sat down. Ed found the remote and turned on the TV to CNN. "I feel more connected if it's on," he said.

"Ed," Stone said, "why did you leave the strong case with Joe Adams?"

"I saw Joe and Sue last summer, when they were on Mount Desert Island, and we talked about what I had. We agreed that I should put together what's in the case as a backup, and I gave it to them before they went to Santa Fe in the autumn."

"What sort of shape was Joe in when you saw him last?"

"He seemed lucid most of the time. Now and then he would call me Tom."

"He did the same with me when I saw him last," Stone said. "Any idea who Tom is?"

"I don't know, maybe one of his Secret Service detail."

"I guess that makes sense. Did Joe know about your archive here?"

"Sort of. I didn't go into detail about my storage area."

"How much does Sue know?"

"She was always there when Joe and I

157

talked — mostly, I think, to kind of translate for Joe, if he lost the thread of the conversation. She could bring him back on track most of the time. When he got tired, he was more likely to wander, and she'd get him off to bed."

"How did they get him up and down stairs?" Stone asked.

"He walked," Ed replied. "He wasn't that far gone."

"When I saw him a couple of weeks ago, he had one of those electric scooters."

"I suppose he was declining." He saw something on TV and turned it up. They were talking about a state funeral for Joe Adams at the National Cathedral, with burial to follow at Arlington.

"That's fitting," Ed said.

"Do you think Sue will come to Maine this summer?"

"I expect so. They have friends on Mount Desert, neighbors they know. They had a boy killed in Vietnam but no other kids."

"It's going to be lonely for her," Holly said.

Mary called them to dinner.

After dinner, as they were moving back into the living room, they heard a siren from a passing vehicle.

"That's the volunteer fire department," Ed said. He went to the front door and looked outside. "Oh, shit," he said.

Stone and Holly joined him at the door. "What is it?"

"It's my house," Ed said, pointing at the flames in the distance.

"It's a good thing you're here, Ed."

"Yeah, I guess they expected me to take another pill and be in bed by now."

"We'd better call the police," Stone said.

"I don't think that's a good idea," Ed replied.

"Why not?"

"Until the place cools down and the volunteers have a chance to poke through the ashes, they're going to think I died there, and that's okay with me."

"I see your point," Stone said. "I think that early tomorrow morning we should get the Cessna over here to fly us to Rockland, then go to New York."

"Why New York?" Ed asked.

"Safety in numbers, real cops, real FBI, should we need them. I have a large house. We'll install you in a suite, and you can watch all the CNN you like while we figure out what to do."

"I hate to leave," Ed said.

"You don't want to stay here now, Ed,"

Holly said, "not until this is over."

"It won't be over until after the election," Ed said. "If then."

"Ed," Stone asked, "are the firemen going to find your archive?"

"Unlikely," Ed replied, "unless they're looking for it. There are two fire doors between the house and the archive, so it wouldn't have burned."

Stone called Rockland airport and arranged for their pickup, then let Seth know their departure time.

They were at the airport at six AM, before the island began stirring, so no one would see Ed's departure. An hour later they were taxiing to the runway in Rockland for takeoff. Stone didn't file a flight plan, and they flew back to Oxford, Connecticut. From there he filed, and they made a normal trip to Teterboro, where Fred was waiting with the car. An hour after that, they were pulling into Stone's garage.

Stone locked the strong case in his safe, then took Ed upstairs to his rooms, then he returned to his office and began catching up on work with Joan.

"Who's your guest?" Joan asked.

"His name is Ed," Stone replied. "That's all you need to know."

"Whatever you say."

When she had returned to her office, Stone called Dino.

"Bacchetti."

"Welcome me home," Stone said.

"Okay, welcome home."

"You two free for dinner at my house this evening?"

"Special occasion?"

"Not exactly, but I think you'll find the company interesting."

"You mean, it won't be just you?"

"Holly's here, and another guest."

"Male or female?"

"I'll let you figure it out. Six-thirty for drinks?"

"We can do that. What are you being so mysterious about?"

"All will be revealed at dinner."

"Really?"

"Well, maybe not all — just enough to keep you engaged."

"Okay, pal, we'll see you at six-thirty." Dino hung up.

24

Stone and Holly sat in the study with the Bacchettis; Ed Rawls had not appeared yet.

"So where's your guest?" Dino asked.

"He'll be along."

"Ah, now we know gender — progress!"

"I think you'll find him an interesting man, if you can set aside any preconceived notions you might have."

"Preconceived notions — more progress! Is it Al Capone? I have some preconceived notions about him."

The phone buzzed, and Stone picked it up. "Hello?"

"I fell asleep, so I'm running a few minutes late," Ed said.

"We'll drink one for you."

"Is he not going to show?" Dino asked.

"He'll show, but he'll be a little late."

"Why don't you fill me in so I can dispel my preconceived notions?"

"Oh, all right, it's Ed Rawls."

Dino stared at him with furrowed brow. "Sounds familiar," he said, then his face fell. "Holy shit, *that* Ed Rawls? Isn't he in a federal pen?"

"No, he was pardoned a couple of years ago. He's been living on Islesboro since then. This is the first time he's been off the island."

"You're having a *traitor* as your guest of honor for dinner?"

"Dino, watch your preconceived notions."

"You mean he's *not* a traitor?"

"He is not. He was the Agency's station chief in Stockholm, and he got in bed with a pretty girl."

"Was the pretty girl Russian?"

"She was, but he thought she was Swedish. The KGB blackmailed him into giving them some information, but he was smart enough to only give them harmless stuff. Kate Lee got on to him and nailed him. He pled guilty and got twenty years, served seven, I think."

"About when he'd be eligible for parole."

"He would have had to serve every day of it, but he was helpful to his government in ways I don't even know about, and Will pardoned him on the last day of his presidency."

"Well, if Will thinks he's okay, I guess

that's good enough for me," Dino said.

"That's awfully good of you, Dino," his wife, Viv, said.

"Sarcasm is unattractive," he replied.

"It was irony."

"Whatever."

Ed Rawls appeared in the doorway, dressed smartly in a blue blazer and a necktie. "Good evening," he said. "I apologize for keeping you waiting."

"You didn't keep us waiting," Stone said, raising his glass. "You just gave us a head start." He introduced Ed to the Bacchettis.

Dino rose and shook his hand. "Thank you for whatever you did that got you a pardon."

"Dino!" Viv said.

Ed laughed heartily. "First thanks I ever had," he said, "whether I deserved it or not." He sat down, and asked for a single malt, one ice cube.

Stone poured him a Talisker.

"Smoky and spicy," Ed said, tasting it. "Perfect. Dino — if I may call you that . . ."

"Sure, it's my name."

"I believe you are this fair city's police commissioner."

"And I thought you had been on a desert island for years."

"The *New York Times* arrives every day in

time for cocktails," Ed said. "I tend to memorize it."

"You have a photographic memory?" Dino asked.

"It's weirder than that," Ed replied. "I just sort of absorb it without thinking about it."

"I could make great use of that faculty," Dino said. "I don't suppose it's transferable."

"No, but it served me well in my work for many years."

"Are you married, Ed?" Viv asked. "Kids?"

"My wife filed for divorce the day I pled guilty," Ed said. "We had a daughter, but she died in the embassy explosion in Nairobi, in '98, one of two hundred and thirty-two who did. It was her first posting for the Agency after she completed her training."

"I'm sorry for your loss," Viv said.

"Thank you. It was an even greater loss for her country. She was a very bright young woman who would have had a spectacular career as a covert officer. She was fluent in French, German, and Swahili."

Fred Flicker entered the room. "Excuse me, ladies and gentlemen, dinner is served in the dining room."

They tossed off their drinks and followed Fred in.

Helene had prepared a mushroom bisque

and a crown roast of lamb, and they drank two bottles of a Dancing Hares cabernet sauvignon, 2010. They moved on to dessert, apple pie à la mode, with a bottle of sauterne, a Chateau Coutet, 1978.

Ed was more relaxed than Stone had ever seen him, and more charming, too. This was a new Ed Rawls, one that Stone liked a lot.

Dino liked him, too. "Tell me, Ed, what really happened at Roswell, New Mexico, when that spacecraft crashed?"

"Dino," Ed said, looking serious, "if I told you that I'd be arrested all over again, and this time, they wouldn't let me go."

They moved back into the study for cognac and coffee. They had just settled down when Stone's cell phone rang. He looked at the number and recognized it. "Excuse me," he said. He left the room and came back five minutes later.

"That was a captain in the Maine State Police," Stone said. "First, I should tell you that Ed's house burned down last night, while we were at dinner at my house."

"Was it an accident?" Dino asked.

"They don't believe it was — there was evidence of an accelerant found. The captain said their preliminary conclusion was that it was a suicide."

Everybody was quiet while digesting that.

"Well," Ed said, "I'm glad it was only a preliminary conclusion. I'd miss me."

Everybody laughed, except Stone. "The body was found in the living room, and the police were puzzled by something."

"I should think they were," Ed said.

"Underneath the body of the man they found an FBI badge in a wallet. His picture ID burned, but the badge survived."

"Well, Ed," Dino said, "you never told us you were an FBI agent."

"They ran the badge number," Stone said, "and it didn't exist. Ed, they apparently believed that you had been impersonating a federal law enforcement officer, which would be a serious crime, if you weren't dead."

"Stone," Dino said, "is this about the strong case downstairs in your safe?"

25

Stone stared at Dino. "How the hell do you know about the strong case?"

"I think Will Lee was concerned about your safety," Dino replied, "or maybe just about the safety of the strong case. I guess he wanted a backup. Anyway, he called me."

Stone relaxed. "You gave me a scare for a minute. I thought I was doing this in the strictest confidence, but apparently not."

"Maybe Will thought it was okay to share it with your best friend in the world."

"Apparently so. I just wish he'd told me."

"Does he know about the fire at Ed's house?"

"Not from me."

"You may not be his only source of information," Dino said.

"Good point," Ed Rawls said. "He might be in touch with someone on the island."

"Or someone in the Maine State Police," Stone pointed out.

"At this stage of the game, I don't think it matters," Ed said.

"And what," Dino asked, "is the game?"

"Politics is my best guess."

"Well, why don't we take a look at the contents?" Dino asked. "We're all good friends here."

"I don't think you want to do that," Ed said.

Dino turned toward Stone. "What is he talking about?"

"I don't know. He told me the same thing, and I took him at his word."

"Maybe you should take him at his word, too, Dino," Viv said.

Dino made a grunting noise and shifted uncomfortably in his chair.

"Contain your curiosity," Viv said. "You might be happier for it."

"I've never been happier for *not* knowing something."

"You might be happier not knowing what happened at Roswell," Ed said.

"I was joking."

Ed grinned. "So was I."

"Ed," Holly said, "just out of curiosity, how did you come to have the strong case? Not what's in it, just the case."

"I was issued it for an operation many years ago," Ed replied, "and somehow it never made its way back to Technical Services."

"Did you have occasion to open it during the operation?"

"Actually, no. Someone else had the key. That person removed the contents and gave me the case and the key."

"But you opened it to place its current contents inside?"

"Yes, I did."

"How did you know how to open the case safely?" Holly asked.

"Safely?" Dino asked. "What does it do, squirt you in the eye if you open it wrong?"

"Something like that," Holly replied, "unless you know the drill."

"What's the drill?"

"Don't tell him, Holly," Stone said.

"Do you know how to open it, Stone?" Dino asked.

"No, I don't, and I don't want to learn."

"So Holly and Ed are the only ones who know how to open it."

"The only ones here," Holly said.

"Well, Stone," Dino said, "if something should happen to you, I'll remember not to open the case."

"Much better for everybody," Ed said.

Stone's cell phone rang, and he looked at it. Blocked number. "Excuse me," he said, and left the room to answer it.

"Hello?"

"Is your friend from Islesboro all right?" Will asked.

"Yes."

"Is he with you?"

"Yes. My other friend is here, too. Apparently, you told him about the package, as well."

"I thought it prudent to do so."

"How did you know about the arson?"

"Someone I know got a call from someone who knew."

"I must say, I'm impressed with your networking skills."

Will laughed. "It comes from a lifetime of keeping index cards and computer files on people I met along the way. I've got a pretty good memory, too."

"What do you want me to do now?"

"Absolutely nothing," Will said. "Secure the package and hang on to it. There is something your friend from the island can do, though."

"What's that?"

"Some people we know down in Virginia would like to have a word with him. Could that be managed where you are now?"

"It could be, if he wants to speak with them."

"Can you think of any reason he wouldn't want to?"

"No, but he might have his own reasons."

"May I speak to him?"

"Hold on, I'll see." Stone put the phone down, went back to the study, and beckoned Ed to join him.

Ed got up and left the study. "What's up?"

"Will Lee is on the phone, and he'd like to speak to you."

"What about?"

"He says some people at the Agency would like to come here and talk to you."

"Where's the phone?"

Stone pointed to the end table where he had left it. Ed walked over and picked it up. "Yes, sir?" He listened for a moment. "No, sir." He listened some more. "I'm sorry, but no, sir." He held up the phone. "You want to speak to him again?"

Stone shook his head.

"Good night, sir." Rawls broke the connection and handed the phone to Stone.

"I take it you don't want to talk to them."

"You take it right."

"Why not?"

"An uncomfortable number of people have already come to know about this situation, and I see no profit in adding to that list," Ed said. "The more people who know

172

about it the more dangerous this gets."

"I understand," Stone said, pocketing his phone. He wondered if Will Lee understood, or if the people at the Agency did.

They went back into the study to finish their brandy.

"You two don't look very happy," Dino said.

"Conversations with powerful people make me nervous," Ed said. He picked up his cognac and raised his glass. "Cheers."

26

Stone worked at being an attorney all day, and at lunchtime, Fred brought him a sandwich at his desk.

"Thank you, Fred. You might ask Mr. Rawls if he'd like some lunch."

"I visited his quarters a few minutes ago, sir, but he was not present, nor is he anywhere else in the house."

"Did you see him leave?"

"No, sir."

"And you have no idea where he's gone?"

"No, sir."

"Please check his suite every half hour and let me know if he turns up."

"Yes, sir." Fred departed.

Stone called Dino.

"What?"

"Ed Rawls has disappeared from the house."

"Maybe he went for a stroll — people do that."

"Ed isn't the stroll type."

"How do you know? On Islesboro he could take a stroll every hour, and you wouldn't know it."

"Nevertheless, I'm worried."

"And you want me to put out an APB on him, is that it?"

"Not exactly. Could you just ask your people to keep an eye out for him?"

"Keep an eye out where?"

"I don't know, exactly, in my neighborhood, I guess."

"You mean you don't want me to block the bridges and tunnels? The airports? Check the hospitals?"

"I don't think that will be necessary."

"I don't think *anything* will be necessary at this point in time. If he doesn't come home for dinner, call me again. You can be such an old woman, Stone." Dino hung up.

Stone buzzed Fred. "Will you take a walk around the neighborhood and see if you see Mr. Rawls?"

"Of course, sir. How far around the neighborhood?"

"A couple of blocks in all directions."

"And if I find him, what shall I do?"

"Just make sure he's okay, and call me if you find him. Just observe from a distance."

"Certainly, sir."

Stone called Ed's cell number, got the usual message, and asked him to call in. He hung up and tried to think ahead. If Ed didn't turn up, what would he do? He would call Dino, that's what. But what would he do about the strong case? Open it? He'd burn that bridge when he came to it.

Joan buzzed him. "An insurance man on line one for you."

Stone picked up the phone.

"Mr. Stone Barrington?"

"Yes."

"This is Marvin Raymond in the claims department at the Steele Insurance Group."

"The claims department?"

"Yes, sir."

"I haven't filed a claim."

"No, sir, but if you had, it would have come across my desk."

"I don't understand."

"The claim was filed by a Mr. Edward Rawls, through our agent in the Penobscot region of Maine. He listed you as his attorney."

"What sort of claim?"

"It seems that someone burned down his house. We've had confirmation of that from the Maine State Police, who investigated."

"That is so."

"What we're concerned about is Mr. Rawls himself."

Stone refrained from mentioning that he was concerned, too.

"What about him?"

"Well, the police told us that they found a male body in the ruins of the house, and they assumed it was Mr. Rawls. If that is so, how did he come to file a claim?"

"The body was apparently that of the arsonist. Mr. Rawls was having dinner with me at my home on Islesboro at the time of the fire."

"Ah. Can you confirm that Mr. Rawls is still extant?"

Stone thought before answering. "He was, at dinner last evening. I haven't seen him today."

"So you can't swear that he is still alive?"

"Having heard nothing to the contrary, I surmise that Mr. Rawls is alive and well."

"In that case, we will proceed with paying his claim."

"Good."

"If you should hear anything, ah, discouraging about Mr. Rawls's continuing existence, I'd be grateful for a call."

"Mr. Raymond, even if Mr. Rawls is not still extant, as you put it, his claim is still a valid one and should be processed as such."

"Quite so," the man said. "Thank you for your assistance and good day." He hung up.

Stone fidgeted through the afternoon, reviewing documents and forgetting what he'd read, then starting over. He didn't get a lot done.

At around six o'clock he heard a small chime that meant the front door had been opened. He buzzed Fred.

"Yes, sir?"

"Did you just come into the house?"

"Yes, sir. I had a thorough look around the neighborhood and saw no trace of Mr. Rawls."

"Thank you, Fred." He hung up.

Ten minutes passed, and he heard the chime again. He went upstairs to check for himself and found Ed and Holly making drinks in his study. "Good God," he said aloud.

"I don't believe he's joining us for cocktails," Holly replied, "but we'd be delighted to have you anyway."

"Ed, where have you been?"

"Shopping," Rawls replied.

"Shopping?"

"At Brooks Brothers. I haven't bought any clothes for some years that didn't come from L.L. Bean, and everything I had went up with the house." Ed raised a glass and took a swig of his Talisker. "Then we took a stroll in Central Park."

"A stroll?"

"A stroll," Ed repeated. "You know, one foot in front of the other? We had a hot dog, too."

Stone poured himself a drink and sat down. "I was concerned."

"About me? How nice of you, Stone, but why?"

"You vanished. We didn't know where you were."

"I'm very sorry. I didn't consider that you might want to know where I was."

"Apparently," Holly said, "you didn't miss *me* at all — not the least concern for my whereabouts."

"I believe that's called being hoist with your own petard," Ed said with something resembling a smirk.

Mercifully, the phone rang before Stone had to reply. "Hello?"

"It's Dino."

"Hello, Dino, what can I do for you?"

"I was calling to ask if I should block the bridges and tunnels, check the airports, and canvas the hospitals."

"What?"

"For Ed."

179

"Oh, no, that's quite all right. He's fine, he just went for a stroll." He said that before he caught himself.

"A stroll?"

"Well, yes, he went shopping, too. Brooks Brothers."

Silence.

"His clothes all burned up in the fire."

"And he wasn't kidnapped or assassinated along the way?"

"He's perfectly all right, Dino."

"I am relieved to hear it," Dino said, then hung up.

Stone hung up, too. "That was Dino," he explained.

"We got that when you called him Dino," Holly said. "I believe you were explaining, or attempting to, how it came to be that you missed Ed, but not me."

"Ah, can I get anybody another drink?"

"We've hardly started on this one." Holly turned to Ed. "He has no explanation."

Stone got himself another drink.

27

The following morning Stone was at his desk again when Joan buzzed.

"Yes?"

"There are two gentlemen here who would like to see you, but they won't tell me who they are."

"Tell them to go away," Stone said.

Joan buzzed back. "That didn't work."

"Tell them to show you some ID, or you'll call the police."

Joan hung up, then buzzed back.

"Yes?"

"They say they're from the Central Intelligence Agency."

"ID?"

"Yes, on both counts."

Joan brought two middle-aged men in business suits into Stone's office. They introduced themselves as Parsons and Queen.

"Let's see some ID," Stone said.

They produced wallets.

"All right, sit down."

"We're here to see Edward Rawls."

"Mr. Rawls isn't seeing callers," Stone said. "I'm his attorney. What's this about?"

The two exchanged a glance. "We can't go into that," Parsons said.

Stone pointed. "There's the door."

"Now, listen, Barrington —"

"Don't let the doorknob hit you in the ass on the way out."

The two didn't move.

Stone buzzed Joan. "Please get me Lance Cabot on the phone." Cabot was director of central intelligence.

Parsons threw up a hand. "Just a minute."

"Hang on," Stone said to Joan, but he didn't hang up. "What?"

"Let's not make this adversarial," Parsons said. "We just want to talk to him."

"And I just want to find out if you're who you say you are," Stone said, "and what the hell you're doing in my office."

"Shall I ring Lance?" Joan asked.

"We'll go," Parsons said, rising.

"Cancel the call," Stone said to Joan, and hung up. "Why are you still here?" he asked the two men.

They shuffled out of his office, and he heard the door close behind them. He buzzed Ed's room.

"Hello?"

"Two guys from the Agency were just here to see you."

"What did you tell them?"

"That you weren't receiving callers."

"I couldn't have put it better myself. I'm sorry you were disturbed."

"Don't mention it," Stone said.

Joan buzzed. "Lance Cabot on one."

Stone pressed the button. "Good morning, Lance, long time no see or hear from."

"Good morning, Stone," Lance said smoothly. Lance said everything smoothly. "I understand you've been rude to two of my people."

"Oh, God, have I violated the National Intelligence Security Act again?"

"You made that up — you know very well there is no such act."

"I just said it to annoy you. What do you want, Lance?"

"We want to speak to Ed Rawls."

"I'm his attorney. You can speak to me."

"These are experienced officers, just doing their job."

"And what is their job?"

"I can't go into that."

"They didn't even want to show me ID."

"They are unaccustomed to dealing with

the general public."

"I'm hurt, Lance, I thought you and I were intimates."

"Sometimes — not this time. Did they show you their IDs?"

"Eventually. I'm a little skittish about that because a few days ago two men identifying themselves as FBI agents, with IDs and badges, presented themselves at my door in Maine. Turned out they were bogus, and so were their IDs."

"I can imagine how upsetting that must have been for you," Lance said archly.

"And one of them turned up dead in the ashes of Ed Rawls's house, complete with his bogus badge."

"That's very unsettling. Did you report this to the FBI?"

"Not yet."

"What are you waiting for?"

"I'm waiting to learn why you want to talk to Ed Rawls."

"I assume you know that already."

"Assume nothing."

"I believe that Ed is in possession of some documents that don't belong to him."

"I can assure you he is not."

"Then you are in possession of documents that don't belong to Ed."

"The only document of Ed's I'm aware of

is the insurance claim pertaining to the loss of his residence by arson."

"Obviously, that is not what I'm referring to."

"Well, if this conversation is to continue you're going to have to tell me what documents you think I'm in possession of."

"I expect you have already read them."

"I have not read any such documents."

"Why must you be so difficult to deal with, Stone?"

"Because you're not dealing with me, you're just badgering me and my client. If you want to deal with me, then deal."

"They are documents of a political nature."

"Then the CIA, being nonpolitical, should have no interest in them. I mean, they're not covered by any act of Congress I'm aware of, including the one I just made up."

"Stone, will you have lunch with me today?"

"Oh, you're in New York?"

"Just for the day."

"I'm not hungry."

"Oh, come on."

"You just want to badger me into betraying my client's confidence, and I'm not going to do it, so why have lunch?"

"All right, tell me how I can get in touch

with Ed Rawls."

"Through me."

"That is, apparently, a dead line."

"Now you're getting the picture, Lance, and it took such a long time."

"Stone, one day soon you're going to call me and ask me to do something for you."

"What would I want you to do for me?"

"Oh, something — very likely something I shouldn't do. Life is a two-way street, Stone."

"That's very pithy. Can I quote you?"

"You can tell Ed Rawls I said that." Lance hung up.

28

Stone hung up and was immediately sorry he had let Lance do it first. Joan appeared in his doorway. "I'm afraid . . ."

Lance Cabot stepped from behind her. "Good morning again, Stone."

"You were in your car all along, weren't you?"

"I was. I didn't want to be intrusive."

"You mean like you're doing now?"

"My more courteous efforts were rebuffed." Lance made himself comfortable in the chair facing Stone.

"Have a seat, Lance," Stone said. "Make yourself comfortable."

"I renew my invitation to lunch," Lance said. "We'll go to that club where we both are members. Then we won't have to fight over the check."

Stone glanced at his watch. "I'm still not hungry."

"You will be by the time we're done here."

"And what are we doing here?"

"Please pick up the phone and ask Ed Rawls to join us."

"I've already told you . . ."

Lance held up a hand. "I don't mind if he's represented by counsel. This is not a legal proceeding, it's just a friendly chat."

"And where is the muscle?"

Lance laughed. "Those two paunchy timeservers? They've gone their own way. I'm glad we're able to get together. I have some things to tell Ed, and it's best if you hear them, too. Saves time."

Stone picked up the phone and buzzed Ed.

"Yes?"

"Lance Cabot is in my office. I think it's best to come down. Don't worry, you won't have to say anything, unless you want to."

"Be right down," Ed said, and hung up.

They sat quietly, trying not to stare at each other, until Ed walked into the office and sat down on the sofa across the room.

"Hello, Ed," Lance said. "It's been a very long time."

"Copenhagen, wasn't it?" Ed asked.

"In the Danny Kaye suite at the Hotel d'Angleterre, the one where the star stayed when they were filming *Hans Christian Andersen.*"

"I recall," Ed said.

"Ed, you've been away from us for a long time, so I thought it might be a good idea if I reminded you of some old Agency practices and, perhaps, informed you of some newer ones."

"I'm here to listen," Ed said.

Stone gave him a thumbs-up by way of agreement.

"You will surely recall that the Agency requires its officers to submit any book or magazine material for approval before publication, even before showing such manuscripts to agents or publishers."

"I have neither an agent nor a publisher," Ed said.

"Only an attorney," Stone said.

"And I am aware, Stone, that, with your wide acquaintance in New York, you are perfectly capable of representing Ed in his dealings with publishers."

"Quite so," Stone replied.

"Ed, our publishing policy has not changed. You may be aware that many manuscripts by former officers have been vetted and published."

"Sure," Ed said, "with a lot of black lines drawn through blocks of text."

"What I hope is that, before you show a manuscript even to Stone, you will go through the text and draw those lines your-self."

"You mean, you don't want me to just blurt out everything I know about the Agency?"

"Certainly not, Ed, and you will know as well as anybody on our committee which passages require redacting."

"I think what you mean, Lance, is that you don't want even your committee to know what's in the unexpurgated version."

"That is so," Lance said. "Information that is very sensitive has its way of spreading, and it spreads in proportion to the number of people who first possess it."

"Perhaps there are things that present-day officers need to know about what their predecessors got up to."

"We compartmentalize," Lance said, "vertically as well as horizontally."

"Every organization has a history," Ed said. "What's wrong with that?"

"We are not every organization," Lance said firmly. "I think you are in a position to know that."

"Oh, I know it very well, but I believe that a system, even a secret one — *especially* a secret one — needs to be periodically purged in order to retain its long-term health."

"Even if so doing would damage people in high places who maintain friendly relations with the Agency?"

Ed shrugged.

"Even if the country is damaged by being deprived of the leadership of some of the best Americans alive?"

"Are you saying that these people should not be held accountable for their actions?"

"Certainly not. I believe the country is well served by knowing what their government has done — *after* sufficient time has passed for the damage to be put into perspective."

"You mean, fifty years after those people are dead? What about the generations between now and then? Are they to remain ignorant of what was done on their behalf?"

"Lance," Stone said, "can you be specific? Give us an example?"

"Why, of course, Stone. May I remind you, as an example, of two events that you are well acquainted with — when an outgoing President, on the morning of the inaugural day of his successor, in, quite literally, the final hours of his service, secretly pardoned two dangerous criminals, one who had assassinated high officials of our democracy, the other who was the most notorious traitor to this country since, perhaps, Benedict Arnold? How, if these things became known, would they affect the political longevity of his successor?"

"Will had very good reasons for his action, and we don't know if Kate had any part in that," Stone pointed out.

"Right on both points, but what does that matter?" Lance demanded. "Her political opposition would immediately assume, perhaps dishonestly, that she did, and so would many members of the public at large, and she would be pilloried. Can you, in good conscience, allow that to happen?"

"I am not in a position to make that judgment."

Lance pointed a finger at Ed Rawls. "*He is!* And you have taken it upon yourself to be his advisor."

"That is not my role in this matter," Stone said firmly. "I have been asked by a person I respect to keep all that from happening by securing . . . whatever is in that package."

"And is it secure?" Lance asked. He pointed at Stone's safe. "I know a dozen people who could unlock that in five minutes, and then it would be insecure."

"I expect you do," Stone replied. "Is that your plan?"

"And there is something else I haven't mentioned," Lance said, ignoring his question. "Even if what you have is destroyed, as Ed's house was destroyed, there is still something I have heard about for years — the legendary memory of Ed Rawls, who, if he lives up to his reputation, could spew every fact in his head into a tape recorder, and then we would be back where we started."

There was a long silence, during which no one wished to speak.

Then Ed Rawls said, "I think what Lance wants is to separate my head from the rest of my body."

With that, Ed got up and walked out of the room. "You two have lunch," he said over his shoulder. "I'll order in."

29

Stone and Lance rode uptown in one of the Agency's omnipresent black SUVs, with inch-thick windows and Kevlar body lining, and neither had anything to say to the other on the way.

The vehicle pulled into the underground garage at a large town house in the East Sixties, and only when the heavy door had closed behind them did the attendants open the car's doors for them.

Shortly, they were seated in the spacious dining room, which used much of the available space to separate the tables, allowing the members to converse in normal tones without being overheard by their fellows.

"Did you know," Lance said, flapping out his huge linen napkin and arranging it in his lap, "that this room is equipped with a kind of electronic noise canceling that makes it impossible to know what is being said at neighboring tables?"

"I did not," Stone replied, wrestling to tame his own napkin.

"And that is why I may speak frankly to you in the midst of our peers, if such exist."

Stone laughed and ordered the gazpacho and the lobster salad.

"The same," Lance said to the waiter. "And a bottle of the Meursault." Then, when the man had retreated from their own little cone of silence, Lance began. "I saw a documentary film this morning that explains the malicious Stuxnet computer virus, of which you have no doubt heard."

"I've read about it in the *Times.*"

"It is called *Zero Days,*" Lance said. "I recommend the film, so that I won't have to explain it to you when next we meet. Suffice it to say that, after a thoroughgoing explanation of what it is and the almost unimaginable damage it could do to our moderately civilized world, if deployed in a cyberwar, it goes on to explain how very secret it has been kept by almost everyone who has any idea of its existence, because all of those people are so terrified by it."

"Sounds like sci-fi," Stone observed.

"It is sci-fi become hellishly real."

"Why are you telling me about this? Does it have something to do with what is in Ed's manuscript?"

"I am giving you an example of what the unintended consequences might be of making Ed's personal knowledge and experience known. I have already told you how it could remove a person I consider to be an excellent President from public life, and preventing her brilliant mind from having any further effect on our history. What I'm telling you now is that there are almost certainly other things in that strong case you're sitting on that could do untold damage to our government and, hence, to our lives."

"Why are you so certain of that?"

"Because I already know much of what Ed knows. And I wouldn't want what I know to become public knowledge. But there is something else to consider, as well."

"And what is that?"

"There is a move afoot for a new, third party to make a run in the next presidential election."

"I've heard something about that," Stone said. "In fact, I made the acquaintance of their putative candidate a few days ago."

Lance looked surprised, something Stone had never before seen happen.

"Good God, Lance, do you mean to tell me that I have learned something you don't already know?"

"Certainly not. I've known about the new party and its candidate for weeks," Lance said reprovingly. "What I didn't know was that *you* knew. How, pray tell, did that come to be?"

"I was invited for a Penobscot Bay cruise on the brand-new yacht of Christian St. Clair," Stone said. "And, incidentally, I believe there is mention of it on Facebook."

"You were in the company of Whit Saltonstall and the *Times* editor and the *Vanity Fair* publisher?"

"They, all of them, abandoned ship when further guests boarded, to wit, Harold Ozick, Clint Holder, and, fresh from a wee-hours infomercial, one Nelson Knott. We shared dinner and breakfast before I, too, scrambled ashore."

At that point, Senator Whitney Saltonstall entered the dining room, in the company of Dino Bacchetti. Lance and Stone raised their glasses, and Saltonstall gave them a little wave. Pointedly, perhaps, he did not come over to say hello.

"Where was I?" Lance said.

"You were being surprised that I knew something."

"Oh, yes. It takes only a cursory tour of our current political situation to know what could happen. We have a strong President and a sadly weakened opposition, and what looks like plain sailing ahead. But consider this: What if, shortly before the Democratic Convention, the matter of the secret pardons became known? And who knows, there may be other things in that manuscript."

"I see your point," Stone said. "We would have to rely on Congress to keep us on a fairly even keel."

"I also happen to know that these people are going to make a determined effort to go for majorities in both houses. They have already recruited several dozen candidates."

"They couldn't ever get majorities in both houses on such short notice."

"They wouldn't need majorities," Lance pointed out. "They could very easily pick up a lot of Republican and even some Democratic votes on crucial issues."

Stone thought about this. "Lance," he said, "the only reason I can think of for why I was invited aboard St. Clair's yacht is that he or some of his guests know that I have the strong case."

"That's very perceptive of you, Stone," Lance said, a sneer in his voice. "Why the hell else would a multibillionaire you didn't know invite you to meet two other multibillionaires you didn't know? Do you think they might have a motive other than enjoying your company?"

"Thank you, Lance, I get your point."

"May I also infer that right around this time, the two bogus FBI agents showed up at your house, and Ed Rawls's house was burned to the ground?"

Stone sighed. "That is not an unreasonable inference to draw."

"I didn't think so."

"Lance, do you think Will Lee knows about all this?"

"I'm certain of it," Lance said. "I told him myself."

"When?"

"A couple of weeks ago."

"I think there's something else I'd better tell you that you don't know," Stone said.

"I hope you're wrong about that."

"All right, Ed has a secret cellar reached by a tunnel from his house that contains his archives — a backup for everything he says in his manuscript."

"Well, I had guessed that something like that existed, but I didn't know where it was."

"Before you do anything about that," Stone said, "let me talk to Ed. It may be possible that he would do the right thing and allow the contents of the strong case and his archives to be destroyed."

"That would be very nice," Lance said.

"Please put that to him." Lance's attention seemed to wander for a moment before he spoke. "Then all we would have to worry about is what's in Ed Rawls's head."

30

Stone decided to walk home and declined a lift in Lance's bulletproof boxcar. It was a lovely day and he meandered to Park Avenue and walked, admiring the tulips, downtown to his own neighborhood, then home, all the way rehashing the situation and deciding what was the right thing to do. As he let himself into the house via his office door, he made his judgment. Joan was not at her desk.

He sat down in his office and buzzed Ed Rawls's room. No answer. He buzzed Fred.

"Yes, sir?"

"Have you seen Mr. Rawls this afternoon?"

"No, sir. I left the house for an hour or so to have a small repair done on the Bentley and returned only a few minutes ago."

"Thank you, Fred."

He heard Joan come through the front door. He buzzed her. "Joan?"

She picked up. "Yes?"

"Do you know where Ed Rawls is?"

"He had lunch in his room. After that, I went to the hairdresser's, as is my weekly wont."

"Thank you." Stone pressed the page button on his phone. "Ed, if you're in the house, please pick up any telephone."

A phone was picked up, but not by Ed. "Stone?" Holly said.

"Funny, you don't sound like Ed Rawls."

"He's not in. I stopped by his room to ask him something, but he didn't respond to my knock."

"Thank you." He hung up, and he had an awful feeling that Ed might have found the pressure too much and done something to himself. He got onto the elevator and went up to the guest floor, then knocked sharply on Ed's door. "Ed? It's Stone. You there?" No response, so with misgivings, he opened the door.

The room was in perfect order, and there was a stack of empty Brooks Brothers boxes neatly piled at the foot of the bed. The small duffel he had loaned Ed was sitting on the bed. He checked the bathroom: in perfect order.

Stone went back to his office, a knot in the pit of his stomach, and tapped in the combination to his safe. He spun the wheel and swung open the big door, checking the contents. The strong case was gone.

He sat down heavily, got out his iPhone, and called Ed.

"Good day," his voice said. "The person you have called no longer exists, and this phone is in a dumpster somewhere. Kindly go fuck yourself."

Stone hung up the phone. The bottom seemed to have dropped out of his stomach. He went into his contacts list, found Lance's cell number, and called it.

No one answered; there was just a beep. "Lance, it's Stone Barrington. Please call me at once."

He put the phone down and tried to think where Ed would go. His only home was a heap of ashes and rubble, so it was unlikely he would go there. Then where? He realized that he had never known Ed anywhere else but Islesboro. His phone rang.

"Hello?"

"What is it, Stone? I'm in a hurry."

"Ed Rawls has flown the coop."

"Which coop?"

"My coop. And the strong case is no longer in my safe. Tell me, is Ed one of those dozen people you know who could open it in ten minutes?"

"Jesus H. Christ," Lance said. "I thought we had this all sorted out."

"So did I, but apparently Ed disagrees."

"Do you have any idea where he could have gone?"

"His only home is Islesboro, and that's burned to a crisp, and I've no idea who or where his ex-wife is."

"I'll call you back." Lance hung up.

Holly rapped on his office door and came in. "Did you find Ed?"

Stone redialed Ed's number and handed Holly the phone. She listened and handed it back to him. "What does this mean?"

"He's gone."

"That's perfectly obvious. What does it mean?"

"I had a long conversation with Lance over lunch, and he convinced me that this whole business with Ed is much worse than I had contemplated."

"In what way?"

"Ed is, apparently, now a danger to himself and others — in fact, a danger to pretty much everything we hold dear."

"Please bring me up to date on that."

Stone recounted his entire conversation with Lance. "I came home prepared to turn over the strong case, but that is as gone as Ed. He got into my safe."

"Oh, shit," Holly said, flopping into a chair. "I'd better call Kate."

"Given your present status at the White House, I don't think you could get through." He called the White House and left a message for Will, adding "urgent" to it.

"Where would he go?" she asked. "Islesboro doesn't exist for him anymore."

"I was about to ask you the same question," Stone said. "I have no fucking idea."

"The ex-wife," she said.

"I thought of that, but I don't know who or where she is, or even if she's still alive. I mentioned it to Lance, and I expect he's looking into it."

"Does he have any money?"

"I've no idea."

The phone rang, and Stone answered it.

"It's Lance. Ed's ex-wife died five months ago, and apparently they hadn't spoken in years. I've got people going through his personnel file, listing people that he might contact."

"Great."

"I'll call you when I know more." He hung up.

Stone's phone rang almost immediately. "Yes?"

"Stone Barrington?"

"Yes, who's this?"

"This is Marvin at the Steele Insurance Group's claims department."

"Yes?"

"I tried to reach Mr. Rawls but got a rather strange message on his phone."

"Yes?"

"I thought perhaps you'd like to know that his claim has been approved, and I've wire-transferred half a million dollars to his bank account. That is the amount his home was insured for. If you could ask Mr. Rawls to send us a list of his furnishings with their replacement costs, we will process that claim separately. We thought he might like to have some cash now."

"Yes, I expect he would," Stone said. "Did you wire it to his Islesboro, Maine, account?"

"Let me see."

Stone could hear computer keys being tapped.

"No, not to the Maine account — one in Georgetown . . . let's see where that is . . . Ah, it's in someplace called the Cayman Islands."

"Thank you, Marvin. I'll give Mr. Rawls your message when I speak to him." He hung up and turned to Holly. "To answer your last question, his insurance claim for his house was approved and the funds wired. He now has half a million dollars in an offshore account."

31

Stone's phone rang again. "Hello?"

"It's me," Will Lee said.

"Bad news, I'm afraid," Stone said.

"Our friend from Virginia has already called and brought me up to date."

"I'm sorry about the package. It was locked in my safe."

"You weren't expected to have him in handcuffs. Do you have any idea where he may have gone?"

"None, I'm afraid. I had lunch with our Virginia friend today, and he convinced me not to allow our other friend to release the contents of the package. When I got home, he was gone. He has no home, now, after the fire, and the only other person I could think of that he might go to was his ex-wife, but I understand she died several months ago."

"What do you think he will do with the package?"

"He's had a lecture, in my presence, from our Virginia friend on the irresponsibility of circulating it."

"Unfortunately, there are many media organs who don't share the responsible view."

"Perhaps it might be time for you to reveal the contents of the package. If you use the period between now and the big event to explain things, the stories might peter out by that time."

"That would be very risky."

"Speak with your lady about it."

"She knows nothing of this business, and I don't feel it's the right time to tell her."

"When would the right time be?"

"On my deathbed, or perhaps much later."

"Are you coming up here soon?"

"Possibly. I'll give you a call, and we'll get together."

"I'd like that."

"Goodbye." He hung up.

Ed Rawls got off the train and, towing his new Brooks Brothers rolling bag with the strong case strapped to it, found the street and got into a taxi. After a brief negotiation with the driver over the long ride, he settled into the rear seat with the *Washington Post* and read until, over an hour later, they arrived.

The house was shuttered, but neat. The lawn service had taken care of the grass and plants. Ed left the real estate sign where it was, then let himself in and locked the door behind him. The house had been built in 1774 and rebuilt several times since, and it made little creaking noises as he walked up the stairs. His late ex-wife's clothes and personal items had been removed by the people he had hired, so he put his luggage in a cupboard in his old dressing room. He tried a lamp, and it worked; the phone did not, but he had half a dozen throwaway cell phones in a shopping bag.

He went downstairs with the strong case to his old study, which had hardly been touched. Myra had never liked it — too cave-like for her, but he felt instantly at home again, his books still on the shelves. He pressed a hidden button and a bookcase swung outward, revealing a large safe. He opened it, stowed the strong case inside, locked it, and swung the bookcase back into place. He switched on the computer and checked his mail — he had kept the e-mail address mostly to deal with the house. When they had divorced, he had given Myra lifetime occupancy, but he had retained title and had gone on paying the utility bills, insurance, lawn service, and the maid who came in twice a week. He switched on his reading lamp, found a book he hadn't read, and started it. He knew they would be here soon.

He had not long to wait. He heard a footstep on the front porch, and he switched off his lamp and stood behind the study door, perfectly still.

"Pretty quiet," he heard a male voice say. "You check upstairs, I'll look around for signs of life down here." Footsteps went up the stairs, others around the living room and kitchen. A man came and stood in the study doorway and played a flashlight around the room. Footsteps descended the stairs, and the two men stood outside in the main hall and talked for a minute.

"I called at the real estate office," one of them said, "and got a key. They've had some interest in the place, but not much. Nobody at the Agency would even look at it because it was associated with Rawls."

"You think there's a Russian radio hidden here somewhere?"

The other laughed. "No, our people went through the place thoroughly after Rawls was arrested and again after the woman died. It's just a house. I ought to buy it myself. It's less than five miles from the Agency." The two men left.

Rawls waited until he heard the car drive away, then he went back into his study, sat down, and resumed reading his book. Late in the afternoon he heard a truck in the driveway, and the clump of something being deposited on the front porch. He waited for the truck to drive away, then put down his book and went to the front door. He had ordered groceries over the phone, using a credit card from his Caymans bank, and they were here: a week's food and two bottles of the Talisker single malt he had enjoyed at Stone's house. He took them into the kitchen, put everything away, and made himself a drink, then returned to his study and his book. After a while he dozed off, and when he awoke it was dark outside. All the shades, blinds, and curtains were drawn, so he didn't need to worry about light leaks. He took one of his new cell phones from his pocket and made a call.

Stone picked up his phone; blocked call. "Hello?"

"Hello, Stone, it's Ed."

"I was worried about you, Ed."

"No, you were just worried about what I'd do. That's why I called."

"What are you going to do, Ed?"

"I'm going to keep my mouth shut. I've already destroyed my archive in Islesboro."

"And how did you do that?"

"There was an incendiary charge set in the pool room. I detonated it with a phone call and a code. It was designed to burn up everything and melt the metal cabinets. No paper would have survived."

"And the case?"

"It's safe, and I'll be out of the country before midnight."

"Everyone who's interested will be glad to hear it. For what it's worth, Ed, I believe it's the right thing to do."

"Maybe," he acknowledged. "You're going to get a check from my offshore bank for your services," he said.

"Not necessary."

"Yes, it is. I don't want to owe anybody anything."

"Oh, by the way, I had a call from your insurance agent. They've paid your claim and wired half a million dollars to your Caymans bank."

"Good to know, thanks."

"That was the insured value of the house. They said you could submit an additional claim for the contents."

"Maybe I'll get around to it."

"I suppose you've already got a throwaway phone. Keep in touch. I'd like to be able to reach you, should there be further developments."

"I'll check in from time to time," Ed said.

"Take care of yourself."

"I always do."

"You're not the subject of a criminal investigation, Ed, so the law isn't after you."

"That hardly matters, since there are enough other people after me."

"And who would that be?"

"Lance Cabot for one, the others are more shadowy."

"I'll see if I can cool Lance down a bit."

"You can try. Goodbye for now, Stone."

As he hung up he heard another car pull into the driveway, and he switched off the lamp. Shortly, the front door opened and he heard voices. He had a gun in a box on a bookshelf, disguised as leather-bound volumes. He quickly retrieved the pistol and stood behind the door again.

32

The front door was unlocked and opened, and Ed heard two, maybe three voices.

"It's really a lovely house," a woman said. "Big rooms for the period and lots of storage space." This, he figured, was the real estate agent.

The other two were a man and a woman, and their voices carried into the living room. Lights were switched on.

"How many square feet?" the man asked.

"About forty-five hundred in the main house. Then there's a fifteen-hundred-foot building with a two-car garage and guest or staff quarters, furnished. The property is available furnished throughout, since the owner was a divorcée with no children. The kitchen is this way."

Ed stood and listened to fragments of their conversation, then they came back and stood in the study doorway. The agent flipped on the overhead light. "Lots of bookcases, as you can see, and lots of books, too."

"Do the books come with the house?" the woman asked.

"They do, but if you don't want them I'm sure a local library would be glad to have them."

"Would you give us a minute to talk?" the man asked.

"Of course. I'll start turning off lights." The agent walked away.

"This is a dead end," the man said. "Except for cleaning, the place hasn't been touched since Rawls's ex died."

"I expect you're right," the woman replied, "but we need to write a report, anyway."

"I'll bet the Agency pulled this place apart after the woman died," the man said.

"If they did, they did a nice job of putting it back together."

"Let's get out of here," he said. "Ma'am?" he called out. "We're ready to leave now."

The agent returned. "Do you have any interest?"

"It's very nice," the woman said, "but we'll need to talk about it. What are you asking, again?"

"Two million, furnished. My instructions are that it's a firm price."

"That may be too steep for us," the man

said. Then the last light was turned off and the door locked. A minute later, the car drove away.

Rawls sat back in his chair, gave them five minutes, and switched his lamp back on. He checked his watch: nine-thirty; pretty late for a viewing. He went back to the kitchen and heated himself a can of soup.

Stone, Holly, and the Bacchettis were having dinner at Patroon. "So," Stone said, "what did you and Whit Saltonstall have to talk about at lunch?"

"This and that," Dino said.

"Come on, Dino, a politician doesn't waste time having lunch and talking about this and that."

"Nevertheless," Dino said. "What did you and Lance talk about?"

"This and that," Stone said, and the women laughed at them.

"I hear your buddy Rawls took a hike this afternoon."

"I think he thought there was no point in hanging around here. He will have prepared a place to disappear to — it's his nature, not to mention his training. He told me he'd be out of the country by midnight."

Dino looked at him sharply. "And this was after lunch?"

"A couple of hours ago."

"After he lit out?"

"Yes. He called me on a throwaway."

"From where?"

"Who knows? He had four or five hours to make himself scarce between the time he left and the time he called."

"I'll bet he's still in the country."

"He said he'd be out of it by midnight, remember?"

"Does he have any money?"

"His insurance company paid him half a million for his house today and wired it to an account in the Caymans."

"Plus whatever he had before."

"He lived as if he had some income, but not much."

"How do he and his ex-wife get along?"

"They don't. She died a while back, having not spoken to him since the divorce."

"I doubt, then, that she would have left the house to him."

"I doubt that, too, but I don't care."

"You don't care that your client is a fugitive?"

"A fugitive from what? He's not a criminal."

"Maybe he burned his own house down."

"Didn't I mention he was having dinner with Holly and me at my house when it happened?”

“He’s tech-savvy enough to have done that with a timer.”

“Why would he do that? It was his only home.”

“That you know about.”

“Granted.”

“You know where I think he’d go?” Dino asked.

“Where?”

“Venezuela.”

“That’s not exactly the garden spot of the Americas these days, you know.”

“Maybe, but nobody could ever find him there.”

“Except the Venezuelan police. They wouldn’t be very hospitable to a retired CIA officer. I think he’s somewhere more comfortable. Ed strikes me as someone who likes his comforts.”

“Who doesn’t?” Holly asked. “By the way, you’re both lousy cops.”

“That’s a terrible thing to say,” Dino said, looking wounded.

“You don’t have any evidence of anything, just suppositions. You can’t find a fugitive with suppositions, especially after the big supposition, the ex-wife, is out of the picture.”

“Well,” Stone said, “he has a nice wardrobe from Brooks Brothers. He wouldn't buy that so he could disappear into the Venezuelan jungle."

"I'll give you that," Dino said.

"Thank you so much."

"Anyway, he's not worried about the cops, and only a little worried about the Agency. He's worried about politics."

"Politics?" Viv asked. "What kind of politics?"

"National politics."

"Is he running for President?"

"No, but somebody is going to run against Kate Lee, and I think Ed knows who and why, or at least he knows enough about the candidate to worry that man and his friends."

"And who would that be?" Dino asked.

"A gentleman called Knott."

"Not what?"

"Not not — Knott, with a *k* and two *t*'s. Nelson Knott."

Dino shook his head. "This is all too fantastic for me."

"It's not as fantastic as you think. The man has already formed a party, called the Independent Patriot Party, and he's got a couple of dozen people to put up for Senate and House seats. He wants the whole ball of wax."

"This is making me tired," Dino said. "I want to go home." He raised a finger. "Check?"

33

Christian St. Clair watched the chopper drift in astern of the yacht, which was moving along at ten knots, lowering the ground speed of the chopper, which set down lightly on the afterdeck roof. The yacht's captain waved St. Clair up to the top deck and walked him to the chopper. They both ducked their heads instinctively, even though they had seven feet of clearance, eight feet for Christian.

St. Clair climbed into the rear seat of the copter, set his briefcase on the seat beside him, and put on his seat belt and headset. "Go," he said into the attached microphone, and the machine rose and peeled away from the yacht, turning to the southwest toward New York.

As they made their way toward the city, Christian reflected on what an important day this was for him. He owned everything a man could want — city houses, country houses, aircraft, seacraft, many cars, and enough art to fill a small museum. There was something else he wanted, though, something that perhaps no one had ever owned: a President of the United States.

Having his own President would make him a kind of benevolent dictator, in his mind. Instead of spending millions a year on lobbyists who conducted subversive campaigns for the legislation he needed, he would simply make a phone call to his President, and his will would be done. Of course, it would still be necessary to buy congressmen and senators, but he had enough of them already to carry any vote, as long as they and the President were of the same party.

He had chosen Nelson Knott carefully and groomed him even more so. Under his tutelage, Nelson had become a man of the people, when he needed to be, and at the drop of a hat. He was also intelligent and well educated, so he mingled nicely with the elite, too. As much at home at a chamber music concert as at the Grand Ole Opry, on a golf course or a NASCAR track, he was ideally suited to command broad appeal, as long as he had Christian's full financial backing.

Over a period of a few years, Nelson and

his wife had found their lot in life becoming steadily more beautiful and luxurious. Whereas they had once stayed at good hotels, now they stayed at great ones, and in large suites. They traveled in what they thought of as their own jet, though it was owned by St. Clair, through a maze of corporations. Their children were at Groton, Mount Holyoke, Harvard, and Princeton. Before the election there would be a gorgeous new concert venue completed in New York City, named Knott Hall, and it would rival Andrew Carnegie's best work.

Her clothes came from Paris and Milan; his from St. Clair's own London tailor, shirtmaker, and bootmaker. They lived in four houses, one of them in Branson, Missouri, and in a Fifth Avenue apartment — all designed by leading architects, and their books and artwork were chosen by Christian and impressed all who visited. Nelson had recently become a member of old-line, prestigious clubs in New York and Washington, and he was already playing golf at Augusta National.

Nelson Knott had a quality that Christian had never seen in another human being: he could take the hand of a man, look into his eyes, and become what that man wanted him to be, whether it be hillbilly or mandarin. He could sit at table in elegant homes bought with old-money fortunes, or at the grubbiest fried chicken joint on the inter-state and relate, in manner and in depth, with whoever was his dining companion.

He could converse on subjects from Jane Austen to Einstein to foreign policy with experts on those subjects and hold his own, or he could produce baseball and football stats in quantity from memory. He could knock the socks off any journalist who sat down to interview him on any occasion.

Nelson had been profiled in *The New Yorker* and *Fortune;* he would soon be on *60 Minutes,* taking up a whole hour, touring his properties, showing off his offices, and unhesitatingly answering any question they could come up with on any subject. When St. Clair had first met him a dozen years before, his mind had been a clean slate, and now, with Christian's careful tutoring, it was a large, impressionist painting of an Ameri-can life well lived.

The chopper settled down at the East Side Heliport, where a very large Mercedes van, with an interior like a luxurious corporate jet, awaited his bidding. Christian bade the driver to take him to the Club, in the East Sixties, where he had arranged a luncheon in a private dining room with ten of the most important but politically unaligned men in the United States. The goal was to impress them deeply but make no demands upon them. Christian would leave it to them to spread the word about this remarkable man they had met, his charm and erudition. Then, when the time came, most of them would form and endow political action committees that would reward Nelson Knott with fame and approbation and punish his enemies with ignominy and debasement.

Christian knew that Nelson had few if any enemies because he was so little known in the world he was entering, but of course he would make them as he made progress. While Nelson could be nearly all things to nearly all men, some would, inevitably, despise him for what he was or wasn't. That was the nature of human beings.

St. Clair entered the Club, took the elevator up to the little dining room, and closely inspected the table, the china, the silverware, and the flowers. Everything had to be perfect. Nelson Knott was announced and entered the room a quarter of an hour before the other guests, as planned. Christian greeted him warmly, but avoided hugging. If he could have changed anything important about Nelson, Christian would have made him a foot shorter. As it was, when the two men stood together, the difference in their heights was stunning, even with the lifts in Christian's shoes. He was careful never to embrace Nelson in the presence of others.

"Nelson, did you receive the briefing papers on our guests?"

"I did, Christian, and I have committed them to memory. I thank you for that courtesy."

"There will be four courses served," Christian said, "and you will change places between each course, so that you may speak individually with each of them."

"I will enjoy that," Nelson said.

"I will begin by saying a few words, and I will leave it with you to say a few words at the closing, to give them something to think about on their way back to their homes and offices."

"That's a good plan," Nelson said. "I had thought I might see Stone Barrington among today's guests," he said. "I was looking forward to seeing him again."

"I'm glad you liked him, Nelson, but he will not be committed to your support between now and the election; he is too close to Kate and Will Lee. After the election, though, I will see that you remake his acquaintance, because he could be useful to you over the years, perhaps as your personal attorney."

"A good thought," Nelson said.

Their guests began to arrive, and Christian managed the introductions.

34

When Christian St. Clair reentered his Mercedes van in the Club's basement, a man was waiting for him inside, by appointment. He was Erik Macher, a former FBI and intelligence agent who now operated as St. Clair's head of security, though few people in general or among St. Clair's many other employees had ever heard of Macher or even knew of his existence. He commanded St. Clair's private security contingent and operated on a very generous budget.

"Good afternoon, Mr. St. Clair," Macher said.

"Good afternoon, Erik. What do you have for me?"

"Since the disappearance of Edward Rawls we have undertaken a broad-based search for him, in this country and abroad, in countries where he served."

"And have you found him?"

"We have not. We have, however, located

what might be thought of as the most likely place he would shelter, even if he hasn't arrived there yet."

"And where would that be?"

"His ex-wife —"

"I told you, Erik, the woman died five months ago, and even if she were alive she would be the last person to offer him help."

"I understand, sir, but we have uncovered an important fact about their divorce."

"And what is that?"

"Although she sought and got the couple's house in Virginia, quite near CIA headquarters, she was not given title, but a lifetime occupancy. That having expired with her, the house still belongs to Ed Rawls."

"Have you checked it?"

"I placed two agents there last evening, posing as prospective buyers. The house has been on the market with a local agency since shortly after Myra Rawls's death. They were shown through it and left the agent with the hope of an offer to come. While there they examined every room and found no signs of occupancy by Rawls or anyone else. They also checked the outbuildings, including a barn and a garage containing a 1985 Mercedes station wagon, also registered in Ed Rawls's name, and connected to a trickle charger. There is a guest or staff flat upstairs. The place is an ideal hideout for Ed Rawls, he just hasn't taken advantage of it — not yet anyway."

"What are they asking for the house?"

"Two million dollars, firm."

"Buy it."

"Forgive me, sir, but unless you require a residence in that part of Virginia, that would be a totally unnecessary expense. It wouldn't even prevent Rawls from using it as a hideout for quite some time, and it would put a large sum in his pocket, upon closing, which he could then use to establish himself elsewhere. He has already collected half a million dollars in insurance money for his house in Maine, so he is awash in cash already. It was wired to an offshore account in the Cayman Islands."

"Can we find out how much is in the account?"

"Very nearly impossible, sir. It would require millions in bribes to bank staff, and it is very likely a numbered account without his name on it."

"The insurance company would have the number, wouldn't they?"

"No, sir. The funds would have been wired directly to the bank, who then, by previous instruction, would have deposited them in the numbered account."

"Is the strong case still with Stone Barrington?"

"We believe it is very likely that Rawls would have removed it from Barrington's custody, one way or another."

"The man's a safecracker?"

"He is a highly trained and experienced intelligence officer. Opening a safe is not beyond his ken."

"Anything else new, Erik?"

"Yes, sir. It appears that Rawls built a concealed storage place adjoining his Islesboro house. We believe he has stored many files there, probably associated with what is now in the strong case."

"Was it destroyed in the fire?"

"No, sir. Apparently it contained an incendiary device that was detonated remotely. We got a look at it as soon as it cooled, and everything inside was completely destroyed beyond recovery."

"Rawls is very smart, isn't he?"

"Yes, sir, he is, and that makes him extremely difficult to find."

"Are police looking for him, too?"

"No, sir, he has committed no criminal act."

"Do we have any competitor in finding him?"

"I'm quite sure the CIA would be very

interested in speaking to him, if they haven't already. Lance Cabot visited Barrington's house while Rawls was in residence, but we don't know if he spoke to the man. Barrington and Cabot had lunch at this club after their initial meeting at the house."

"What, now, is your recommendation?"

"I have taken the liberty of placing two of my agents in a house within sight of Rawls's Virginia place, with instructions that one of them must have visual contact with the house at all times. Should he arrive there, we will know."

"If we find him there, then what?"

"It seems highly likely that Rawls will have a secure place in the house that would contain the strong case. We will find and open it. Also, it would be an ideal place to interrogate him, obviating transporting him to another location for that purpose."

"Erik, it is extremely important that no permanent harm come to Rawls. That would only make him more interesting to the police, the Agency, or anyone else who is looking for him."

"As you wish, sir."

"We have already lost three of your men to this investigation, and that has been a major inconvenience to me, not to mention a major expense, what with having to pay the families large sums of money for their silence."

"I am quite aware of that, sir, and you may rely on their silence."

"I should bloody well hope so."

"Sir, it would be helpful to me if I had some idea of the contents of the case."

"It would be very helpful to *me* to have that, as well, Erik."

"Of course, sir."

"Suffice it to say that I believe it contains evidence of secret pardons, one of them that of Rawls, granted by Will Lee late in his second term, and that public knowledge of these might be an insurmountable impediment to the reelection of Katharine Lee."

"Who was the other pardon for, sir?"

"I don't know, but I would certainly like to. Beyond the pardons, there may be inflammatory information concerning our friend Mr. Knott."

"Sir, I and my people have searched his background thoroughly, to the point where no one, in my view, could find anything derogatory that we have not already expunged from his various records."

"I am aware that there are limits to what one man may learn of another, Erik. It is always possible to miss something, and I cannot afford that."

"I understand, sir."

"Keep me posted on Rawls."

"Yes, sir." Macher got out of the van and left on foot as it drove away.

35

Ed Rawls kept the lowest possible profile for the first week. He used one light at a time, double-checking to see that the blinds were drawn, and he stayed out of the living room, which fronted the road. But then he ran short of scotch, and as an afterthought, groceries. It would take too long to get the scotch delivered, so he made plans to go to the village.

Shortly after midnight he grabbed a flashlight and made his way to the garage. He pulled the cover off the old Mercedes and disconnected the battery charger, all this without turning on a light. The car started immediately, and he let it run for a couple of minutes with the garage door open, then backed it out and pointed it at the main road, up close against the tall hedge, then he switched it off, closed the garage door, and went back into the house.

As he walked to the front steps he froze,

then stood behind the big oak tree out front. A light had gone on in the house across the road, a hundred yards away, and as far as he knew, nobody lived there. It was a weekend place for the owners, and not every weekend, and tonight was not a weekend.

Keeping the oak tree between him and that house, he made his way to the driveway, then around back, letting himself in the rear door. He locked it behind him and went to lock the front door, as well. He got his binoculars from the bookcase in his study; they were high-powered, and he went to a front window and trained them on the light across the road.

The light was in a kitchen window, and a moment later a blond woman opened the refrigerator and took out something. He had caught a glimpse of her through the crack of his study door when the couple had come to look at his house. They must have liked the neighborhood, he thought.

He got his throwaway cell phone, looked up the number for the sheriff's substation in the village, and called. As expected, he got a beep. "There are intruders in the Denton house on County Road 6," he said into the phone. "I just passed by there and saw somebody inside. Please look into it." He hung up and hoped the call had wakened the deputy, who would be asleep on the sofa in the squad room.

Deputy James Garr woke from a light sleep and heard someone recording a message. He got up, went to the machine, and played back the message.

"Shit," he muttered to himself. He went outside and started the patrol car, then picked up the radio microphone. "Central, this is car three. Come back."

"What's goin' on, James?" a woman's voice said.

"I'm leaving substation four. Got a call of intruders at the Dentons' place on County Road 6."

"You want backup?"

"Not yet. I'll call you from my handheld if I do."

"Sorry they woke you up, James."

"Screw you, Suzie." He hung up the microphone and started driving. It took him four minutes to reach the Denton house, and he drove past at thirty miles an hour, then pulled over and turned off his lights. Looking back, he could see the kitchen window, and there was a light on.

He walked back to the house and had a look in the front window; all he saw was the light from the kitchen. He unsnapped the keep on his Glock and walked quietly around the house to the kitchen window. There was an empty recycling bin at the foot of the steps to the back door, and he turned it upside down and stood on it. He took off his hat and peered through a corner of the kitchen window. There was a blond woman in a pantsuit sitting at the kitchen table, working on a crossword puzzle. There was a half-empty glass of orange juice beside her on the table.

Now, he asked himself, what would a woman be doing sitting at a kitchen table in a pin-striped suit at one o'clock in the morning? He got down from the bin, re-installed his hat, walked up the back steps, and rapped sharply on the pane in the door with his high school class ring.

He heard something resembling a scuffle from inside, and the woman called out, "Farrell!" He rapped again. "Sheriff's office," he called out. "Open up, please!"

"Farrell!" she shouted again.

Garr tried the door, found it unlocked, and let himself in. "Sheriff's office!" he called out again, and unholstered the Glock.

"What the hell is it?" a man's voice demanded.

Garr stepped into the kitchen, the weapon at his side, and found himself staring into somebody else's Glock. A man in a gray business suit was pointing it at him.

"Drop your weapon," Garr said. "I'm a uniformed sheriff's deputy, can't you see that?"

The man didn't drop it. "What the hell do you want?" he asked sourly.

"Drop the weapon," Garr said. "I won't tell you again."

The man lowered the pistol. "What's this about?"

Garr walked over to him, his Glock in plain view but pointed at the floor, and took the pistol from the man's hand. "This is about you showing me some ID, both of you, and explaining what you're doing in this house."

The woman put a hand to her breast. "Oh, you scared me half to death," she said.

"Both of you, put your ID on the table and step back."

They both came up with driver's licenses, set them down, and stepped back.

"Tell me what you're doing here."

"Well," the woman said, "the owners are in the Bahamas for a couple of weeks, and they offered us the house while they were gone."

"You have anything in writing to confirm that?" Garr asked.

"I'm afraid not," the man said.

"What's their cell phone number?" Garr asked.

The man began slapping his pockets. "I've got it somewhere," he said.

"Then let's have it." He was going through his pockets now. Garr picked up the two licenses; one was New Jersey, the other, Connecticut. The names were Drake and Solberg. "Are you two married?" he asked.

"Yes," the man said, "but not to each other."

"Oh, it's like that, is it?"

"It's like that."

"Where's that number?"

"I appear to have left it in another suit."

"Why are you dressed in business clothes in the middle of the night?"

"We were watching television and hadn't got sleepy yet," the woman said.

"You weren't watching television," Garr said, tapping the crossword, "and neither was he."

"Oh, yes, I was watching the news in the living room," the man said.

"The Dentons don't own a TV," Garr said. "Now, both of you grab the table, and don't make any sudden moves." He began patting them down. "And let me see the license for the Glock."

"I have a Connecticut license," the man said. "You want to see that?"

"Nope, that doesn't work in Virginia." Garr cuffed the man and told the woman to sit down. He pressed the PTT button on his radio. "Suzie," he said, "I'm going to need another patrol car. I've got a couple of B&E's on my hands."

Ed Rawls watched through his binoculars as a second sheriff's car pulled up, and two people were stuffed into the rear seat. He would sleep better, now.

36

Erik Macher arrived at his office in Washington, D.C., at nine sharp. His secretary, Ilsa, was already at her desk in the small office building where Christian St. Clair housed his lobbyists and other D.C. personnel.

"You'd better sit down," she said, pouring him a cup of the strong coffee he liked.

Macher sat down. "Okay, I'm sitting, what is it?"

"Drake and Solberg got themselves arrested in Virginia last night."

"What?"

"Breaking and entering. Apparently they weren't exactly renting the house they were using to surveil the Rawls place. They're being held in a sheriff's substation in a wide-place-in-the-road village in Fairfax County."

"First, find them a lawyer."

"There's one on the way. I told him we're good for bail money."

"Good, now find out who owns that house and get them on the phone for me."

"A couple named Mark and Debby Denton. He's an attorney on the legislative staff of the American Bar Association. She does something not too big at State. Before I call them, Solberg told me their story to the deputy was that the Dentons were on vacation in the Bahamas, and they offered them the house while they were gone."

"Do we know anybody who knows the Dentons?"

"My sister works at State. Want me to call her?"

"Yes, please."

"I already did. Debby Denton has offered to call the sheriff down there and tell them that she and her husband just got back from a vacation in the Bahamas and loaned the house to the couple for a tryst."

"Why did she agree to say that?"

"My sister is her boss."

"Tell her to make the call," Macher said, "and tell Solberg I want her and Drake in this office by ten-thirty."

"Right."

Macher looked up from his coffee. "You're a gem, you know."

She grinned. "I know."

■ ■ ■ ■

At ten-thirty Solberg and Drake were in Macher's outer office. "Send them in," he said to Ilsa.

The two didn't look very fresh. Solberg's hair needed doing, and Drake needed a shirt and a shave. Macher didn't ask them to sit down. "You broke into that house? Why?"

Drake shrugged. "Because it was there, exactly where we needed it, and we didn't have time to find the owners and rent it."

"You know how long it took Ilsa to find the owners and get them to back your story?"

Neither spoke.

"Ten minutes." Macher wasn't sure if it happened that fast, but it sounded good.

"We're sorry," Solberg said.

"Were you two screwing when the deputy arrived?"

"We were *not,*" Solberg said. "He caught us out when I said we'd been watching TV. There wasn't a TV in the house, and the deputy knew that."

Macher shook his head in disgust. "What about Rawls?"

"No sign of him," Drake said, "but he's there."

"And what evidence do you have of that?"

"He doesn't have anywhere else to go. And besides, I can feel him there."

"You can *feel* him there?" Macher demanded. "Are you psychic or something?"

"Sort of," Drake replied.

"Define that."

"I look at the available evidence, and my mind forms a conclusion from that."

"And how much available evidence did you have?"

"Rawls owns the house, his only other home burned down. It's familiar territory for him, he would be drawn to it. Rawls is also known to be cheap, and it wouldn't cost him anything to go back to his own house."

"And that's enough evidence to conclude he's there?"

"Yes, sir. I'm not trying to convict him of anything, just establish his whereabouts. What I've got is enough for that, and there is no contradictory evidence to put him anywhere else. Ergo, the house is our best shot."

Macher looked at the young man with new respect. "You're right," he said. "What do you propose we do from here? And no breaking in — we don't need more trouble."

"We can either surveil the house by a live satellite feed, or we can go back down there and sit on it until he shows his face. The satellite is too expensive."

"Has Rawls seen you two?"

"We were in the house with the real estate agent. He might have watched us from some hiding place."

"And being an old spy, he might just have such a place in the house," Macher said.

"Yes, sir."

"All right, you two go home and get cleaned up, get a good night's sleep, have some breakfast, if you haven't already. I'll put somebody else on the place."

The two thanked him and shuffled out.

"Ilsa, please get me a longitude and latitude of the Denton house, will you?"

Ilsa walked into his office and placed a slip of paper on his desk. "There you go."

Macher turned to his computer, opened a program that gave him access to satellites, and entered the coordinates. The program looked for a satellite, found it, and Macher watched the screen as the eye in the sky zoomed in on the Denton house. He clicked a couple of times on the zoom-out tab, and lo, the Rawls place appeared on the other side of the road. Then he zoomed in on that. There was a car parked between the garage and the house, hard up against a hedge. It wouldn't have been visible from the Denton place.

"Ilsa, bring me Solberg's report on their visit to the Rawls place."

Ilsa placed a file on his desk, and he read it. Rawls or his ex-wife owned an old Mercedes that was reported in the garage. Ilsa was still standing there. "Please check the Virginia DMV and see if a car or cars is registered either to Rawls or his dead wife, and if so, make and model."

Ilsa returned to her desk, and he could hear her computer keys clicking. She returned and handed him a slip of paper.

"A 1985 Mercedes E500 station wagon," he read aloud. "Tan metallic paint." Macher zoomed in tight on the car on his screen. "Bingo!" he said.

"You want me to put another team on the place?" Ilsa asked.

"He's there," Macher said. "Put two teams on him. If he drives someplace, follow him."

"How far?"

"To the ends of the earth, but my guess is he'll just go out for groceries."

37

Ed Rawls went grocery shopping. There was no car in sight when he pulled out of the driveway, and he headed for the village. Fifteen minutes later he was patrolling the aisles of the supermarket with the store's biggest shopping cart. He loaded the goods into the station wagon, went into the liquor store and bought a mixed case of booze, half of it Talisker.

He drove back to his house, and as he passed the Denton place he saw a van parked out front, emblazoned with a logo: "Jiffy Window Washers." He was suspicious, but there was actually a man on a ladder washing the windows, so he continued home and put the car into the garage. It took four trips to get all the boxes and bags into the kitchen and the liquor into the study bar. He put everything away, then went into his study, switched on his reading lamp, and got out his throwaway cell phone.

"Martin Real Estate," a woman said.

"Good morning, this is Edward Rawls. You have my house listed."

"Yes, Mr. Rawls, we showed it a few days ago. I've been expecting an offer, but I've heard nothing. The couple loved the place."

"Well, I've decided I love it, too, so I'm going to take it off the market with immediate effect."

"Certainly, sir. I'll move the file to our inactive list."

"Just shred the file, and we'll say no more about it. Thanks very much. Oh, and don't forget to pick up your sign." He hung up. On the drive home from shopping, he had begun to feel like a free man. He got up and walked around the house, opening the blinds and curtains, letting the light in. What the hell, he thought, what do I care if they know I'm here? I'm not going to spend the rest of my life running from these bastards.

He called the phone company on his cell and asked them to reinstate his old number, and an hour later it was working. He was reading the *Washington Post* when the doorbell rang. He got up, took his pistol from its hiding place, and tucked it into his waistband at the back, pulling his sweater over it. When he opened the door a man in white coveralls stood there.

"Good morning," Ed said.

"Good morning," the man replied with a ready smile. "We're doing some window-washing in the neighborhood, and I wondered if you'd like us to do yours. I'd be happy to look around and give you a price, inside and out."

"Thanks, but I have a contract with a local firm that takes care of the place, including the windows."

"I see."

"Apparently not. If you'd seen, you'd know the windows are clean."

"Oh, yeah, right. May I ask your name?"

"No, you may not. Good day." Ed closed the door and watched through the sidelight as the man walked away. Ed noted that he was wearing well-polished wingtips, instead of the rubber boots a window washer would more likely wear. Well, he thought, I've now announced my presence here, let's see what they do about it. He went back into his study and picked up his book, Conrad Black's biography of Franklin Roosevelt, which he thought was pretty damned good.

He had been reading for nearly two hours when his phone rang, nearly lifting him out of his seat; he had forgotten that it had been reconnected. He picked it up. "Hello?"

"Mr. Rawls, I'm glad to catch you," a man's voice said.

"Who is this?"

"My name is Erik Macher. I operate a security service out of Washington, D.C."

"I've already got an alarm system and a monitor," Rawls replied.

"No, I'm not calling about that."

"Then tell me why you're calling, and stop wasting my time."

"I wish to make you an offer for the strong case."

"What strong case?"

"The one you have hidden in your house. I have a client who is willing to pay you half a million dollars for the case and its key."

"Then your client is a goddamned fool," Rawls replied, "and you can tell him I said so."

"That's very foolish of you," Macher said.

"I'm old enough to figure out for myself whether or not I'm a fool," Rawls said, "and I find myself of sound mind and superior judgment. What was your name again?"

"Erik with a *k,* Macher, spelled the German way."

"I'll make a note of that so I can hang up on you immediately if you should call back," Ed said. "And if you send your fucking window washer around here again, I'll shoot the son of a bitch on sight."

"That would be unwise."

"I'll tell you what's unwise," Ed said, "burning down my house, that's what. But I appreciate your calling, because now I know who the bastard is who did it. Tell me, do you have a nice house somewhere that I can burn down for you? And I promise not to leave a corpse in the living room." Ed hung up.

He was angry, and he needed to blow off some steam. He looked up the number of the builder in Islesboro who had built his house there.

"Bill Haynes," the man said.

"Bill, it's Ed Rawls. How you doing?"

"Just fine, Ed. I heard about your house."

"Yeah, so did I. You want to rebuild it for me?"

"Sure, glad to."

"You still got the plans?"

"Yep."

"Well, get out there and get to work. By the way, there's a secret cellar next door, with a tunnel running from the house. I'd like that sealed off, please. It's of no further use to me."

"It will be done."

"How long is it going to take to finish the place?"

"Well, let's see, I'll get some people out there tomorrow to clean up what's there, and, assuming the pad is in good shape, we'll start framing early next week. After that, I'll need a couple of months, I guess, if you want it built exactly like before."

"I do."

"Then I'm on it, Ed. It's going to cost you more per square foot than it did when I built it the first time, but that's just inflation."

"I'm okay with that. Give me a price."

Haynes did.

"Agreed. You can send me a contract at my place in Virginia." He gave the man the address and phone number. "Call if you have any questions as you proceed."

The two men said goodbye and hung up. Ed felt better than he had in weeks. He went to the little study bar and poured himself a drink, then turned on the TV. The satellite was still working; he had forgotten to turn off that service. He switched to the D.C. CBS station for the news, just in time to see a promo for *60 Minutes*. They were devoting the entire show to Nelson Knott. He went to the listings and set the show to be recorded on the DVR.

This is going to be interesting, he thought.

38

Stone and Holly took an afternoon run, and when they got back to the house the message light was flashing on his phone. "Don't miss *60 Minutes* tomorrow," Will Lee's voice said. "If you're going out, be sure and record it. I'll be in town tomorrow. I'll call you for lunch."

"What's on *60 Minutes*?" Holly asked.

Stone switched on the TV and looked it up. "Financial skullduggery, baseball, and children with wild pets."

"I wonder which of those Will found so fascinating."

"We have only to wait until Sunday at seven to see."

"By the way, I'm headed back to Washington tomorrow," Holly said. "Maybe I can get a ride with Will. Will you ask him?"

"Have you served your sentence already?"

"Almost. I've got some things to do around the house that I've been postponing for nearly four years. Here's my chance to do them without guilt."

They got undressed and into the shower together. Somehow, being clean was a turn-on for them both. When they had exhausted each other they talked.

"Here's a thought," Stone said. "Don't go back to Washington at all."

"That's a surprising thought."

"After all, they've had time to forget about you at the White House. If you didn't go back they'd never miss you."

"Thank you so much, what a compliment!"

"I'd rather have you here with me."

"On what basis?"

"All the sex I can manage at my advanced age."

"And that's it? That's all you want from me?"

"Didn't I mention marriage?"

"You did not."

"Funny, I thought I did."

"You could mention it now, if you're so inclined."

"All right, marriage."

"What about it?"

"Doing it."

"Doing it is sex, not marriage."

Stone searched for the words: "Marriage,

together."

"You just can't bring yourself to say the words, can you?"

"If I do, will you accept?"

"Try it and see."

"Oh, all right. Will you marry me?"

"No."

"You were just leading me on, weren't you?"

"Certainly not. I just needed to know your clear intentions before —"

"Before turning me down?"

"Stone, you know I love you, and I know you love me."

"That's right, I do," Stone said, sounding surprised.

"But we lead such different lives."

"Not for the past two weeks. We've led pretty much one life together, and I think we did it very well."

"I can't argue with that," Holly said.

"Then what are you arguing about?"

"You know I love my job."

"All right, I propose a compromise."

"Go ahead."

"Do the job for the rest of Kate's term, then ditch Washington once and for all and devote yourself to me forever."

"Devote myself to you, instead of to my country?"

"I'm a better catch."

"I'll concede that, for the purposes of argument."

"We'll live a free life in New York, Santa Fe, England, and Paris," he said. "We'll see the world, live well, and fuck each other's brains out."

"I'll tell you what — if Kate isn't reelected, I'll marry you and we'll do everything you just said, especially that last part."

"Now you're putting me in an impossible position," Stone complained.

"How so?"

"I can no longer support Kate for reelection, or even vote for her."

"Don't be ridiculous."

"That would be against my own self-interest," he said. "I may even have to support another candidate."

"That's crazy talk."

"I know it is, but how could I want her to be reelected if that caused me to lose you."

"I didn't say you'd be losing me."

"But I'd have to wait another four years, when she can't run again."

"Four years isn't such a long time," she said.

"You sound as though you don't believe that."

"All right, it's a long time, but there's the

promise of something new for me, if she's reelected."

"A promise from Kate?"

"Sort of a promise."

"You mean a *hint* of a promise."

"If you like."

"And what is Kate dangling before you, like a ball of yarn before a kitten?"

"The Agency."

"Are they going to shoot Lance?"

"No, but he might get kicked upstairs."

"Director of Homeland Security?"

"Could be."

"Do you think Lance would take that? He'd probably have more fun staying where he is."

"No doubt, but there could be something else for him in the offing."

"What else is there?"

"Think about that for a minute."

Stone thought about it. "No!" he said after a moment.

"Why not?"

"The VP slot on the ticket?"

"Why not?"

"Lance would hate that — there's no power involved."

"How about if he were VP, but were given the whole national intelligence system to play with?"

Stone thought.

"And after that . . ."

"Oh, God, Lance for President?"

"I'm just guessing, but he'd only be VP for four years."

"Do you think he would take it?"

"Do you think Lance could possibly see himself as President?"

"I've no doubt of it," Stone said. "And you'd replace him at the Agency?"

"Possibly."

"But then I'd never see you again."

"Not necessarily."

"You mean, like now — a couple of times a year?"

"We could do better than that."

"How?"

"The country might like it better if the director of central intelligence were a stable married woman."

"You mean, instead of a wild and crazy single woman?"

"Well, yes."

"But you couldn't live in New York or any of those other places where I've gone into the housing business."

"Well, not all the time."

"Now I get it," Stone said, "you want me to move to Washington."

"Or the Virginia suburbs."

"That is a breathtakingly bad idea," Stone said, shivering.

"I'm sorry you think so."

"It's not personal."

"Oh, then what is it?"

"I'm not sure I could make that sacrifice, even for my country."

"Could you make it for me?" she asked.

"I think my offer is the better one," Stone said.

She said nothing.

"Well?"

"I'll think about it."

39

Stone, uncharacteristically, didn't sleep well. He was out cold for about an hour, then he jerked awake. The Virginia suburbs? Waiting for Holly to come home from work every day? The thought made the rest of his night nearly sleepless, whereas Holly remained exquisitely somnambulant. A marriage proposal was an extremely rare event for both of them, but it didn't keep her awake.

The next morning she began packing, and he was surprised at how much stuff she had.

"Why don't you leave some things here?"

"Why?"

"So that when you come back, you won't have to bring so much stuff."

"Now, Stone, be realistic. You know you don't want a lady's things hanging in the guest closet, for all the world to see."

"All the world?"

"All right, just the other ladies."

"There aren't any other ladies."

"At the moment," she said. "But before I land in Washington there'll be somebody new scratching at your door."

"You wound me."

"Nonsense. We both know who you are."

"Are you saying I would be an unfaithful husband?"

"Certainly not. If I thought so for a moment, I'd poison your bourbon. But, an unfaithful fiancé . . . ?"

"That's a terrible thing to say. When I was married to Arrington I was absolutely faithful."

"I accept that, though it wasn't for very long, was it? Your engagement, I mean."

"She was living here."

"Well, that would cramp your style a little. I, however, would not be living here — if we were betrothed."

"I hate that word."

"I'm not surprised. I don't like it very much myself, I was just making a point."

The phone rang, and Stone didn't wait for Joan to get it. "Hello?"

"How about the Boathouse restaurant in Central Park, one o'clock? I'll book." It was Will Lee.

"Okay. If you're going back today, there's somebody here who'd like to catch a ride."

"I can do that. Have him meet me at the

263

East Side Heliport at four o'clock."

"I'll tell him." He hung up. "You're to meet Will at the East Side Heliport at four o'clock."

"Perfect. On the way down I can feel him out about getting back to my job."

"What are you going to do until four?"

"I'll do a little shopping and catch some lunch somewhere. There's a nice restaurant at Barneys."

Stone gathered her into his arms and kissed her. "I was perfectly serious last night."

"Last night? I thought that was a dream."

"You have to learn to distinguish your dreams from reality."

"I do that at work, not in your bed."

"And when will you be back in my bed?"

"Probably not until I've achieved world peace."

"Swell."

"But my failure to do so shouldn't keep you out of *my* bed."

Stone let it go at that.

He took a cab up to Central Park, got out at Seventy-Second and Fifth, and walked over to the boat lake. He looked around the restaurant and saw only one man alone at a table.

"He's keeping it warm for us," Will said from behind him.

They shook hands and walked over to the table. The Secret Service agent made himself scarce, but stayed within easy reach. Nobody seemed to notice a former President in their midst. Must be the casual clothes, Stone thought.

They ordered lunch and a bottle of chardonnay.

"So, how have the last couple of weeks gone?" Will asked.

"They've been very strange."

"Did you enjoy your time with Ed Rawls?"

"Actually, he was a little more companionable than he has been in the past."

"He's back at his house in Virginia," Will said, taking a sip of his wine.

"Did his wife leave it to him?"

"He never gave it to her, just lifetime occupancy, and her lease has expired. He was hunkered down for a week or so, but now he's living there quite openly."

"I don't get it — he seemed fearful in Maine, especially after they burned down his house."

"He's already started rebuilding it."

"What's changed?"

"His attitude, I guess. As far as I can tell, nothing else has."

"He's still got the strong case?"

"I don't see him ditching it, do you?"

"He had a cellar next to his Maine house with all his files in it, until he set off an incendiary device."

"Well, that's news," Will said. "Maybe that made him feel more devil-may-care."

"Do you think he's in any real danger?"

"*He* doesn't seem to thinks so, and I guess that's all that matters."

"What's on *60 Minutes* tonight?"

"A last-minute programming change — they're going to spend the whole hour introducing Nelson Knott to all the people who normally sleep in the wee hours."

"I thought his whole business plan was based on insomnia."

"Until now. He's making his evening debut, so to speak. I want to hear what he says when they ask him if he's thinking of running for office."

"Why else would they give him the hour?"

"I've heard a rumor that Christian St. Clair may be making a bid for CBS News. Maybe they don't want to piss him off." Will took another sip of his wine.

"Is this his first big move, then?"

"No, his first big move was a luncheon last week for ten high rollers at your club on the East Side."

"How'd he do?"

"Word is, four of them have promised to start a PAC with a hundred million dollars each, and a couple of the others are leaning that way."

"Times have changed, haven't they, since twenty of us put up a million each to get Kate started?"

"Times have certainly changed."

"Is Kate worried about Knott?"

"No, Kate's not a worrier, but I am. I mean, we can match his fund-raising, but there's never been an independent candidate with that kind of war chest at the outset. I find it scary, especially since he's got St. Clair for a sponsor. Christian loves nothing better than a puppet, and this one's going to be the most expensive one ever put together."

"How does the strong case play into all this?"

"Hard to say. What's important is that Christian thinks it's important."

"Is it all about the pardons?"

"At least partly."

"I'm sorry I ever asked you to pardon Teddy Fay."

"Don't worry about it."

"What I don't understand is why Ed Rawls would do something that might undermine Kate. He owes her a lot, or rather, owes you a lot."

"I have my own theory about that, but it's just a theory."

"Tell me."

"I believe Ed thinks that what's in the strong case would help Kate, and what's more, I believe Christian St. Clair thinks so, too."

"Perhaps we'll know more tonight."

"Perhaps." They finished their wine, and Stone chose to walk home while Will went east, toward his chopper.

40

The house seemed oddly empty; Holly was gone, and the staff were out or at home in Stone's second house next door. He found a book that he had left unread for weeks and plowed into it.

In the early evening he went upstairs and asked Helene to send his supper up in the dumbwaiter, then he got into a nightshirt and switched on *60 Minutes.*

Martin Shawn, who he had read was near retirement, conducted the interview with Nelson Knott. The show opened with a helicopter tour of his Virginia estate, then Shawn was greeted on the front porch by the Knotts for a tour of the house. Finally, the two men settled into comfortable chairs before a cheery fireplace in a large library, bursting with books.

Shawn got right to the point. "Mr. Knott, there have been strong and persistent rumors that you are considering a run for President. Anything to them?"

Knott smiled. "There is usually something to a strong and persistent rumor, isn't there?"

"Then you're considering a run?"

"I am. I haven't made a final decision yet, but I seem to be thinking about it more and more."

"Have you been thinking about your qualifications?"

"I've been thinking about my qualifications since high school."

"And you think you're ready to be commander in chief?"

"At first, I just read a lot, especially about American history. For about the past decade I've been engaged in an intensive, personal quest to learn everything I can about foreign and domestic policy, and I've devoted a good deal of time to military history and current thinking. I think I'm probably better prepared for high office than anyone in this country who hasn't made a career of politics, and a great many who have."

"If you're interested in the presidency, why haven't you made a career of politics, worked your way up through elected office?"

"Because I think that the Senate, and to

an even greater extent the House, produces too many people who think they're ready to be President, and not nearly enough who really are ready. The real work there is done by staff, and the elected members spend most of their time raising money for their next election. They have too little time to read, to study in depth, and to think. I made myself financially secure by building a company in my youth, so I've been able to set aside time to study and to learn from people who've been there and done that, whereas most businesspeople just devote themselves to making more money they don't really need."

"How do you divide your time?"

"I start at eight AM with a staff meeting to review the products we're offering that day on television, then I have some lunch and spend my afternoon reading or studying policy. Around midnight I review what I have to say on our nightly television program, then I go on air, and afterward read some more."

"And when do you sleep?"

"I have a peculiar lack of a need for deep sleep. It's genetic — my father was the same way. I don't sleep more than a couple of hours a night, though I catch a catnap or two during the day. Since I'm in excellent physical condition, I'm able to devote myself to a much longer workday than anyone I know. My business staff is divided into day and night people, and I have another staff that is devoted entirely to researching policy and political issues. If I should run for President and win, that group would form the core of a White House staff, and they'd be ready to go on day one, as would I."

They talked on, then came to the end of part one of the program, and Shawn announced that they would continue the program from Knott's Washington, D.C., offices.

Then the third part moved to Knott's New York City apartment.

Near the end Shawn put another question to Knott. "What do you think of the performance of Katharine Lee in office?"

"Between the Lees, I'm a bigger fan of her husband's presidency. I think the current President Lee is too caught up in intelligence matters, having spent her working life at the CIA, and she's not nearly as good on domestic matters. Her husband helps out with that, of course, but he's very rightly enjoying his new son and his retirement."

"And you think you could do a better job than Katharine Lee as President?"

Knott laughed. "If I didn't think that, I wouldn't even be considering a run."

"And why are you forming a new party, instead of running as either a Republican or a Democrat?"

"I've never been strongly attracted to either party. I'm fairly liberal on social issues and conservative on fiscal policy. I'm not an ideologue, I'm a pragmatist, and I believe in what works. Also, Katharine Lee is assured of her party's nomination, so there's no room for me in the Democratic Party, and the Republican Party is so exhausted from the last election and are such hidebound ideologues that I wouldn't fit in there. There isn't an existing party that has any real standing, so starting from scratch seems the best way to the general election."

"That route has never worked before," Shawn pointed out.

"We've never had quite the same conditions before," Knott replied evenly. "Also, there's never been a candidate with roots in broadcasting. If I run I'll produce a number of hour-long films that will explain exactly what my policy goals are across the policy spectrum. They'll be available online, and people can watch them at their own pace and as many times as they wish."

"It sounds like a tutorial," Shawn said.

"A tutorial on what I believe, what I know, and what I plan to do."

The program ended, and Stone was surprised to find that he had been impressed. His meeting with Knott on St. Clair's yacht had been brief, but now he knew a great deal more.

His phone rang. "Hello?"

It was Will Lee. "What did you think of Mr. Knott?"

"Well, he was very nice to you, wasn't he?"

Will laughed. "Come on, what did you think?"

"I was impressed, when I hadn't expected to be. I think he did a very good job of presenting himself as somebody who might make a good President."

"I'm really sorry to hear that, because it confirms my own judgment," Will said. "I think Mr. Knott is going to be a formidable candidate."

"Do you think Kate can beat him?"

"Yes, but she's going to have to take a fresh look at the campaign and how it's going to work, and she's going to have to anticipate his every move and counter it."

"She'll be on the defensive, then?"

"Every candidate for reelection is on the defensive — that's the nature of the beast."

"I don't know what I can do to help,"

Stone said, "but please know that I'll do whatever I'm asked."

"You've already proven that with your help on this strong case thing, Stone. It's not your fault that we've lost control of the situation."

"How do we get control back?"

"I'm not sure that we can, but I'm thinking about it. If I come up with something and you can help, I'll let you know."

The two men said goodbye and hung up.

41

Stone spent the next day with a feeling of unease. It disturbed him that he had been so easily impressed, when he thought of himself as a skeptic. If he could be swayed, why not a great many others? The idea of Kate having to leave office without a second term was painful to him.

Late in the afternoon, his cell phone rang. "Hello?"

"Stone, it's Ed Rawls."

"What a surprise," Stone said wryly. "Are you enjoying being back in your own home?"

"I'm impressed that you know that."

"I think everybody who wants to know probably now knows. I hear you're rebuilding your Islesboro house, too."

"There's only been one phone call on that subject, and that makes me wonder how you know."

"I have friends, too, Ed, some of them

276

remarkably well informed. In a recent conversation with one of them I asked a question you might be able to answer for me."

"What's your question?"

"Why would you want to release or even possess information that might be harmful to Kate's presidency? Do you have something against her and Will, or are you just ungrateful?"

"I have no intention of doing anything that would harm either of them."

"You're kind of slow getting around to telling me that, aren't you?"

"I have my reasons, and I can't explain them over the phone."

"You were in my house for three days — you could have told me face-to-face."

"Once you know everything, you'll understand my reticence."

"What, exactly, do you plan to do, Ed?"

"Not over the phone."

"Did you watch *60 Minutes* last night?"

"I did."

"What did you think of Knott?"

"Creepy and dangerous."

"Is there anything in your strong case that would bear on his candidacy?"

"There is something, and St. Clair's people have done such a good job of sanitizing his past that I might be one of only two or three people left alive who know about it."

"Were the others very old or very unlucky?"

"Very unlucky. Three, perhaps four people are dead because they knew."

"This is beginning to sound like a conspiracy theory, Ed."

"It isn't a theory, and it's spelled out, with supporting evidence, in my manuscript."

"And what do you intend to do with it?"

"Publish it."

"You have a publisher?"

"I'm the writer, editor, and publisher, and it's ready to go."

"If you're self-publishing, you're still going to need a printer."

"There is new equipment that can print, bind, wrap, and put postage on a book. All I have to do is to plug a thumb drive into its computer, then walk around to the other end and collect the finished books in envelopes, already stamped."

"How are you going to distribute it?"

"I have a mailing list of two hundred opinion makers. All I have to do is take the boxes to a post office. You're on my list, so you'll get a copy, so will Holly Barker."

"And when can I expect it?"

"When I think the moment is right."

"And how will you decide that?"

"By weighing all the factors in play. I don't have any trouble making decisions."

"Something else I don't understand, Ed."

"What's that?"

"Why are you suddenly living openly in your own home, where anyone can walk in, kill you, and take your strong case?"

"They've found me three times," Rawls said. "In Maine, at your house, and now at my house, and I'm still alive. They're being run by a man named Erik Macher, out of his security business office in D.C. Have you ever heard of him?"

"No. Who is he?"

"He's Christian St. Clair's personal policeman. He's offered me half a million dollars for the strong case, and I think I told you he has more people than a lot of police departments. Two of them showed up in the house, escorted by a real estate agent with whom I had listed the place. Another turned up yesterday, clumsily disguised as a window washer. I'm just tired of running."

"When are you going to print the book, Ed?"

"I printed it this morning," Rawls said. "It's ready for mailing."

"Do you think this Macher guy knows that?"

"No. I got it all done without being rumbled."

"And where are the books?"

"They're at a packing and shipping place in D.C., which is waiting for my call. I dropped them off an hour and a half ago."

"Are you going to be able to stay alive until you can make that call?"

"I expect so. I can text them in less than a minute."

"Ed, why did you call me?"

"To give you the phone number of the shipping place. If you hear that something has happened to me or that I've disappeared, I'd be grateful if you'd make the call for me. I've told them you could be the one to give them instructions."

Stone didn't say anything for a minute.

"I can hear the lawyer's wheels turning in your head," Rawls said. "You're trying to figure out whether making that call might make you liable."

"Not legally liable."

"Liable to get killed for your trouble."

"You swear to me that your book isn't going to hurt Kate or Will?"

"One of the two pardons that Will made — mine — will become public knowledge, but not the other. Kate can honestly deny all knowledge of mine, and Will can offer justification."

"What justification?"

"An old KGB hand defected to the Agency during Kate's run for the presidency, and he spilled the whole story from the KGB point of view. It makes me out, correctly, to be a victim, not a willing collaborator. That gave Will justification for my pardon. If the story comes out, others will verify what the Russian guy spilled to the Agency. I may not end up smelling like a rose, but I won't be thought of as a traitor anymore. And it won't damage Kate."

Stone sighed. "Okay, what's the name and number of your pack-and-ship place in D.C.?"

"I've already texted it," Rawls said. "It's in your phone. If for some reason I don't survive this, I'll thank you now for your help, Stone. Otherwise, I'll see you in Islesboro next summer, if not sooner."

Rawls hung up.

Stone checked his messages; the phone number was there.

42

Holly called from home. "I wanted to thank you for our time together," she said. "I loved it, I really did, and Kate was right, not being in touch with the White House allowed me to reset my brain. It made me a woman again, something I had almost forgotten, instead of just a functionary."

"I never forgot you were a woman," Stone said.

"Thank you for that, and thank you for the proposal, however unconventional it may have been."

"You're welcome."

"How long is the offer going to be open?"

"I'm afraid I can't answer that. I can't see into the future."

"I guess I'll have to accept that answer."

"Or my proposal."

"An important part of me wants to, and right now, but my head is getting in the way."

"I understand that. It's the other part I love most."

"Thank you for that, too."

"Have you seen *60 Minutes*?"

"No, I missed it. I wasn't here to record it. I've talked to a friend who saw it, so I know pretty much how it went."

"I was impressed."

"You *were*?"

"So was Will."

"He hadn't seen it when we talked."

"How was the trip back?"

"Will said that Kate is looking forward to having me back, and that was a relief."

"Did you ever doubt it?"

"I'm afraid I did, getting suddenly cut off like that. Will told me that Ed Rawls is living in his old house in Virginia."

"And rebuilding his Maine house."

"Sounds like he's optimistic about the future. He thinks he might be alive to enjoy it."

"He's not sure about that," Stone said.

"What happens to the strong case if he's suddenly not around?"

"I think he's made plans, just in case."

"That's scary. Will won't like to hear it."

"I don't think Will has anything to worry about, nor Kate."

"It sounds like you and Ed have been talking."

"He did most of the talking."

"Can I ask you what he said?"

"Not yet, maybe later."

"Has a new woman come scratching at your door?"

"Not yet."

"Don't worry, it'll happen soon."

"I don't much care at the moment."

Holly laughed. "When it happens, you'll be responsive — you always are."

"I'm not sure whether to take that as a compliment or a condemnation."

"Take it as a compliment, you'll feel better."

"I'll try."

"Don't try too hard. I have to go now. The pizza deliveryman is ringing the doorbell."

"Bye-bye."

"Bye-bye." They hung up.

The phone rang a minute later.

"It's Dino. Dinner at P.J. Clarke's at seven?"

"Done."

"See ya." He hung up.

Dino, scotch in hand, was ogling the women at the bar when Stone arrived.

"I guess Viv is out of town."

"She is. She has an early meeting in L.A. tomorrow morning."

Stone looked around. "Don't let it go to your head."

"Just browsing," Dino said. "Hey, I've been getting a lot of questions about you."

"From Christian St. Clair?"

"Yep."

"I didn't know there was anything about me he doesn't already know. I'm sure he has copies of my medical records and tax returns."

"I'm sure he could get them if he wanted them," Dino replied.

"Did you see *60 Minutes*?"

"I did. That guy is something, isn't he?"

"Knott or St. Clair?"

"Both, I guess."

"Let me ask you something. Do you think St. Clair is capable of murder?"

Dino froze. "What makes you ask that?"

"Because I've heard he had three or four people taken out who knew stuff about Knott."

"Jeez, I don't know. He seems like the most civilized guy in the world."

"Do you think he would remain civilized if somebody tried to take away something he wanted?"

Dino shrugged. "People can change in a flash."

"I'm not sure it would represent a change," Stone said. "I think when a man has that much money, when he's completely in control of his own destiny, he starts wanting to be in control of other people's destinies, too."

"Certainly Knott seems to be entirely Christian's creature."

"Entirely," Stone said. "If Christian could get him elected, then Christian would be, effectively, President of the United States."

"He's too short to be President," Dino said.

"Yeah? Napoleon was too short to be emperor of France, too, and we know how that ended."

"Well, Christian has chosen a very tall guy to be his surrogate, maybe he's compensating that way. What do you think St. Clair would do if he had that power?"

"I think he'd make it a lot easier for him to be Christian St. Clair. When you have that much money, only government can impede your progress. That's why the super-rich give so much money to political races."

"I suppose so."

"I heard just today that Christian invited ten super-rich guys to lunch at the Club to meet Nelson Knott."

"Yeah? What happened?"

"Four of them have agreed to start PACs with a hundred million each, and two others are considering it."

Dino choked on his scotch, and Stone pounded him on the back. He was finally able to speak. "Four hundred million in the bank, just like that?"

"Six hundred million, maybe, and that's not counting whatever Christian is spending. Knott might be playing the game with a billion in the bank."

"Then Kate is in trouble."

"Maybe, maybe not."

"But to go back to your original question about St. Clair, if he's invested a couple of hundred million of his own money in Knott, then yes, I think he might kill people to protect his investment."

"Well," Stone said, "I don't want to be one of them."

43

That night, Stone dreamed exotic, dramatic dreams that seemed to involve Christian St. Clair and his political surrogate, but when he awoke, he could only remember fragments.

He breakfasted, showered, shaved, dressed, and went downstairs to his office. He opened his cell phone and went to Ed Rawls's text with the information on the pack-and-ship place in D.C. and dialed the number. He had decided to take the distribution of Rawls's books out of Ed's hands and into his own.

"Yes?"

"My name is Stone Barrington. Do you remember that name in relation to Ed Rawls?"

"I do. I'm to accept your instructions for delivery, should you call."

"I'm calling. Do you have a van in your business?"

"I do, and the twenty boxes will fit into it."

"I'd like you to load all the boxes into the van and deliver them to the following address. Got a pencil?"

"I have. Give me the address."

Stone gave him the address of his New York house.

"That's going to be expensive, if my van has to go to New York. It might be cheaper to put the boxes into bigger boxes, then ship them by Federal Express Ground."

"I need the boxes here today," Stone said. "How much to deliver them?"

The man did some math and mentioned a number.

"Done," Stone said. "How long will it take to get them here?"

"We can have the van loaded in about an hour, then four to six hours, depending on traffic."

"I'll give you a credit card number," Stone said. He did, then hung up.

Joan came in with the mail. "Good morning."

"Good morning. This afternoon, probably around three o'clock, a van is going to arrive and deliver twenty boxes. If I'm not here, I want you to secure them."

"How big are the boxes?"

"They each hold about ten books."

"There won't be room enough in your safe for that many."

"Then lock them in the wine cellar." The wine cellar had a steel door in a steel frame, and the lock operated four bolts on each of the three sides.

"Okay. This is all very peculiar," Joan said.

"You are quite right."

"It will be done." She went back to her office.

Stone riffled through the mail and found an envelope from a law office in Virginia; that struck him as odd, and he opened the letter inside.

Dear Mr. Barrington,

I am an attorney with offices in Virginia. One of my clients is Edward Rawls. I assume you will receive this letter on Tuesday; I will be in New York that day, and I would like to see you on an urgent matter as early in the day as possible. I will phone for an appointment.

Carson Rutledge
Rutledge & Rutledge

Stone buzzed Joan, and she answered. "I'm expecting a call from a Mr. Carson Rutledge, and —"

"He's on the other line and wants an appointment."

"Invite him to come as soon as he can."

She went back to her call, then buzzed. "He's on the way over here now — be here in fifteen minutes."

"Thank you."

Carson Rutledge was a tall, slender man in a well-tailored, chalk-striped suit, with a head of thick gray hair. Stone offered him a chair and coffee. He declined the coffee, and Stone thought that a good thing, since he seemed to be pretty wired already.

"Thank you for seeing me on such short notice," he said.

"That's quite all right, Mr. Rutledge. What can I do for you?"

"Ed Rawls has asked me to deliver this package to you by hand," he said, opening his briefcase and handing Stone a padded envelope. "It contains two copies of a book Mr. Rawls wrote and the originals of some documents that are reprinted in the book."

Stone accepted the package and put it on the coffee table. "Is this a book that Ed has recently written?"

"It is, and I must tell you, I'm glad to have that material off my hands. I suggest that you keep it in a safe, or at least under lock and key."

"I shall do so."

Rutledge heaved a deep sigh. "I feel greatly relieved," he said.

"Why is that?"

"Because during the time those things have been in my possession, I have come to fear for my life, and that is not an emotion I am accustomed to."

"And now that you have given them to me, should I fear for my life?"

"I don't know that for a fact, but it's my strong feeling that you should be, if anyone other than you, me, and Ed Rawls should learn about this transfer."

"Do you have a malefactor in mind?"

"Mr. Barrington, do you have any concern that your office might be under electronic surveillance?"

"I have enough concern that I have it electronically swept at regular and close intervals."

"Let's just say that my suspected malefactors are a very rich man, his protégé, and his private security force."

"I believe I get the picture."

"I'm glad of that." He stood. "And now, if you'll excuse me, I'd like to return, posthaste, to my usual dull and uneventful existence."

"Can I have my secretary call some transportation for you?"

"Thank you, no, I have a car and driver waiting outside, and it's a long drive to Virginia." They shook hands; Rutledge took his briefcase and walked out.

Stone sat down, found a small box cutter in his desk, and sliced open the package. He found two bound copies of a book entitled *A Great Storm Coming,* by Edward Rawls, a longtime officer in the Central Intelligence Agency.

Stone picked up the phone and called Dino.

"Bacchetti."

"It's Stone. Are you going to be in your office for the next couple of hours?"

"Yeah, I'm having a sandwich at my desk for lunch."

"I'm going to send you something that, once you open it, you should treat as if it were a bomb."

"But it's not a real bomb?"

"No, but read it as soon as possible, then lock it in your safe and don't speak to anyone about it, except me."

"You promise it won't explode?"

"I promise." Stone hung up the phone and gave the second copy of the book, in its envelope, to Joan. "Ask Fred to deliver this as soon as possible. He is to place it in Dino's hands and no one else's."

"You betcha," Joan said, taking the package and leaving his office.

Stone opened his copy of the book and began to read.

44

At around 3:30 PM Joan came into Stone's office. "The boxes you told me about are here. Can I have the man bring them in?"

Stone thought about that. "No, there's a hand truck in the garage. Ask the man to unload them in the front hallway and give him a hundred bucks, then ask Fred to come down here and put them in the wine cellar."

It was done, and Stone watched the whole time, then locked the wine cellar door himself.

He opened the envelope containing the original documents Rutledge had given him; they were two Virginia birth certificates, one seventeen years old, the other twelve. He checked Rutledge's phone number on his letterhead, then called him.

"Rutledge & Rutledge," a man's voice said.

"Mr. Rutledge? This is Stone Barrington."

"Yes, Mr. Barrington?"

"You'll recall that we met in my office this morning."

"No, sir, that would have been my father. I'm Carson Rutledge Junior."

"May I speak to your father, please?"

"I'm afraid he's not in. We expected him in from New York a couple of hours ago, but he hasn't turned up yet, and he's not answering his cell phone."

"Could you ask him to call me at my office when he returns? He has the number."

"I'm afraid . . ." the man began, then stopped. "We've been having some trouble with our phone lines, so he will need to go to another location to return your call."

"All right, thank you." Stone hung up and called Dino.

"Bacchetti."

"Did you read it?"

"I did. I was about to call you, but I wanted to check on something."

"What do you think of Rawls's book?"

"Ordinarily, I would think that the guy was just some conspiracy nut — the whole business seems so improbable — but having met him, he doesn't seem like a nut."

"I don't believe he is."

"I've got somebody checking on the two birth certificates."

"Checking what?"

"Checking to see if there are corresponding death certificates."

"In Virginia?"

"No, in New York. I had someone run them down, and both the mothers now live in the city. Hang on a minute." Dino put him on hold. "You remember our conversation last night at Clarke's?"

"I do."

"You asked me if I thought Christian St. Clair was capable of murder?"

"I remember."

"I've just had it confirmed that the older child and her mother are deceased — a traffic accident nearly two years ago."

"And the other?"

"No record of a death on the twelve-year-old or his mother, but they have moved from the address we had, and we haven't been able to find a new one."

"What kind of a traffic accident happened to the seventeen-year-old?"

"They ran off the road on the New Jersey Turnpike and slammed into a bridge abutment. The state cops thought she probably fell asleep at the wheel."

"Anything that made anyone doubt that?"

"Not until now," Dino replied.

"Let me call you back," Stone said.

"I'll be here."

Stone asked Joan to find a number in Virginia for Ed Rawls and waited while she made the call.

"No answer," she said. "I left a message on his answering machine to call you."

"Thanks." He hung up and dialed the law offices of Rutledge & Rutledge again. This time he got an answering machine and left a message.

He called Dino again. "Do you have anything further on the second mother?"

"No, but I saw something on the birth certificate I hadn't noticed at first."

Stone picked up the original copies of the two certificates. "I've got the originals. What did you see?"

"Well, first of all, the father on both of them is listed as one N. R. Knott."

"I see that."

Joan buzzed him. "Hang on, Dino. Yes, Joan?"

"A Carson Rutledge Junior for you on one."

"Dino's on two, tell him I'll call him back." He pushed the button. "Yes, Mr. Rutledge?"

This time, his voice sounded younger and a little shaky. "Mr. Barrington, I've just heard from the police that my father died in a car crash on the interstate an hour and a half ago."

"I'm very sorry to hear that," Stone said.

"His driver was killed, too. The police think he fell asleep, then crashed into a bridge abutment."

Stone was stunned into momentary silence. "I'm very sorry for your loss, Mr. Rutledge. When your father was here this morning he told me that he had recently begun to fear for his life. Do you have any idea why?"

"I think it may have had something to do with a client's business."

"And who was the client?"

"I'm afraid I can't divulge that."

"Might it have been Edward Rawls?"

The young man paused. "I believe so."

"Mr. Rutledge, I'm sorry to bring it up at this time, but I think it might be a good idea if you asked the police to run a tox screen on your father's driver."

"You think he might have been drugged?"

"I don't know, but the circumstances are very much like another accident that I'm aware of."

"All right, I'll do that."

"Again, I'm very sorry for your loss."

"Thank you. I'll call you if I have any further information." He hung up.

Stone called Dino. "Anything new?"

"We've learned that the mother of the twelve-year-old left her apartment shortly after the deaths of the other mother and her daughter."

"So when she heard, she ran."

"Sounds like it."

"I've got something, too. The lawyer who delivered the books and birth certificates to my office this morning was very glad to be rid of them and pretty nervous. He told me he feared for his life. I've just spoken to his son, and the man and his driver were killed in a crash on the interstate earlier this afternoon. The police think the driver fell asleep, and they hit a bridge abutment."

"Tell the son to ask the police to run a tox screen on the driver," Dino said.

"I have already done so."

"Somebody just handed me a note," Dino said. "The Virginia state documents office has no record of either of the two birth certificates having ever been registered."

"They're numbered."

"Neither number exists. Apparently, they screw one up now and then and list the certificate as destroyed. Both certificates with those numbers are listed as having been destroyed."

"Oh, shit."

"Yeah. It's a good thing nobody knows you have those documents."

Stone thought about the "trouble" Rutledge & Rutledge were having with their phone lines. "I'm not sure that's true," he said.

45

Stone had Joan call Ed Rawls's number every half hour, until she was done for the day. He was beginning to think that he was going to have to go to Virginia and check his house, but then he had a thought.

Holly had thought that Lance Cabot might be a candidate to run with Kate as her vice president. If so, that would explain why Lance was so interested in Rawls and the strong case. He called Lance and got him as he was about to leave his office at Langley.

"What is it, Stone?"

"There have been serious developments," Stone said.

"Developments with what?"

"The contents of the strong case."

"What developments?"

"For one, Ed Rawls, after living openly in his old house for a few days, is unreachable. He's not answering his phone or responding to messages left, and I don't have a cell phone number for him. He's been using throwaways."

"When did you last call him?"

"I've been calling him every half hour since midafternoon. The last time was ten minutes ago."

"His place is sort of on my way home from work," Lance said. "I'll go by and check on him."

"He has a car, an old Mercedes station wagon. Check his garage, too, will you?"

"All right." Lance hung up.

Dino called again. "Any news on Rawls?"

"None. I just spoke to Lance Cabot, who has taken a great interest in the contents of the strong case. He's going to drive by Ed's house on his way home from work."

"Why is Lance so interested? Does he want Kate to be reelected so much?"

"Kate gave Lance his job as director of central intelligence," Stone pointed out, "and if loyalty weren't enough to get him involved, there's something else — Holly told me she thinks Kate might be considering him as a running mate."

"Well, *that* would certainly get Lance interested. What's your next move, if Ed Rawls can't be found?"

"Ed printed two hundred copies of his

manuscript and had them stored at a pack-and-ship place in D.C. He told me that if anything happened to him, to call them and tell them to mail the books. He said he has a mailing list of two hundred opinion makers. I guess that means newspapers and TV news people, columnists, and like that."

"Have you done that?"

"I had them trucked up to me this afternoon. They're locked in my wine cellar."

"I don't think it's a good idea to have those books so close at hand," Dino said.

"I know. If Ed can't be located by morning, I'm going to see that the books are mailed."

"You want me to send a couple of cops up there to sit on them until you can get them out of the house?"

"I don't think that'll be necessary."

"Did you discuss the books with anybody on the phone?"

"I called the pack-and-ship place and arranged to have them brought here."

"When was the last time your phones and your office were swept?"

"I don't know, maybe last week."

"A lot has happened since last week. We've talked about the birth certificates on the phone, too."

"I'll get Mike Freeman to send somebody

over in the morning."

"You could call Bob Cantor and have him do it now."

"I'm not ready to panic yet, Dino."

"What's it going to take for that to happen?" Dino asked.

"If Ed Rawls turns up dead, then I'll panic."

"Well, when you get around to it, call me and I'll help."

"Thank you, I appreciate that."

"You want dinner at Patroon?"

"You think I ought to leave the house?"

"I think leaving the house might be a good idea," Dino said.

"I'll see you at Patroon at seven-thirty, then."

"I'll pick you up at seven-fifteen. Don't hang around out front, wait until you see the car."

"All right."

They both hung up. Stone tidied his desk and made a to-do list for the following day. He was about to leave when he decided to call Ed Rawls's house one more time. He dialed the number, and it rang three times.

"Hello?"

The voice was not that of Ed Rawls.

"Who is this?"

"It's Lance, Stone."

"Any sign of Ed?"

"I'm in his study. A lamp has been knocked over and a drink spilled. The room smells like scotch."

"What about his car?"

"It's in the garage."

"So he didn't leave under his own power."

"Apparently not. I haven't searched the whole house yet, but I've got a team of specialists on their way here now."

"I don't think Ed is a morning or afternoon drinker," Stone said. "If he was having a drink, it was probably last night."

"That's a good point."

"I'm on my way out for dinner with Dino. Will you call me on my cell when you know more?"

"I will. Enjoy your dinner, I'm not going to enjoy mine for some time." Lance hung up.

Stone saw Dino's SUV outside and walked out Joan's office entrance and into the car.

"Anything new?"

"I called Ed's house and Lance answered. A lamp had been knocked over in Ed's study and a scotch spilled."

"Sounds like last night."

"That's what I said. His car is in the garage, so if he's gone, he left with somebody else."

"I don't like the sound of that," Dino said.

"Neither do I."

They arrived at the restaurant, sat down, and drinks were brought immediately. Ken Aretsky, the owner, came over. "You two don't look happy," he said. "Anything I can do?"

"Station somebody to keep an eye on our glasses and fill them when they get empty," Dino said.

"You will not run dry." Ken went about his business.

"When is Viv back?" Stone asked, for lack of anything else to say.

"Tomorrow."

The two were uncharacteristically silent. They finished their drinks, and they were instantly refilled.

"We'd better not drink dinner," Stone said. "Let's order."

They ordered and were waiting for dinner when Lance called.

"Hello, Lance."

"My people are here and are still going through the house. Ed is not present, and they say that the house has been gone through by pros. They got Ed's safe open in the study, but I don't know if they got the strong case. There's still some cash in there."

"What do you think, Lance?"

"I think that, best case, Ed is in the trunk of somebody's car. Worst case? Well . . ."

46

Ed Rawls gradually came to. They had injected him with something, and he felt numb all over. Gradually, it became clear to him that he was in the trunk of a large car, driving over smooth pavement. He was not bound or gagged, for which he was grateful. Probably, they had thought the drug would keep him out until they reached their destination.

As he became more conscious he began to explore his surroundings with his hands. He found a tire iron, which he put under his body, where he could reach it when he needed it.

There was a bit of light at the upper-right-hand corner of his space. He felt that surface, and it seemed to be the back of the rear seat. He pressed very slowly on the seat and a seam of light opened from top to bottom. Finally, he could see the back of a man's head in the front passenger seat.

He continued to push the seat back, running his fingers down the crack of light slowly. The seat continued to give. Soon, light opened in the middle of the rear seat, which meant that it was not a bench, but divided. He could see the back of the driver's head now, and the two men were talking, something about sports.

Ed stopped pushing on the seat. It was clear that he could press on it until it would leave half the trunk exposed, but the driver might catch that in the rearview mirror. He pushed again, but the seat back came to a stop, as if there were an obstacle to its opening. Ed got his whole hand through the opening, feeling for the obstruction, and he found it.

He ran his hand over the surface and suddenly, he knew what it was. The butt of a rifle or shotgun. He got a good grip on the stock and twisted it, to free the barrel from any obstruction; he swung the weapon and shortly, the barrel was in the foot well, and he had a firm grip on the stock. He worked the barrel along until it was touching the rear door, then he tightened his grip on the stock and pulled it into the trunk. A couple more pulls and he had possession of a police riot gun, the kind with an eighteen-and-a-quarter-inch barrel. He slid the action back far enough to reveal a shell in the chamber, then let it close.

He got a good grip on the seat back and pulled it closed. All was dark again. He arranged his body so as to be comfortable, with the shotgun lying along his right side, so that it wouldn't be seen when the trunk opened, then he relaxed and waited for developments.

The car seemed to leave a limited-access highway, perhaps an interstate, and made a right turn. A couple of minutes later, they made another right turn onto a road that was noisier and a little rougher, probably gravel or dirt. The road wound left and right and finally made another right turn onto crunchier gravel, then it pulled up.

Ed heard the two front doors slam and footsteps on both sides of the car. He closed his eyes and made an effort to relax and let his mouth hang open. The trunk door opened.

"Let's get him inside," one of the men said. Somebody grabbed his left arm and pulled, and he used the opportunity to bring the barrel around and rap the knuckles sharply, raising a cry of pain.

"Oh, shit, Manny, he's got your shotgun," one of them said.

"That's right, I've got your shotgun," Ed

311

said. "You should know that it's loaded and the safety is off, and my finger is on the trigger. Take one big step back, both of you."

The two men obeyed. While keeping the shotgun trained on them, Ed got an elbow under his body and pushed himself upright. He swung his legs over the threshold of the trunk and pushed until he could rest his feet on the ground.

"Now," Ed said, "you're going to do exactly as I say, and the punishment for not doing what I say is going to be a shotgun blast to the knee. You'll survive, if your buddy can get a tourniquet on you fast enough, but you'll likely lose the leg when you get to a hospital. Everybody got that?"

"Yes, sir," both men said simultaneously.

"Now, put your hands on top of your head and interlink your fingers."

Both men complied.

Ed searched the one on the left and found a pistol, a flashlight, and a pair of handcuffs on his belt. He relieved the man of those implements and tossed them into the open trunk. "On your knees," Ed said. The man complied, and Ed searched the other one, finding the same items, along with a spare magazine. "On your knees," he said. The man complied.

Ed drew back the shotgun and clipped

first one, then the other on the back of his head. They both fell forward onto their faces and lay very still. He searched both men's pockets and found keys on both of them, then he cuffed them with their own handcuffs and threw both sets of keys into the woods. He tossed their wallets into the trunk, then he turned over both men and found a cell phone and a handheld radio on each of them and tossed those into the trunk.

He pulled both men away from the car, pocketed a gun, a phone, and a radio, closed the trunk, and walked around to the driver's side. The keys were in the ignition. He looked into the backseat and saw the strong case, then he got into the car, started the engine, and got turned around. He followed the dirt road back to the pavement, then turned left and drove to the interstate. He headed south and was now reoriented. It was a thirty-minute drive back to his house.

He slowed as he approached, then saw lights on. There wouldn't have been so many on last night, he reckoned. He was about to drive past when he saw Lance Cabot come out of the house and sit in a rocker on the front porch. He slammed on the brakes, pulled into his driveway, and got out of the car, taking the shotgun and the strong case with him. "Good evening, Lance," he called out, and climbed the porch steps.

Lance didn't get up. "Good evening, Ed," he said. "You didn't need to bring a shot-gun."

"It's borrowed, like the car and this stuff." He emptied the pistol, phone, and radios onto the table beside Lance's rocker.

"What time did they take you?"

"Very late, I think. I must have fallen asleep in my chair in the study when they rousted me and injected me with something. While I was out they must have searched the place, found my safe and got it open, and taken the strong case. Their wallets are in the trunk, if you want to know who they are."

"Do you know who they work for?" Lance asked.

"My guess is a man named Erik Macher, runs a security service in D.C."

"And works for Christian St. Clair. I know him. He used to be with us."

"Could you use a drink?" Ed asked.

"I could, and something to eat, if you have it. We hadn't got around to raiding your fridge yet."

Ed went into the house and returned with a bottle of Talisker, ice and glasses, a slab of

Brie, and a box of crackers. He set the tray on a table between the two rockers, poured them both a drink, and sat down. "Your health," he said, raising his glass.

Lance took a big swig. "Stone called me. He couldn't raise you."

"I came to in the trunk of the car and managed to get the shotgun out of the rear seat. They took me to the proverbial cabin in the woods, and there the tables were turned. I left them unconscious and handcuffed. If you want them I'll give you directions."

"Let's let them find their own way home," Lance said. "It'll be a good experience for them."

"Right." They ate the cheese and crackers and drank much of the scotch.

"I'd better call Stone," Lance said finally. "He'll be worried about you."

"You do that," Ed said, "and give him my best. I'm going to bed. I'd be grateful if you locked the doors behind you."

47

Stone and Dino had finished dinner and were on cognac when Stone's phone vibrated. Number blocked.

"Yes?"

"It's Lance. Sometime in the wee hours of last night two men invaded Ed Rawls's home, sedated him, opened his safe, and retrieved the strong case. They stuffed him in the trunk of a car and took him to a cabin in the country about thirty minutes from his house. While en route, Ed regained consciousness and managed to retrieve a shotgun from the rear seat. When they opened the trunk they were surprised to find their own shotgun pointed at them. Having cuffed the two men and thrown away the keys, Ed is now in his bed. The strong case is with him."

"I'm relieved to hear all of that," Stone said. "You sound a little drunk, Lance."

"Funny, so do you."

Stone laughed. "Does the fact that Ed still has the strong case indicate a disinterest on your part in possessing it?"

"Pretty much. As I told you before, I believe I know everything that's in it."

"Did you know that Nelson Knott fathered two children with black mothers, respectively seventeen and twelve years ago, and that the elder child and her mother are dead from an accident described as the mother falling asleep and striking a bridge abutment on the New Jersey Turnpike, and that the other mother and child have disappeared?"

Lance drew in a quick breath. "What evidence exists of this?"

"I have both the original birth certificates."

"I did not know about this."

"I didn't think so. Also, the attorney who gave me the birth certificates earlier today was killed on his way back to Virginia in an accident described as his driver falling asleep and crashing into a bridge abutment on the interstate."

"Have you called the police?"

"I'm sitting next to the police right now, and he's just as drunk as I am."

"Let me speak to Dino, please."

Stone handed the phone to Dino. "Lance

wants to speak to you."

Dino took the phone. "Yes? Yes. Yes. I understand. Go fuck yourself, Lance." He handed the phone back to Stone.

"Yes?"

"I tried to persuade Dino not to deal with this information in such a way that it might immediately become public knowledge."

"I heard his answer to that request," Stone said.

"Stone, when you and I, and perhaps Dino, have all sobered up, we should have a conference call on this subject. I believe I can convince you both that it is not in the interests of anyone, particularly the President, for this information to leak, unless we release it at just the right moment."

"Okay, call us both at ten tomorrow morning. Dino and I should be sober by then. I don't know about you."

"Thank you, Stone, I'll do that. Is there anything else?"

"Yes, there is. Ed Rawls has printed and bound two hundred copies of his manuscript and they are awaiting mailing now, addressed to as many 'opinion makers,' as Ed likes to describe them."

"Jesus God. Where are they?"

"I am not at liberty to divulge that information, and neither is Ed, since he doesn't know, himself. Perhaps you would like to include that subject in our conference call tomorrow morning. Good night, Lance." Stone hung up.

Dino smiled. "Did Lance shit a brick?"

"I think that is not an inaccurate description of his reaction. He's going to call us tomorrow morning at ten and beg us to come to our senses."

They paid the bill and made their way gingerly back to Dino's SUV. When they were inside the cop in the front passenger seat sniffed the air and said, "I should issue both you gentlemen with a summons for traveling in the rear seat of a motor vehicle while under the influence."

"There's no such charge," Dino said.

"Lucky for you, Commissioner," the cop replied.

Stone awoke an hour later than usual the following morning and managed not to throw up immediately. He drank an Alka-Seltzer, ate half his breakfast, and eventually arrived at his desk.

Joan came in with the mail. "Good morning," she said. "You look like you were hit with a baseball bat."

"That is an approximation of the way I

feel," Stone replied. "Do you have any aspirin?"

"How many do you want?"

"Many, please."

She brought an aspirin bottle and set it on his desk beside a glass of water. He shook four into his hand and got them down. "I'm expecting a conference call with Lance Cabot and Dino at ten, and I'd appreciate it if you'd hold all my calls until we're finished."

She nodded, then fetched a pitcher of ice water and placed it on his desk. "You're going to need this, if you expect to survive until lunchtime."

Lance called promptly at ten o'clock. "Are you both there?" he asked.

"In a manner of speaking," Dino said.

"Same here," Stone replied.

"Now listen to me carefully. I am assuming that you would both prefer to see Kate Lee reelected than have Nelson Knott replace her?"

"Yeah."

"Right."

"We have seven months to go before the election. If these birth certificates are published now, Christian St. Clair will have plenty of time to discredit these women or prove that they never existed."

"One of them *doesn't* exist," Dino said.

"The other may not, either," Stone chipped in.

"If she's alive, then she's in hiding somewhere," Lance said, "and if she learns on television or in the *National Inquisitor* that we're looking for her, she may vanish again, and we may never find her."

"A good point."

"Yeah, okay."

"Dino, if you start looking into the New Jersey car crash or treat the disappearance of the second woman as a crime, that information will make its way to St. Clair and put us at a disadvantage."

"Oh, all right," Dino said, "I can take the position that there's no evidence of a crime. I'll sit on it until there is."

"Stone, if Ed Rawls's book is published, the same thing will happen."

"Oh, all right, I'll see if I can delay the mailing."

"Good. Now, in anticipation of your acceptance of my advice, I have gratefully dispatched to each of you a bottle of the CIA's secret hangover remedy, which has saved the life of many an agent in difficult circumstances. One swallow every four hours, and you will regain your health by dinnertime." Lance hung up.

Joan came in and set a medicine bottle on Stone's desk. "This came, hand-delivered, from Lance, while you were on the phone."

Stone picked it up, unscrewed the cap, and took a big swallow.

48

Stone, fortified by periodic doses of the magic CIA remedy, had regained his health by midafternoon, so he was healed when Ed Rawls's call came in.

"Hello, Ed. How are you feeling after your ordeal?"

"Just fine, thank you. Lance sent over some stuff that cured my hangover."

"I'm happy for you."

"Where the fuck are my books? My pack-and-ship place told me they took them to New York on your orders."

"To my house, yes," Stone said. "Now they are in a different place, a very safe one."

"I was afraid that when I disappeared, you'd ship them."

"Those were your instructions, but you turned up just in time to stop me."

"I want them back."

"No. They cannot be released until exactly the right moment. If they were sent now,

St. Clair would have time before the election to discredit your work."

Ed was quiet for a moment. "You have a point," he said finally.

"I have some questions," Stone said.

"Shoot."

"Where is the mother and her twelve-year-old?"

"In a safe place," Ed said. "They moved to a new house a few weeks ago."

"Are you in constant touch with her?"

"I know how to find her. My place in Maine is being framed as we speak, or I'd send them there."

Stone thought about that. "Perhaps they might be safe in my house in Dark Harbor, with security people to help."

"I like the sound of your house for them, but security people would be noticed on arrival, and there would be talk in the village."

"How about after Labor Day, when the summer folk go home?"

"Better, but the lack of people would make the security types even more noticeable."

"How about this — we get Mike Freeman at Strategic Services to come up with an operative, and the three of them openly move in as a family."

"I like it," Ed said. "Maybe there could be

a woman, too — her sister, say."

"I expect that could be arranged."

"Who pays for all this?"

"I do. Mike will give me the in-house rate. Maybe we could station somebody there to keep an eye on who arrives on the ferry."

"Not on the island. Station somebody at the other end, in Lincolnville. He'd be less noticeable and nobody gets off on Islesboro who didn't get on in Lincolnville."

"Good."

"Of course, there's still a little pond called Penobscot Bay. Lots of boats out there, lots of places to come ashore on Islesboro."

"There is that," Stone said.

"Think of something else."

"How about another country?"

"Which one do you have in mind?"

"France or England. I have houses in both."

"I like that better."

"And there's a private airstrip on my English property."

"Can it take a jet?"

"Yes. Perhaps you should get ahold of the lady and ask her to obtain passports for her and her son. I'm not going to smuggle them across any borders."

"I'll do that right away. I know a passport service that can get it done in a couple of days. How will you get them to England?"

"Strategic Services has a Gulfstream that's back and forth all the time. They can hitch a ride."

"Let me make a call, and I'll get back to you. I'll have to go buy another throwaway phone. I've run out."

"I'll wait to hear from you."

"Did you get your phones and your house swept?"

"They were due today but haven't arrived yet."

"Good. See you later." Rawls hung up.

Joan came into his office. "How are you feeling?"

"Very well, thank you."

"You know, if we could get that stuff analyzed we could bottle it, sell it, and make a fortune."

"I suspect that it may contain ingredients that can't be bought over the counter."

"Oh. By the way, the Strategic Services people are here. I started them upstairs, and Fred is with them."

"Good."

A couple of hours later the team leader from Strategic Services came into Stone's office. "You're clean," he said, "house and phones. We're going to have a look next door, too, if that's okay."

"Go right ahead," Stone said.

Ed Rawls called. "I have news."

"Go ahead, my house and phones are clean."

"The lady got married eighteen months ago, to a retired army master sergeant, so they have a new last name. More good news — they took a Mediterranean cruise last year and got passports, so they can leave whenever you like."

"Wonderful. Let me look into transportation. I'll get back to you." He hung up and called Mike Freeman at Strategic Services.

"Hi, Stone, are my people finished?"

"Yes, and we're clean here, thanks very much."

"Everything else all right?"

"I need to get three people to my place in England on the quiet."

"Are they legal?"

"They are, and they have passports — father, mother, and a twelve-year-old son."

"I'm going to Brussels early on the day after tomorrow, eight AM departure. I could drop them at your place."

"Ideal."

"I'll need their names and addresses and copies of their passports first thing tomorrow morning. We have to file a passenger list with the FAA."

"I'll get them to you. Mike, once they're there, they're going to need armed security to watch over them."

"How many?"

"Two should do it."

"I'll get them down from London."

Stone hung up and called Rawls. "We're set for an eight AM the day after tomorrow. Where are they located?"

"In southern New Jersey."

"Good. I'll arrange for a car to pick them up and take them to Teterboro."

"Great."

"Mike will need their names, address, and dates of birth, and copies of their passports tomorrow morning." Stone gave him a fax number for Freeman.

"I'll get it done." He gave Stone an address in Cape May, New Jersey.

"Tell them the car will be there at six AM. They'll be going to the Strategic Services hangar at Jet Aviation, Teterboro."

"Right."

"What are their names?"

"Henry and Martha Parker. The boy's name is Thomas. They're known as Hank, Marty, and Tommy."

"Got it. Text me when they've been briefed, and tell them they'll have security at my house when they get there." Stone hung up and called Major Bugg, his estate manager.

"How are you, sir?"

"Very well. I'm sending you some guests, a family of three. They'll be there in the evening, day after tomorrow."

"Where would you like them?"

"Where do you suggest?"

"We've finished renovating Sir Charles's cottage. They'd be very comfortable there, and we can feed them from the main kitchen, unless they'd like to do their own cooking." Sir Charles was the previous owner, from whom Stone had bought the property.

"Sounds ideal." Stone gave him the names. "And give them a car to use for sightseeing and shopping."

"As you wish."

"Have you got a dog that could stay in the cottage? I'll bet the boy would like that."

"Of course. We're never short of dogs."

"Thank you, Major."

Stone hung up, satisfied that all was well.

49

The following morning, Joan buzzed Stone. "There's a Mr. Henry Parker to see you. He doesn't have an appointment."

"Send him in."

A large African-American man in a business suit came into his office, and Stone rose to greet him. He was a good six-three and something over two hundred pounds, fit-looking.

"Good morning, Mr. Parker," Stone said.

"Please call me Hank."

"And I'm Stone." He pointed the man to a chair. "Coffee?"

"Thank you. I got up early this morning and missed mine."

Stone poured him a mugful and set it on his side of the desk. "Tell me what I can do for you."

"You've already done plenty for us," Parker said. "I want to thank you for that."

"You're very welcome."

"I just need to know something about the place we're going. I don't want it to be too big a surprise to my family."

"I have a house in the south of England, not far from the English Channel. It's on about a hundred and twenty acres of land. There's the main house and half a dozen cottages. I've asked the estate manager, Major Bugg, with two *g*'s, to put you in the recently updated cottage where the previous owner lived while the main house underwent a renovation. I thought you might be more comfortable in something smaller than the big house, but when you see it, if you don't think it's the thing, speak to Major Bugg and ask him to put you in the main house."

"A cottage sounds better for us."

"They can bring your meals from the main kitchen, or you can cook your own, or some combination of the two. I've asked Major Bugg to make a car available to you for shopping or sightseeing."

"Wonderful. How far is it from London?"

"About ninety miles. It's an hour and a half's drive, but it might be easier to take the train."

"I'd like for Marty and Tommy to see London. I was stationed there some years ago."

"What did you do in the army?"

"Special ops. I retired two years ago, after thirty years."

"How do you feel about dogs?"

"Love 'em — we all do. Ours is staying with friends while we're gone."

"I thought Tommy might like to have a dog as a friend while you're there, so he will. By the way, there are a pool and a tennis court behind the main house, and there are bicycles and horses for riding, if you're so inclined."

"Wow! Tommy will be very excited." Parker arranged his features to something more serious. "How long will we be there?"

"Hard to say. It might be best for you to stay until the election, in November."

"Then Tommy will miss some school."

"I'll ask Major Bugg to arrange a tutor for him. I expect it would be helpful if you can get a curriculum from his school."

"That's very kind of you."

Stone buzzed Joan. "Please bring me a thousand pounds sterling."

Joan came in with an envelope and Stone handed it to Parker.

"You'll need some local currency. If you want to open a bank account while you're there, Major Bugg can arrange it."

"Thank you. I'd like to take a couple of

guns with me. We've been warned these people have already committed murder."

"You can't do that. The firearms laws are much stricter in Britain than here, but you'll have two armed security people watching over you at all times. They work for the London office of a company called Strategic Services. It's their airplane you'll be flying on, and the CEO of the company, Mike Freeman, will be aboard. He's flying to Brussels, and he'll drop you on my private landing strip on the way."

"Private landing strip?"

"It was a bomber base during World War Two. Customs and Immigration people will meet you there and clear you in."

"What's the weather like this time of year?"

"Cooler than here, and with more rain. You might take sweaters and a raincoat. There'll be umbrellas in the cottage. If you're there until November, you might need a warmer coat, or a liner for your raincoat."

"Is there any sailing available?"

"The property is on the Bewley River, spelled B-e-a-u-l-i-e-u, and you can probably rent a sailing dinghy in the village of the same name. There's a rubber dinghy with an outboard on my dock, and you're welcome to use that on the river. It's quite a beautiful place."

"This sounds like it's going to be a wonderful vacation."

"I hope so. You can stay as long as you like, even after we get the all-clear."

"Once again, I'm very grateful to you."

"Hank, you're right to take this seriously. As you say, these people have already committed kidnapping and murder. Listen to your security people. They know the territory, and they know what they're doing."

Parker stood and offered his hand. "I won't keep you any longer."

"Enjoy the flight. It's a comfortable airplane. Oh, after you arrive, if you make any calls to the States, use the landline in the cottage, instead of your cell phones, and be circumspect about your location. Don't even mention the country."

"I'll be careful."

"Does your house have a garage?" Stone asked.

"Yes."

"Open it tomorrow morning to let in the car that's picking you up. Strategic Services is providing an SUV and armed men up front. Load the car in the garage."

"Got it." Hank Parker left.

Stone called Ed Rawls and told him about

his meeting with Parker. "He's thoroughly briefed about what to expect, and there will be two security people with them at all times."

"That's a relief," Ed said.

"Have you had any further contact with St. Clair's people?"

"No, but I'm ready if they show up."

"Don't kill anybody if you can help it. That would be a lot more trouble than it's worth."

"I'll keep that in mind."

"I expect they won't bother you again, but if they do, they'll send more than two people."

"I've still got their shotgun, and a little arsenal of my own. You might think about going armed yourself, Stone, until this is over."

"That's good advice."

"My house in Islesboro is already framed. They're moving fast."

"When you go back, use my place until you get yours in shape."

"Thank you, I'll take you up on that. Now, if we can just get the Parkers out of the country, we'll be in good shape."

"I hope you're right."

50

Erik Macher arrived in Cape May, New Jersey, late in the evening and spent the night in a motel. At dawn the following morning he got a call on his cell phone.

"Yes?"

"They're stirring in the house."

Macher had had the Parker residence under surveillance since noon the previous day, shortly after his search had proved fruitful. "I'll be over there in a few minutes. Call me if anybody goes out."

"Yes, sir."

Macher cleaned up and got dressed, then drove to the quiet neighborhood where the Parker family lived in a small Victorian house. He pulled up behind the surveillance van half a block away and got inside. "What's going on?" he asked the two men.

"Nothing yet. The boy came outside and got the newspaper, then went back inside.

"Was he dressed?"

"Yes."

"Then they're moving," Macher said. "Why else would a man who's retired get his family up this early?" He looked at his watch: five-fifty. Then, as he watched, a black SUV with tinted windows approached the house and turned into the driveway. A garage door opened, the vehicle drove inside, and the door closed.

"That's pretty weird," one of his agents said. "Is something being delivered, do you think?"

Ten minutes later the lights went off in the house, the garage door opened again, the SUV backed out, and the door closed. The vehicle drove away.

"I'll get my car," Macher said. "You keep that SUV in sight." He ran back to his car, the van made a U-turn, and Macher followed. His cell phone rang. "Yes?"

"We've got the vehicle."

"We'll change places from time to time."

The SUV turned north, and the two cars followed. Macher was getting hungry. They drove north for more than an hour, and the SUV made a few turns, ending up on Highway 17 North. Shortly, it turned off the four-lane road and headed east. A mile later, it turned into the entrance of Teterboro Airport. The van and Macher followed.

They were both stopped at a security guard's booth.

"Destination?" the guard asked Macher.

"We're following the SUV ahead."

"Let me see some ID, please."

Macher showed him a driver's license. Up ahead he saw the SUV turn right.

"Go ahead."

Macher made the same turn the SUV had, just in time to see the vehicle drive through a security gate. From his knowledge of Teterboro, that was unusual; cars weren't allowed on the ramp. He parked his car and ran inside and through Jet Aviation in time to see the SUV drive past on the ramp. He stood at the rear windows and watched as the vehicle drove behind a hangar. He walked out to the ramp, where a shuttle bus was waiting, its door open. A driver sat inside.

"Excuse me," Macher said, "do you know whose hangar that is?" He pointed. "The biggest one."

"Yeah, that belongs to Strategic Services."

What the hell? Macher thought. He stood on the ramp and watched. Shortly, the main door opened, and a tug arrived and pulled a Gulfstream jet out onto the ramp. Macher jotted down the tail number, got out his cell phone, and called his office.

"Yes, sir?"

"I'm at Teterboro. A Gulfstream is on the ramp, starting its engines." He gave the man the tail number. "Check the system and see what destination that airplane has filed a flight plan for. I'll hold."

A couple of minutes later the man came back on the line. "The aircraft has filed for Brussels, nonstop."

"Track it." Macher hung up and walked quickly toward the hangar. As he approached he could see the black SUV inside with the doors open. The Parkers had to be on that airplane. What the hell? He glanced at his wristwatch: 7:55. He went to his contacts and dialed a number.

"Yes?"

"It's Erik, sir. I'm at Teterboro Airport."

"What are you doing at Teterboro?"

"We were surveilling the Parker residence in Cape May when a large black SUV drove into their garage, apparently loaded them up, then departed. We followed the SUV to Jet Aviation at Teterboro, where it drove into a hangar owned by Strategic Services. The family apparently got aboard a large Gulfstream jet, which was towed out of the hangar and is taxiing as we speak. The jet has filed a flight plan for Brussels."

"Brussels? Why would they go to Brussels?"

"I don't know, sir."

"Are you sure the family is aboard?"

"I haven't had eyes on them, but all signs point to their presence. What are your instructions?"

"Do you have contacts in Brussels?"

"Yes, sir."

"Have the airplane met and the family identified as being on board, then followed to their destination."

"Yes, sir." Macher began looking up a Brussels number.

Hank Parker looked around the big airplane. He, his wife and son sat in a group of four seats, all buckled in.

"This is fantastic, Dad!" Tommy said.

"It sure is."

"Where are we going again?"

"To England. I'll show you on the map as soon as the seat belt sign goes off."

The airplane taxied onto a runway, and the engine noise increased. Hank was pressed into his seat from the acceleration, and a moment later they lifted off, and he heard the landing gear come up. Half an hour later the airplane was above the clouds and leveling off. The seat belt sign went off.

Hank got out a map he'd taken from an atlas and unfolded it. "You see this town right here? It's called Bewley, but it's spelled the French way. We're headed for a big estate just south of the town, and it has its own landing strip."

Mike Freeman, who had introduced himself when they boarded, walked over to their seats. "We're at fifty-one thousand feet now, headed for England, with a hundred-and-fifty-knot tailwind. Would you folks like some breakfast?"

"We ate at home," Hank said, "but Marty and I could use some coffee."

"I'll send it over." He walked forward, toward the cockpit.

A moment later a flight attendant appeared with coffee on a tray.

When she had gone, Marty said, "I feel better now — there's no way they could find us where we're going."

"You're right," Hank said, but in his heart, he wasn't sure about that.

51

Stone watched the tracking app on his computer until the Gulfstream was at cruising altitude, then went back to work. Joan came in with a FedEx envelope.

"This came for you from Cape May, New Jersey," she said, setting it on his desk. "You open it."

"Getting nervous?" Stone asked.

"You betcha."

Stone unzipped the envelope and removed an unlabeled DVD with a Post-it stuck to it. *Thought this might come in useful. Hank.*

Stone slipped the disc into his computer and started it. An African-American woman sat on a chair in front of a white background, probably a sheet. She was fortyish, handsome, beautifully coifed. "My name is Martha Shivers," she said. She gave the date and time. "I'm forty-one years old. When I was in my twenties I worked for Knott Industries in Washington, D.C. I started as a receptionist but was promoted over the seven years of my employment there, ending up as one of two executives to the chief executive officer, Mr. Nelson Knott. During the time I worked for him, Mr. Knott seemed to find me attractive, but he was married, so I resisted his overtures. Finally, one night when I was working very late on a special project, Mr. Knott and I were alone in his office and he pressed himself upon me. I protested and struggled, but he pushed me down onto a sofa and raped me. Shortly after that he went to the studio to do his daily broadcast, and he told me not to leave, that he would come back and do it again. He said this as though I had consented to sex, which I had not.

"As soon as he left the room I got my clothes back on and went home. Before leaving I typed a letter of resignation with immediate effect, signed it, and left it on his desk. I went home, and the next day I started looking for another job.

"A couple of months later I found myself pregnant. Before my encounter with Mr. Knott in his office I had not had sex since my divorce, four years before that, and I had not had sex since my resignation.

"I had lunch shortly thereafter with a former coworker at Knott Industries who told me that something similar had happened to another woman, Helen Trimble. She had a daughter from that experience. I was put in touch with her in New York City, where she had gone to live, and we compared our experiences. She had also been raped by Mr. Knott. She had received a monthly check for two thousand dollars from a New York bank since the birth of her child, but she had not seen or spoken to Mr. Knott since she had resigned from his employment, shortly after she became pregnant and revealed it to Mr. Knott.

"She helped me find an apartment in New York, and I moved there, using up most of my savings. I found employment as a seamstress with a dress manufacturer. Shortly after I gave birth, I began receiving a monthly check from the same bank as Ms. Trimble had. She then told me that she had recently phoned Mr. Knott and asked for more money and an educational fund for her daughter, who was very bright and good in school. He told her to go to hell, and immediately after that the monthly checks stopped coming. She told me that Mr. Knott had threatened her, and that she was frightened.

"Shortly after that she went to visit her parents in New Jersey and, driving back to

New York, she collided with a bridge on the turnpike. The police said it was an accident, that she had fallen asleep at the wheel. She and her daughter were both killed instantly.

"I immediately took my newborn baby and left New York City, fearing for my life. I moved to a small town in southern New Jersey called Greenwich, where I went to work for a sailmaker, who trained me to sew sails.

"Two years ago I met a retired army master sergeant, and eventually we married and he adopted my son. We bought a house in another town and moved there. Recently, I learned that two men with badges had visited my former employer in Greenwich and were looking for me, and remembering what had happened to Helen Trimble, I became frightened. My family and I have now moved to a location that will remain undisclosed until I feel safe in returning to my home."

She held up a photograph. "This is a picture of Nelson Knott," she said, then held up another photograph. "This is a picture of my son, who is now twelve years old. As you can see, he strongly resembles his biological father. He has given a blood sample which may be used to compare my son's DNA with that of Nelson Knott."

After another minute, the image faded.

Stone took the disc from his computer and buzzed Joan; she came in. He shook the FedEx envelope and a tube, labeled, dated, and identified as Thomas Parker's blood, fell out. He handed Joan the disc. "Please call Bob Cantor and have him make two hundred and ten copies of this DVD ASAP. When they arrive, put one in each envelope in the wine cellar and the rest in my safe." He handed her the vial. "Please call my doctor and find out where a DNA profile can be made of this blood and send it there."

"You betcha," she said. She took the disc and the vial and went back to her office.

Stone thought for a moment, then called Lance Cabot.

"Yes, Stone?"

"Ed Rawls has located the mother of the twelve-year-old, who is now remarried. I have spirited her, her son, and her husband out of the country, where they will remain until it is safe for them to return."

"That's good news. We'll need to get her interviewed at once."

"I don't think that will be necessary. She sent me a DVD, on which she relates how she worked as an executive assistant to Nelson Knott, who raped her in his office.

She later gave birth to a son, now twelve. She knew the other mother, whose name was Helen Trimble, whose story was much the same as the second mother's. I am having the DVD duplicated and I will include one with each of Ed Rawls's books. She also sent me a vial of her son's blood for DNA purposes, which I am sending out for a profile."

"That is excellent news," Lance said.

"Will you find a way to let Will know?"

"I have a meeting in Washington later today, and he will be there."

"Good. You might discuss with him when would be a good time for me to have the books mailed."

"Certainly."

"Lance, you employ a lot of people who are sneaky for a living, do you think one or more of them might contrive to get a DNA sample from Nelson Knott?"

"What a good idea," Lance said, but he didn't say he was going to do it. "E-mail me the DVD, and I'll get back to you." He hung up.

Stone called Ed Rawls.

"Hello, Stone."

"The family is off," Stone said. "They're about halfway across the Atlantic as we speak."

"Great news."

"There's more." Stone told him about the DVD. "I'll send it to you."

"That is fantastic. I wish I'd thought of it."

"I wish I'd thought of it, too. And," he said, "she sent a blood sample from her son. I'm sending it out for a DNA profile, and Lance is working on getting a DNA sample from Nelson Knott."

"Wow! What a great woman!"

"Lance has a meeting with Will today. He'll get back to me."

"And you get back to me," Ed said.

52

Erik Macher got back to his office, switched on his computer, and brought up his aircraft tracking software. He found the Gulfstream, identified by its tail number, halfway across the Atlantic. He estimated the distance to Brussels and calculated that the flight would land at about ten PM, European time. He called his contact in Brussels and conveyed that information to him.

Brussels? Why Brussels? It seemed an unlikely place to hide a family, but perhaps that was reason enough to choose it. He set his iPhone alarm to warn him when the aircraft would be approaching Brussels. It was very important that the family be intercepted and followed at the airport, because once in the city, they might be impossible to find.

At eight-thirty PM his alarm chimed, and he went back to the tracking software to recalculate the Gulfstream's landing time. Its tail number was nowhere to be seen. He rebooted the software and looked again; the aircraft was not on the line between its former mid-Atlantic position and Brussels. He felt a rising wave of panic; if he lost these people St. Clair would kill him.

Then he saw the tail number, not over the English Channel, where he would have expected it, but over southern England. He got out an aeronautical chart of the area and put the position of the airplane between the Bournemouth and Southampton airports, headed west. He watched as the aircraft made a 180-degree turn back to the east, and a couple of minutes later it stopped moving. That was impossible; the airplane couldn't hover, and there was no airport where it had landed. You didn't put down an aircraft of that size on a grass strip somewhere; you needed pavement, and a lot of it, if you ever planned to take off again.

He continued to stare at the symbol, and perhaps ten minutes later it began to move again, very slowly. It was taxiing back to the west end of what must be a runway for takeoff. Sure enough, as he watched it picked up speed and left, turning toward the Channel. Clearly, the family had been dropped off in an area with no airport.

He brought up the opposition research file on Stone Barrington and looked for a connection with England. There it was: he owned a house called Windward Hall, on land just south of the village of Beaulieu. He Googled Windward Hall and found a history of the house, including the information that, during World War II, British Bomber Command had had a base on the property, with a seven-thousand-foot runway. It had been used mainly for intelligence and surveillance flights, and as a departure point for Special Operations executive agents being parachuted into France. That would have kept it off aeronautical charts; that and camouflage would have made it difficult for the Germans to locate.

He picked up the phone and called Christian St. Clair.

"Yes?"

"It's Erik. I've found the family," he said. He explained what had happened.

"It's damned clever of you to figure that out, Erik," St. Clair said.

"Thank you, sir. How do you want to proceed?"

"You know who to call in my London office," St. Clair said. "The two of you should assess the situation and take action."

"How extreme an action?"

"I don't want them returning to the United States," St. Clair said. "And I don't want them making calls to people in the States. Is that perfectly clear?"

"Perfectly, sir," Macher said. It was late in London; he looked up the cell phone number of his counterpart there and made the call.

The Gulfstream set down gently on the runway at Windward Hall, rolled down the runway, then taxied back to the ramp in front of the hangar. The pilots shut down the left engine, and the flight attendant opened the forward door and dropped it into place as an airstair.

The Parkers gathered their things, and when they reached the tarmac a Land Rover pulled up and loaded their luggage. A man in the front passenger seat got out and came toward them. "I'm Major Bugg," he said, offering his hand. "Welcome to Windward Hall."

As they got into the vehicle the left engine of the airplane restarted, and the big jet began taxiing back to the end of the runway.

"You're being housed in Chestnut Cottage," Bugg said to the family. "It has three bedrooms, and you may decide which of them you wish to use."

They drove along a dark road, made a turn, and pulled up before the cottage. Two men in dark clothing walked toward them out of the darkness. "These are your security people," Bugg said, "Dan and Walter." Everybody shook hands.

"We'll be working outside the cottage," Dan said.

The driver handled their luggage, while Bugg escorted them inside. A yellow Labrador retriever welcomed them in the foyer, wagging all over.

"This is Maggie," Bugg said. "She's everyone's favorite dog on the estate. Her food is in the pantry, and she has a cup of food and a biscuit three times a day."

Tommy and Maggie appeared to already be in love.

They walked into a living room where the lamps were on. Bugg took them from room to room and their luggage was put in the two bedrooms they chose.

"The fridge is stocked, and so is the pantry," he said. "There's a laundry room just behind the kitchen, and the bar in the living room has also been stocked." He showed them how to use the telephone system, which was much like that of a hotel, with buttons for calling various extensions. "I'll be back at work tomorrow morning at eight, and the kitchen help begin arriving at six." He handed them some keys. "These are the cottage keys and the key to the car, which is in the garage. Sleep as late as you like — you have no schedule to keep here. You can drive into the village or see the countryside. There are maps in the car and a GPS system, as well. Please let me know tomorrow if you have any questions."

They all shook hands with him and the major left in the Land Rover.

"Hank," Marty said, "this is better than home."

"This is Alfred Brand," a voice said.

"Alf, it's Erik Macher. We met when you were in New York last time."

"Ah, yes, Erik. I've had a text from the chief that you would call and to give you every assistance. What's up?"

"A family of three has arrived in the south of England this evening, from the United States," Macher said. "In short, the chief doesn't want them to return."

"Ah, yes. How do you wish to handle it?"

"I wish *you* to handle it," Macher said, "since I'm in the United States. I can't be of much help there, I'm afraid."

"What is the time frame?"

"As soon as possible, but not so hurried

that mistakes are made."

"Where are they?"

"At a country house called Windward Hall, south of Beaulieu, in Hampshire."

"I know the area, but not the house."

"Neither do I. I should think your first move would be to reconnoiter the place and determine their exact location."

"Does the chief have a means in mind?"

"Well, he doesn't want them shot in the head."

"An accident, then?"

"I think that would be best."

"Do they have a car?"

"I don't know. This operation is a clean sheet of paper. Reconnoiter, then get back to me with questions or a plan." Macher gave him his cell number. "Please remember that it's five hours earlier here than where you are. No middle-of-the-night calls, except in an emergency." He gave the man the names and descriptions.

"I'll have people there by dawn to take a look at the situation," Brand said. "Can I have a week to get it done?"

"Let me know your schedule tomorrow."

"I'll do that." He hung up.

Macher hung up, too, glad not to have to deal with the operation himself.

53

Stone had a call the following day from Major Bugg, reporting that the family was settled in and comfortable.

"Is security in place?" Stone asked.

"Two men, armed. They'll work shifts, and there will always be two on duty."

"Thank you, Major."

Shortly, Ed Rawls called.

"Good morning, Ed."

"Good morning, Stone. How'd the transfer go?"

"I've just had a call. They're comfortable and happy, and security is on the job."

"Good. I've had a call myself, and it's disturbing. The next-door neighbor of the Parkers in Cape May called to say that two vehicles were watching the place very early yesterday morning, around five-thirty AM — a gray van and a black sedan."

"Uh-oh."

"Exactly. The Strategic Services car arrived just before six and pulled into the garage, as planned. It left ten minutes later and both the van and the sedan made U-turns and followed. I think they must have followed them all the way to Teterboro, and if they did, they probably got a look at the airplane's registration number, and if they got that, they could use tracking software to follow it to a landing."

"That's okay, Ed. The crew filed for Brussels, then, when they were in British airspace, they would have requested a new destination to my property."

"Stone, that software works as well over land as over sea, unless the pilot was clever enough to turn off his transponder before making the turn for England."

"No, he wouldn't have done that. ATC would have been all over him — that's how they track flights."

"Then we're faced with the distinct possibility that St. Clair's people know about where it landed."

"There's no airport there on the aeronautical charts."

"But they would see the airplane stop moving, then start again."

"Well, shit."

"I know how you feel, but you'd better

tighten security over there."

"I'll get on it, Ed." The two men hung up.

Alf Brand went online and found a satellite photograph of Windward Hall, which showed the main house and all the outbuildings. This was bad; these people could be in the main house or any one of the half-dozen cottages he could see. Clearly, this was going to be an on-the-belly-in-the-grass operation. He rousted four of his men out of their beds and put them on the alert, setting a meeting at a country pub south of Beaulieu at noon, then he packed some clothes and a weapons bag and got into his car, a dark green Range Rover.

Two hours later, he was climbing over a stone wall and onto the Windward Hall estate. He had chosen a wooded area to breach the wall and he sparingly used a pinpoint flashlight to make his way through the trees toward the main house. He wanted to get a close-up view of every cottage on the place before believing they were in the big house.

The woods ended thirty yards from the largest, southernmost cottage, and a single light burned in what was probably the living room. Brand sat down and leaned against a tree just inside the tree line and dug a sandwich out of his kit. He sat, munching and drinking coffee from a thermos jug while the moon came up.

He finished the sandwich, then used night binoculars to sweep the property. To his surprise, he caught a movement in the moon shadow of the nearest cottage and trained his glasses there. A man sat cross-legged on the ground, leaning against the cottage, eating a sandwich and drinking coffee from a thermos jug. A short automatic weapon rested on his lap. "One guard and counting," Brand muttered to himself. This would be a much simpler job, he reflected, if he could just put a round into that man's head, then enter the cottage and shoot everybody. Well, at least he knew where the family was sleeping. Nobody would guard an empty cottage.

Stone finally got Mike Freeman on his cell phone in Brussels.

"Hello, Stone."

"Hello, Mike."

"We dropped your people last night, and all was well when I left them."

"I'm afraid we have a problem. We've learned that two vehicles followed them from Cape May to Teterboro, and it's likely that they got the tail number of your airplane and tracked it."

"That's bad news," Mike said. "I think we're going to have to increase security."

"My very reason for calling," Stone said.

"I'll put six men on each shift — that way they can spread out and have a wider field of fire. I'll also put two of them inside the cottage."

"That sounds good."

"I should think that any attempt would be made after dark."

"I agree."

"Then I'll have everybody in place by nightfall. Is that satisfactory?"

"It is."

"I'll give you a ring when everything is complete."

"Good." Stone hung up.

The Parkers slept late; it was eleven o'clock before they were up and dressed.

There was a knock on the front door, and Hank answered it.

"Good morning, Mr. Parker," one of the guards said. "We're changing shifts now. I just wanted you to know."

"Thanks very much. Say, do you know the area around the estate?"

"I grew up near here."

"Is there some nice place in the country

where we could go for lunch?"

"Yes, there's a very cozy country pub a couple of miles up the road toward the village. It's called the Rose & Crown, and the food is very good."

"That sounds ideal."

"Just turn right out the gate and you'll come upon the pub on your left a couple of miles up. A couple of our men will go along and show you the way, then tail you wherever you go."

"Thanks so much." Hank went back inside. "How about lunch at a country pub?" he asked his wife and son. They were agreeable.

"Can we take Maggie?" Tommy asked.

"I expect so, the Brits like their dogs."

Alf Brand arrived at the pub for his meeting at noon. Two of his men were already at a table in a nook by the fireplace, and he joined them. A couple of minutes later, the other two came in and sat down.

"Now listen," Alf said, and his group turned quiet.

One of his men who faced the door put a hand on Alf's arm and stopped him. "Don't look now, but a man just entered the pub, and he's casing the place. From the look of him he's packing, and he's a pro."

Alf shifted his chair so that he could get the man into his peripheral vision. "Confirmed," he said. Then, as he watched, three black people entered the pub, one of them a boy, along with another obvious pro. "The gang's all here," Alf said.

Across the room, one of the family's guards kicked his partner under the table. "Group at a table next to the fireplace," he said.

"Got 'em," the man replied.

"Those guys are pros," the first man said.

54

Mike Freeman listened carefully to the report from his man at Windward Hall, then hung up and called Stone Barrington.

"Yes, Mike?"

"Two of my men accompanied the family to a nearby pub for lunch, and they spotted five men there who were obvious pros."

"Any trouble?"

"Not yet. They left a man to watch from a distance and the leader of the group left in a green Range Rover. He ran the plates, and the vehicle is registered to a London company owned by Christian St. Clair."

"What steps have they taken?" Stone asked.

"They're returning the family to their cottage soon and a crew of six will be guarding them, two in the house."

"Do you have a recommendation?"

"I thought of moving them to the main house, but that would be just more area to patrol. I think it's better that they stay where they are for the moment."

"All right. Something you should know — Hank Parker is ex–special ops. He retired as a master sergeant. It might be good to arm him. He'd be an extra man for you."

"I'll have it done. You'd better decide if you want to leave them at Windward Hall or move them to Paris or New York."

"Do you have a recommendation, Mike?"

"If St. Clair could follow them to Beaulieu, he could follow them anywhere, so I don't think moving them would help. I think they're well enough guarded, and I'd recommend leaving them where they are for at least a few more days."

"All right, let's do that." Stone thanked Mike and hung up.

Stone thought about it for a few minutes, then called Lance Cabot.

"Yes, Stone?"

Stone explained what had happened and the steps he had taken.

"I think that's sensible."

"Did you discuss the situation with Will at your meeting?"

"Yes, briefly."

"Did you talk about when I should have the books mailed?"

"Yes, and the answer is not yet."

"I think I disagree. The safety of this family is at stake, and the sooner we go public, the sooner the pressure will be off them. Once the story is out, St. Clair can't afford to harm them."

"You have a point," Lance said.

"What's more, I think we should express-mail the books to the mailing list for overnight delivery."

"Let me make a call," Lance said, and hung up.

Stone waited impatiently for half an hour, then Lance called back.

"What's the word?"

"I've had word that Nelson Knott is going to release a video announcement this afternoon, in time for the evening news shows."

"An announcement that he's going to run?"

"What else would he announce? That he's not going to run?"

"I guess you're right."

"Then I think you should overnight the books. We'll give Knott the day to do follow-up interviews, then we'll have it in the media's hands in time for tomorrow's evening news. Ed's book will make a very nice hand grenade to toss into the mix."

"All right. Have you made any progress

with getting a DNA sample from Knott?"

"My people are working on it. I'll keep you posted."

"All right, you let Will know that we're going, and I'll let Ed Rawls know."

"Right." Both men hung up.

Stone called Ed and brought him up to date.

"I didn't expect an announcement this soon," Ed said.

"Neither did I."

"Still, it's good that we're ready to go. Are you going to tell me where the books are now?"

"On their way to the post office, for overnight mail."

"Okay."

"Lance's people are working on getting a DNA sample from Knott."

"The sooner the better."

"Gotta run." Stone hung up and buzzed Joan.

"Yes, boss?"

"We need to get the books to the post office right now, and they should be sent express mail, overnight."

"I'll call and get them to pick up the books," she said. "They'll do that for large mailings."

"Great. Go!"

Stone called Dino and told him the news. "I'm astonished that St. Clair found the family as quickly as he did."

"I was, too."

"I'll be sure to watch the evening news," Dino said. "Dinner afterward? Viv is back."

"Sure."

"Rôtisserie Georgette at eight. I'll book."

"You're on."

Joan came into his office with an envelope. "The post office will pick up the books by noon, and they'll be delivered by three tomorrow afternoon." She handed him an envelope. "And the DNA profile came back from the lab."

Stone opened the envelope and looked at the report. "It's Greek to me," he said. "E-mail it to Lance Cabot, please."

A van pulled up at Nelson Knott's Washington office shortly after lunch, and a television reporter and a crew got out and went inside. They took an elevator to the executive floor and presented themselves at the reception desk.

"Mark Whittaker, from *60 Minutes,*" the reporter said. "We have an appointment."

"One moment." She made the call. "Go right in," she said, pointing at the double doors behind her.

Nelson Knott rose to greet them.

Whittaker introduced himself. "Thank you for seeing us on short notice, Mr. Knott."

"I was expecting Martin Shawn," Knott said.

"Martin's out of town. When we heard you were releasing a statement today, our executive producer thought we should try and get ahead of the game."

"Fine, but you can't release this interview until after seven PM this evening."

"We're good with that." He turned to his crew. "Let's do this with Mr. Knott behind the desk. Get set up." He turned back to Knott. "Do you think I could have some coffee?" he asked. "My throat is a little scratchy."

"Of course." Knott went to a sideboard and poured two cups. "Cream and sugar?"

"Black is fine, thanks."

Knott handed Whittaker a mug and set his own on his desk. It was emblazoned with one word, "BOSS." He sat down and sipped his coffee while the makeup man dabbed at his face, then they were ready.

"All set," Whittaker said.

"Then let's do it," Knott said, taking the last swallow of his coffee.

Whittaker moved Knott's coffee mug across the desk. "Let's get this off camera."

55

Don, from the family's security team, called a colleague at the cottage.

"Beta here."

"This is Alpha. We've spotted opposition at the pub, and we'll be heading out shortly for the cottage. We're going to need backup before we depart."

"Roger."

"Put two of you in a car and watch our ass on the way back. Leave the other two inside the cottage. The opposition is in a green Range Rover. We'll make the transfer to the cottage from inside the garage. Call me when your vehicle is in place at the pub parking lot."

"Roger, wilco." He hung up.

"Okay, everybody," Don said, then he looked up to see the five men across the room throw some money on their table and leave the pub. "We're going to finish our lunch, then get into our car and drive back to the cottage. We'll have other men in another car following us. Take your time."

Everybody went back to eating, and Don got up and had a look out the front window, then called Beta again.

"Beta."

"Be advised the opposition has a second vehicle, a Toyota 4Runner, the big one."

"Roger."

Don went back to the table and made idle chatter while everyone finished lunch.

When everybody was done, Don went outside and surveyed the parking lot and the road beyond. He saw their second vehicle waiting, then went back inside. "The vehicles in question have left," he said, "and our second vehicle is in place. Let's load up now and try to be quick."

He got the family outside and into his Land Rover, then headed back toward the cottage.

Don's radio crackled. "Alpha, we have a black Toyota SUV one hundred meters behind."

"Beta, let me know if they close on us."

Two minutes later they were through the gate and headed for the cottage.

Alf Brand watched from the shelter of the woods as the two cars arrived at the cottage, one entering the garage and closing the door behind them. The other car emptied, and the men all went inside.

Alf called Erik Macher in the States.

"Yes, Alf?"

"Bad news," he said. "I had a meet with my people at a local pub, and the family came in with professional protection, and they spotted us. The family are now back in their cottage, and six opposition are inside with them."

"Shit," Macher said. "What's your recommendation?"

"We're blown, no getting around that. The opposition is on full alert and we will not — repeat, *not* — be able to stage anything that looks remotely like an accident. Also, it's likely that more opposition have been summoned. If we attempt an assault on the cottage we will have a war on our hands and the police on us in approximately four minutes."

"So, basically, we're fucked."

"That's an affirmative."

"I'll get back to you on this number."

Alf hung up and leaned against a tree. St. Clair was not going to take the news well — he had worked for the man long enough to know that. If Macher came back with orders to assault the cottage, he would walk. He liked working for St. Clair, but not well enough to die for him or go to prison.

Ten minutes later, his phone buzzed.

"Alf here."

"All right, we accept your assessment of the situation. Your orders are to withdraw your team, but maintain surveillance on the cottage. If conditions change, and you feel you have an opportunity to take them without a shooting war, call me back. Otherwise, wait for my call."

"I understand," Alf said. "Withdrawal is under way." He called his number-one man.

"Yes, sir?"

"I'm in the woods near the cottage. We have orders from home to withdraw — the opposition is too great to attempt an operation without a firefight. Get your men back to the pub or other nearby accommodation and wait for a call from me. Have one of your people relieve me in two hours. After that we'll maintain visual contact with the cottage and hope for a change of circumstances. No one is to be out of contact, clear?"

"Clear, sir. I'll issue the orders now."

Alf hung up and settled down to watch and wait.

Stone reached into his jacket pocket for

something and struck hard metal. He came out with the key to the strong case. He walked out to Joan's office. "FedEx this to Ed Rawls in Virginia for earliest possible delivery, please." He handed her the key.

Joan looked at it closely. "I've never seen anything quite like this," she said.

"You don't want to know." He went back to his desk and sent Ed an e-mail, advising him the key was on its way.

In England the sun was setting. Don called his men together. "Establish a rough, square perimeter around the cottage, with one man at each corner, full body armor," he said quietly, so the family wouldn't hear. "We'll be relieved in four hours by another team. At any sound of gunfire withdraw to the interior of the cottage and prepare for an assault."

The men did as they were instructed.

At three PM, fifty-one media outlets in New York, Washington, Los Angeles, and Atlanta nearly simultaneously received a DVD from Knott Industries, together with a press release with an activation time of seven PM EST, announcing a press conference on the Capitol steps at 6:45 the following evening.

■ ■ ■ ■

Stone was watching the evening news when the story broke. Nelson Knott, sitting in the library of his Virginia home, made a three-minute statement announcing his candidacy for President of the United States, and the formation of the Independent Patriot Party, with offices in every state and sixty of the country's most populous cities, which would be open for business at eight o'clock the following morning. Knott looked relaxed and comfortable in a V-necked cashmere sweater and appeared to be speaking without notes. He also announced that he fully expected the new party to have candidates on the ballot for all House and Senate seats by Labor Day. At least fifteen of these would be converts from the Republican rolls in both houses.

Stone met the Bacchettis at eight at Rôtisserie Georgette, and they ordered drinks. "Did you watch the news?" he asked them.

"You bet your sweet ass," Dino said. "Knott's announcement was very slick. Is anybody from the administration going to comment?"

"I expect so."

"Are the books on their way?"

"They'll all be delivered by three PM, Eastern, tomorrow."

"I can't wait," Dino replied.

56

The following morning, Ed Rawls was having breakfast in the kitchen when the doorbell rang. He felt for the small 9mm pistol in the pocket of his robe, then went to the door. A man in a Federal Express uniform stood at the door. Ed put his hand inside his robe pocket and thumbed back the hammer on the weapon, then opened the door.

"Good morning," the man said. "I have a delivery for you, and I need a signature."

Ed looked over the man's shoulder and saw the FedEx truck. He slowly released the hammer on the pistol, then signed for the package.

The driver handed him a stiff FedEx envelope. "Have a good day," he said, then left.

Ed went back to the kitchen, opened the envelope, and shook out the key to the strong case. He put it into the other pocket of his robe, got the mail from the mailbox on the porch, and went back to his breakfast. When he was done he cleaned up after himself, then went into his study, switched on the TV for *Morning Joe,* and started opening the mail.

He was absorbed in a copy of his investment statement when he looked up and found a man standing in the door. What with Joe Scarborough in mid-rant, he hadn't heard him enter the house. He thought of going for his pistol, but the man already had one in his hand, equipped with a silencer. Ed pressed the mute button on the TV remote control. "What the fuck do you want?" It occurred to him that, having published and circulated his book, there was nothing pressing remaining in his life, and it might be as good a time as any to die.

"We want the strong case," the man said. "And if you don't give it to us without a fuss, you're going to die here and now."

"Oh, all right," Ed said. "Can I get up and get it without being shot?"

"Go ahead, but carefully."

Ed got up, swung back the bookcase hiding his safe, entered the code, and opened the door.

"Don't reach inside," the man said, "just step back two paces."

"Sure thing," Rawls said, and followed orders.

The man motioned to a companion behind him. "Get the thing out of the safe." The man stepped past Rawls and retrieved the strong case.

"We'll say good morning to you, then," the man with the silenced pistol said.

"And to you," Ed replied.

The man turned to go.

"Oh," Ed said.

The man turned. "What?"

"It occurs to me that you might like to have the key, since the case can't be opened without it."

"Where is the key?"

"In this pocket," Ed said, pointing at it.

"Take it out very, very carefully," the man said.

Ed did so, then tossed it to him.

The man caught the key without taking his eyes from Rawls, impressing him. "Thank you. Now sit down and don't move for five minutes."

Ed sat down, picked up his investment statement, and started to read.

The man with the silenced pistol vanished, and Ed heard the front door close softly. He picked up the remote and restored Joe Scarborough to speech in mid-rant. He was now on the subject of Nelson Knott's announcement and its potential effect on the coming election.

Stone was having his own breakfast in bed, watching *Morning Joe,* when the phone rang. "Yes?"

"It's Ed Rawls."

"Good morning, Ed."

"I thought you'd like to know that I received the key, and just in time."

"In time for what?"

"In time for two of Christian St. Clair's thugs to walk, armed, into my house and demand the strong case on pain of death."

"Well, since you're still alive, I assume you either killed them both or gave them the case."

"I gave them the case, and the key, which had arrived only a few minutes before."

"So, there's an end to that," Stone said.

"Not quite," Ed said, "they still have to get it open."

As the two men drove away from Rawls's house, one of them said to the other, "Are we going to open the thing?"

"That's above my pay grade," the man said. "I'll pass it up the line, and somebody else can make that decision."

They drove into Washington, went to Erik Macher's office, and delivered the case and its key to him. "Rawls didn't give us an argument," the man said.

When they had gone, Macher sat and stared at the case. Weeks of trouble, he reflected; how many dead? He had lost track. He inserted the key into one of the two locks.

"No," he said aloud. He put the key back into his pocket and called Christian St. Clair.

"Yes, Erik?"

"Good morning, sir."

"Have you heard anything further from our people in England?"

"No, sir. It's mid-afternoon there, so I expect there has been no change in the circumstances, or I would have heard."

"Then what can I do for you?"

"I have the strong case, sir."

There was a sharp intake at the other end of the line. "Bring it to me, unopened," he said.

"Where are you?"

"At my home in New York."

"I'll leave immediately, sir. It should take me four or five hours to drive the distance."

"I'll expect you." St. Clair hung up.

Macher left his office, stowed the strong

case in the trunk of his car, and drove away. He turned on the satellite radio and selected CNN. All the news was of Nelson Knott's announcement of his candidacy the previous day. He found some classical music.

Stone went down to his office in time to get a call from Will Lee.

"Good morning, Will."

"Good morning, Stone. Have you had any news of the delivery of your packages?"

"Not yet. They are all supposed to be delivered by three PM, or so the post office promises."

"In time for the evening news."

"Should be plenty of time."

"I'll look forward to it," Will said.

The two men hung up.

57

Around noon, Stone got a call from Ed Rawls.

"Hello again, Ed," he said.

"Hello, Stone. If it sounds like I'm in a car, I am."

"Your old Mercedes?"

"No, that's a short-range car, it's tucked away in my garage. I'm driving a rental."

"Is this a long-range trip?"

"It is. I'm headed to Islesboro. I'll drive as far as Augusta, then get a lightplane charter to the island. It occurred to me that when the mailing hits the media I'm going to be getting a lot of phone calls and interview requests that I want no part of."

"I expect you're right. Would you like to stay at my place until yours is finished?"

"Thank you, that would suit me very well."

"I'll call Seth Hotchkiss and tell him and Mary to expect you. Knock on his door when you get there, and he'll let you in."

"Perfecto. Have you had any blowback from the mailing yet?"

"No, and I don't expect any, since nobody will associate me with your book."

"Well, there are a couple of mentions of you."

"I'd forgotten about that, but they were innocuous."

"I guess that describes them. What are you going to do with the Parkers now? Once the news is out, they'll no longer be a threat to Nelson Knott or Christian St. Clair."

"No, but the press will be looking hard for them. They'd be a hot interview."

"The DVD will cover that. They've got enough quotes for a week, anyway."

"I'll just leave them where they be, I think. I'm sure they're enjoying the vacation, and I don't want to cut it short."

"Good idea. Let me give you my latest cell number."

Stone wrote it down.

"You might give that to the Parkers, too, should they want to reach me."

"You know, Ed, you might have saved their lives by figuring out that St. Clair had people following them."

"Maybe, who knows?"

"What are you going to do for the rest of

the year?"

"I'm going to finish my house and furnish it, then I'm just going to sit around and watch the election campaigns on TV. When it's over I won't have anything else to do."

"You'll think of something," Stone said.

"Maybe I'll take a look at the new crop of widows up there. We seem to get three or four a season."

"I'm sure the attention would make them happy."

"Okay, you take care."

"Give me a call when you're in the house, and I'll give you some tips on how to run the place."

"Will do. Bye." They both hung up.

Stone had a sandwich for lunch and was reading a contract later when Joan buzzed. "A producer at *60 Minutes* is on one for you."

"Did he say what it was about?"

"Nope."

Stone picked up the phone. "This is Stone Barrington."

"Mr. Barrington, we've received your mailing, and —"

"My mailing? What mailing?"

"The Ed Rawls book and the DVD. I'd like to ask you some questions about it."

"It's nothing to do with me. Call Ed Rawls. Goodbye."

He hung up, and Joan buzzed again. "Somebody from MSNBC," she said, "a producer on the Chris Matthews show."

"Tell him I'm busy, to call Ed Rawls." Before he could hang up, she said, "Somebody from Fox News on line two."

"I don't want to speak to anybody about the books," he said. "Refer them all to Rawls." He hung up and wondered how the hell he had been connected to the mailing. He buzzed Joan.

"Yes?"

"You didn't put my name on those envelopes, did you?"

"Nope, just the address, in case we got returns."

Stone groaned. "Okay, then, you handle the calls. There are going to be two hundred of them."

"But how would they know the books are from you?"

"You ever hear of a reverse directory, Joan? You look up an address, and it tells you who lives there."

"Oh, my God, I'm so embarrassed."

"You can convey your embarrassment to the two hundred callers."

She buzzed back a few minutes later to

say Dino was on line two. Stone pressed the button. "Hello."

"You must be getting a lot of calls," Dino said. "I hear your address is on every envelope."

"Yeah, Joan screwed up, something she doesn't often do. She'd never heard of a reverse directory."

"What are you doing about the calls?"

"Referring everybody to Ed Rawls."

"And where is Rawls?"

"On his way to Maine, driving a rental. He didn't want the calls."

"Will they track him down there?"

"I don't think so," Stone said. "His phone was destroyed with his house, and he's using a burner. He's staying at my place until his new one is finished."

"Is the Parker family okay?"

"They're fine. They're at my place in England."

"So everybody's battened down for the big moment, huh?"

"Everybody but Nelson Knott and Christian St. Clair. They'll be getting the first calls soon."

"Yes, that could ruin their day. Have you heard anything from Lance Cabot?"

"Not since yesterday. Will Lee called this morning, and we had a brief chat. He seemed calm."

"Heard anything from Holly?"

"Nope. I think she's back at work by now and probably doesn't have the time to call."

"Why don't you get her to quit the job and marry you? Viv thinks you're made for each other."

"Tried that, didn't work. She's married to the White House, and I'll tell you a secret — Lance is a candidate for Kate's running mate this time."

"What's wrong with what's-his-name, the VP?"

"He's unwell, something serious, I think."

"Has Holly got a shot at Lance's job, if he runs with Kate?"

"I believe she has."

"Well, that means she's not going to marry you until she's old and gray, and you're nearly dead."

"That crossed my mind," Stone said. He hung up and watched the lights flashing on his phone, as people called in.

58

Erik Macher got out of his car and tried to see as far forward as possible. He was stuck on I-95 in New Jersey and had been for half an hour. His cell phone rang.

"Yes?"

"It's Alf. We're stumped here. Another half-dozen armed people have arrived and are now deployed. Even if we just wanted to shoot this family, we wouldn't have a chance, without fifty percent fatalities of our own. Only a mortar or a rocket-propelled grenade would give us a chance at them. How long do you want to go on paying us to watch the grass grow?"

Macher made his own decision: "All right, pull your people out and go home. If I hear that anything has changed, I'll call you, and we can start all over again."

"Right. We are aborting this mission."

Macher hung up and ran for his car. Traffic had started to inch forward.

Joan buzzed Stone. "Yes?"

"Lance Cabot on two."

He pressed the button. "Yes, Lance?"

"We've processed Nelson Knott's DNA sample from his coffee mug. It's a match for Martha's son — no doubt."

"What do you think we should do with it?"

"Get it to your mailing list as soon as possible," Lance said.

"I don't have the mailing list, it was on the envelopes."

"Come to think of it, Stone, neither do I. But we have a list of contact and fax numbers for several hundred media organizations worldwide."

"I think fax is a good idea. Send it to all the U.S. numbers, and who cares if it's overkill."

"Okay, I'll get our lab to type up a suitable letter, and we'll attach the report to it."

"Somebody is going to reach me eventually about this, and they're going to ask how we got the DNA sample. What do you want me to say?"

"Well, for God's sake don't say my people got it. Say that someone in Knott's organization managed to obtain it and sent it."

"Sent it to whom? Not to me!"

"A law enforcement agency."

"That would slow them down for about half a second, Lance. Which law enforcement agency?"

"Let me talk to somebody at the FBI, maybe I can get them to release the results."

"They're a criminal investigative body — they would process it only if the commission of a crime were involved."

"Rape is a crime," Lance pointed out.

"Yes, but not a federal crime."

"Where did the alleged rape take place?"

"In Knott's office in Washington, according to her DVD testimony," Stone said.

"I'll send the whole package to the D.C. police chief and see if we can get them involved. They're the proper investigative authority."

"Good idea!" Stone hung up.

A group of men and women sat in a screening room at the D.C. police department and watched Martha's statement. It ended, and the chief looked around the table. "Since receiving the book and the DVD, we've received a lab report saying that there's a DNA match between Nelson Knott and the boy. My question is, do we have the basis for an investigation here?"

"Certainly we do," her deputy replied, "if it occurred in the District, and the woman says it did, and it would have occurred within the statute of limitations." There was general assent around the table.

"The book and the DVD, but not the DNA report, have been sent to two hundred media outlets around the country. Should we send out the DNA report?"

"We're not exactly ahead of this story," her deputy said. "Sending out the report might give us some catch-up."

"We have a list of press and media fax numbers, don't we?" the chief asked.

Her public affairs officer raised his hand. "We do, Chief, and I can have it out to them in a matter of minutes. We can robo-dial all the numbers."

"Fine, do it, and let's get an investigative team assembled right now and start substantiating everything."

In New York, at CBS Television, another group sat watching Martha's testimony on the DVD. It ended, and everyone was quiet for a moment.

"Okay," the executive producer said, "how do we go forward?"

"We get it on the news, pronto," somebody said.

"Why us?"

"Because we gave Knott *60 Minutes* last week. All of it."

"That doesn't make us accomplices in a rape. Is this cause to disrupt a presidential campaign?"

"I'll give you a better reason to get it on the air now," the youngest member of the group said.

"Go ahead."

"This package didn't just come to us, every media outlet in the country is going to know about it in no more than an hour. We don't want to be the only one not broadcasting it."

"That's a very good reason. Get a report together, call Knott for a comment, and we'll lead with it on the evening news. Then let's get it on *60 Minutes* Sunday night, the whole statement. Go!"

Erik Macher was now doing forty miles an hour; he called St. Clair, and his secretary answered. "It's Macher. Let me speak with him."

"He isn't taking any calls this afternoon. He didn't feel well after lunch, and he's lying down. And there have been many calls from the media."

"I'm not surprised, given yesterday's announcement. Let him know that I was delayed by traffic accidents on the interstate, and that I'll be there in two hours."

"I'll tell him as soon as he wakes up."

Macher hung up and tried to see into the future. Getting ahold of the strong case had given them a leg up, he thought. Knott's announcement had been received respectfully by the media; now they would start digging into Knott's past. He'd been working for years to make sure that there was nothing in that past that would cloud the man's political future, even to committing murder. With the handing over of the strong case to St. Clair, Macher would be the hero of all their efforts, and he intended to make the most of it. He would go from being in charge of an at-arm's-length security company to being an important executive in St. Clair's business empire. They couldn't afford not to give him that, because he knew too much to be cold-shouldered. He was going to place that case in St. Clair's hands personally, and reap the attendant rewards.

Traffic was clearing; he picked up speed.

59

Stone got a call from Mike Freeman.

"Yes, Mike?"

"My people in England tell me that all opposition around your estate has disappeared. They've apparently been withdrawn."

"I expect that St. Clair has heard about Martha's statement by now, and if so, she would no longer be in danger."

"Should I withdraw my people, then?"

Stone thought about it. "Wait until tomorrow morning, but leave two people with them. If they can find out where the family is, the press and media are going to want to interview Martha, and they will be very pushy about it."

"All right, I'll do that." He hung up.

Joan buzzed. "Ed Rawls on one."

Stone pressed the button. "Yes, Ed, where are you?"

"North of Portland. I'll get a room in

Augusta and fly tomorrow morning. The forecast is good."

"What's up?"

"I was just wondering if you'd heard anything from St. Clair or his people?"

"Nothing at all?"

"Not a peep," Stone said.

"How about Knott?"

"Nothing from him, either, but I haven't expected any of them to contact me."

"I just wondered," Ed said. "Good night." He hung up.

Stone went upstairs to his study and poured himself a drink. He glanced at his watch. Half an hour to go.

Erik Macher pulled up before Christian St. Clair's double-width town house. One of his people was guarding the door. He got the strong case out of his trunk and trotted up the stairs.

"Good evening, Mr. Macher," his man said.

"Don't let them give me a ticket," Macher replied, and rang the bell. Another of his people answered it. "Where is Mr. St. Clair?" he asked the man.

"I believe he's in his study," the man replied. "He just woke up from a nap. He's been down all afternoon."

"Thank you," Macher replied, and walked up the curving staircase from the marble hall to the second floor, to the double doors of St. Clair's study, which was where he worked when he was in New York. He rapped on the door.

"Who is it?" St. Clair called from inside.

"It's Erik, sir."

"Do you have the strong case?"

"I do, sir."

"Then come in!" His voice sounded excited.

Macher let himself into the two-story room, which was filled with pictures and books. St. Clair sat at his desk. The only light on in the room was the lamp that illuminated its surface.

"I'm sorry I'm late," Macher said. "There were accidents on the interstate. I did the best I could, and I did call you." He walked toward the desk.

St. Clair beckoned him. "I had a migraine and was down for a while. What do you hear from England?"

Macher stopped and set down the heavy case. "The family are surrounded by armed men, and have been since this morning. There was no opportunity to stage an accident, and even an all-out assault would not have worked, so I sent our people home, until circumstances have changed."

"Damn it!" St. Clair said. "Set the case up here." He cleared the desk of papers and patted the desktop.

Macher placed the case on the desk and turned the opening side toward St. Clair. "Here you are, sir."

St. Clair examined the case. "Jesus, it's pretty substantial, isn't it? How does it open?"

"I'm sorry, sir, here's the key." He dug it out of his pocket and handed it to St. Clair.

"How does it work?" he asked.

"I don't know, sir, I haven't opened it."

"Obviously your curiosity isn't as strong as mine." He waved Macher to a chair across the desk from him and inspected the locks. "This brings an end to our problems," St. Clair said, inserting the key into a lock and turning it.

"I'm delighted to hear it," Macher said.

St. Clair inserted the key into the other lock and turned it. "Come November, I'll have my man in the White House." He set down the key and reached forward with both hands to open the case.

Macher was looking directly at St. Clair's face when the strong case exploded. His chair and he in it were knocked backward several feet, and he was stunned by the force. St. Clair was screaming. Macher got up on one elbow and looked at the man: he was flat against the bookcase behind him and on fire from the shoulders up. So was the bookcase.

Macher struggled to his feet and tried to find a way to help St. Clair, but there was nothing he could do. He looked around and saw a fire extinguisher near the door to the room and ran for it. He expended the entire charge in St. Clair's direction; when it ran out, he went looking for another and found one in the kitchenette where St. Clair's lunches were prepared. He ran back into the room and emptied the second extinguisher. St. Clair had fallen to the floor behind his desk.

Macher knew at once that the man was dead; his arms, shoulders, and face were stripped of clothes and his flesh was burned black. The phone on the desk was gone; he found another on a table across the room and called 911.

"Nine-one-one operator, what is your emergency?"

"An explosion and fire," he replied.

"Anyone injured?"

"One fatality. I could use some first aid." He gave her the address.

"Police, EMTs, and an ambulance have

been dispatched."

Macher hung up and began plotting how he might go to the board and be placed in charge of St. Clair's business interests. And Nelson Knott. He couldn't let the man think he was free to act as he pleased.

Stone watched the evening news: Ed Rawls's book and Martha Parker's statement took up the first ten minutes, then came this:

"In a related story, Mr. Knott's principal financial backer, Christian St. Clair, was killed this afternoon by an explosion in his home on New York's Upper East Side. A business associate, Erik Macher, was slightly burned and was treated at a local hospital and released."

The rest of the program was taken up with interviews and political reports connected to St. Clair's death.

"St. Clair's death comes at a very difficult moment for Nelson Knott," a reporter was saying. "Knott has sequestered himself at his Virginia estate and released a statement saying that he is devastated by the death of Christian St. Clair and will have no other statement until tomorrow. He has called a news conference for ten am, at which time he is going to have to address these accusations of the rape of two women when they were employed by him."

Stone watched the news all evening, switching from CNN to the networks to MSNBC. He fell asleep with the TV on.

60

Nelson Knott awoke from a fitful sleep to the ringing of a telephone. The bedside clock said seven AM. He rolled over and grabbed the phone. "What?"

"Mr. Knott," his secretary said, "I'm getting a flood of calls from the media for you."

"I told you last night — refer them to the press conference at my office at ten this morning."

"I've done that. There's something else, sir."

"What is it?"

"The morning television shows are all reporting that several women have emerged, accusing you of charges similar to the one on television last night. Your attorney called and requested that you cancel the press conference this morning and not give any interviews until you and he have met."

Knott was unable to speak.

"Sir, what would you like me to do?"

"Cancel the press conference," he replied, "and don't call me again." He hung up. He reached for his wife, but he had forgotten that she was in New York, shopping. He got out of bed and paced the room, naked and in a panic. It was obvious to him that his presidential bid was at an end, and Christian St. Clair was dead, so he couldn't ask him what to do next.

He went into his study and looked out the big windows with their view of the Virginia countryside. It was pouring rain, and the wind was whipping the trees on his lawn. It seemed a metaphor of what had suddenly happened to his life, and there was nowhere to go from here.

He sat down at his desk, still naked, opened a drawer, and removed a beautiful, handmade .45 semiautomatic pistol, one of a considerable collection. He racked the slide, thumbed the safety off, put the barrel into his mouth, and pulled the trigger.

Stone overslept, not waking until nearly nine o'clock. The TV was still on to MSNBC, and Mika Brzezinski was speaking into the camera and a banner beneath her read: "Breaking News."

"The Virginia State Police, called to the home of Nelson Knott, found him at his desk, dead of an apparently self-inflicted gunshot wound. His death came after multiple reports of accusations of rape by former female employees of his company. Thus ends perhaps the shortest presidential campaign in American history."

The phone rang.

"Hello?"

"Stone, it's Ed Rawls. I'm back on Islesboro, at your place. Just got in."

"Have you heard the news?"

"I've heard nothing else," Ed said. "I'm in your living room, and it's on right now."

"You heard about St. Clair, too?"

"Yeah, at bedtime last night, in Augusta."

"Ed, do you know anything about that explosion?"

"Well, I know that if you don't follow the proper procedure when you open a strong case, you get a strong reaction."

"Did you mention that to the people who took the case from you?"

"Nope. They didn't ask me."

"Ed, there's something I've got to know."

"I'll help if I can."

"What was in the strong case?"

Ed chuckled. "Nothing. Not a thing."

"And for how long had that been true?"

"Well, I emptied it before I left it with Joe Adams," Ed said. "I was trying to finish my book at the time, and I needed a red herring to keep people busy and off my back until it was done."

"Did Joe know it was empty?"

"Nope, he never asked me what was in it."

"And all the time it was in my possession, it was empty?"

"Yep. You never asked me, either."

AUTHOR'S NOTE

I am happy to hear from readers, but you should know that if you write to me in care of my publisher, three to six months will pass before I receive your letter, and when it finally arrives it will be one among many, and I will not be able to reply.

However, if you have access to the Internet, you may visit my website at www.stuartwoods.com, where there is a button for sending me e-mail. So far, I have been able to reply to all my e-mail, and I will continue to try to do so.

If you send me an e-mail and do not receive a reply, it is probably because you are among an alarming number of people who have entered their e-mail address incorrectly in their mail software. I have many of my replies returned as undeliverable.

Remember: e-mail, reply; snail mail, no reply.

When you e-mail, please do not send attachments, as I never open these. They can take twenty minutes to download, and they often contain viruses.

Please do not place me on your mailing lists for funny stories, prayers, political causes, charitable fund-raising, petitions, or sentimental claptrap. I get enough of that from people I already know. Generally speaking, when I get e-mail addressed to a large number of people, I immediately delete it without reading it.

Please do not send me your ideas for a book, as I have a policy of writing only what I myself invent. If you send me story ideas, I will immediately delete them without reading them. If you have a good idea for a book, write it yourself, but I will not be able to advise you on how to get it published. Buy a copy of *Writer's Market* at any bookstore; that will tell you how.

Anyone with a request concerning events or appearances may e-mail it to me or send it to: Publicity Department, Penguin Random House LLC, 375 Hudson Street, New York, NY 10014.

Those ambitious folk who wish to buy film, dramatic, or television rights to my books should contact Matthew Snyder, Creative Artists Agency, 9830 Wilshire Boulevard, Beverly Hills, CA 98212-1825.

Those who wish to make offers for rights of a literary nature should contact Anne Sibbald, Janklow & Nesbit, 445 Park Avenue, New York, NY 10022. (Note: This is not an invitation for you to send her your manuscript or to solicit her to be your agent.)

If you want to know if I will be signing books in your city, please visit my website, www.stuartwoods.com, where the tour schedule will be published a month or so in advance. If you wish me to do a book signing in your locality, ask your favorite bookseller to contact his Penguin representative or the Penguin publicity department with the request.

If you find typographical or editorial errors in my book and feel an irresistible urge to tell someone, please write to Sara Minnich at Penguin's address above. Do not e-mail your discoveries to me, as I will already have learned about them from others.

A list of my published works appears on my website. All the novels are still in print in paperback and can be found at or ordered from any bookstore. If you wish to obtain hardcover copies of earlier novels or of the two nonfiction books, a good used-book store or one of the online bookstores can help you find them. Otherwise, you will have to go to a great many garage sales.

ABOUT THE AUTHOR

Stuart Woods is the author of more than sixty novels, including the *New York Times*–bestselling Stone Barrington and Holly Barker series. He is a native of Georgia and began his writing career in the advertising industry. *Chiefs*, his debut in 1981, won the Edgar Award. An avid sailor and pilot, Woods lives in New York City, Florida, and Maine.